A DARKENED DOORSTEP

MATT FREEMAN

DEATH MASK PUBLISHING

CONTENTS

The world is the world and Kythira is another world.
— ANCIENT VENETIAN SAYING

1
THE VISITOR

Reece and Amaya ended the last day of their vacation over a bottle of wine, shared on the balcony of their rented room overlooking Kapsali's twin bays. Sailboats dotted the harbor, the lights atop their masts painting pale streaks across the darkened waters. The marina below the harbor's modest lighthouse blushed with golden light so that it looked from a distance like fire burning in the rocks. There was beauty everywhere, and that should have been enough. But Reece found himself oppressed by dread—not his usual dread of an ominous future stalking his present joys like a horror movie killer, but the dread one feels when one knows the killer is already in the house and they've just heard the first of his footfalls upon the steps.

Amaya was holding her glass by its stem like an adult of many years instead of the newly minted twenty-year-old she was. "This wine is so good," she said, examining its color by the candlelight. "And I love that it's made right here in Kythira." She stretched her legs as far as they would go and then dropped her feet into Reece's lap. "What a romantic place."

He'd chosen their destination well. These were the moments Amaya would remember once they were back at sea, where for one final agonizing deployment he'd pretend not to know his rank-and-file paramour. "Makes sense. After all, this is the island where love was born."

"Mm, right. Aphrodite." Amaya swirled the last of the wine in her glass. "I wonder if this place is so magical because she was born here, or if her folks chose this spot because it was already like this." She drank the rest of her wine, and a blush came to her cheeks.

Reece began rubbing her feet. "Well, as legend has it, it all began when the titan Kronos severed his father's genitals and threw them into the sea. They say Aphrodite was born off these shores in the foam created by that divine seed."

Amaya raised her eyebrows. "Severed genitals? That isn't quite the romantic tale I was hoping for, Reecey."

"Well, that's her story. Unless you want to take Homer's word for it."

"I'll ask him the next time I see him. But for now, I'll settle for the word of the Greek Mythology major who's been following me around for the past six months."

Reece laughed. "Well, at least my degree is doing me some good."

"Hey, it allowed you to become an officer. You don't think I'd be interested in Seaman Reece Holloway, do you, Lieutenant?"

Joking or not, that was the last thing Reece wanted to hear. "I should hope not," he said with a forced grin. He patted Amaya's foot to let her know he was finished and then laced his fingers behind his head in case there was any doubt.

She watched him for a moment before withdrawing her feet and leaning in to plant a kiss on his lips. "I'm gonna go get washed up."

The darkness of the room devoured her. The moment she was gone, Reece turned the wine bottle upside-down and tapped the bottom as if he were trying to knock loose a stubborn gob of ketchup. Once the final drop had fallen, he stood with glass in hand and leaned against the railing. With his other hand he made a quick check that the ring was still there. It'd been burning a hole in his pocket all week, but he still hadn't found the perfect moment to spring the question of forever on her. Somehow it hadn't been the right moment when they'd been camping in the pine forest near the shore. Nor had it been the right moment when they'd been standing in awed silence outside the cliffside Church of St. John, the low sun sparkling off the pristine water. What on earth was he waiting for? A wink and a nod? A promise that she wouldn't shred his heart into confetti the moment he laid it all on the line?

Reece set his glass on the table and stepped into the room, closing the balcony door behind him. The only light was that which spilled from the open space of the bathroom door, and the only sound was the falling water mingling with the hum of Amaya's favorite tune. Reece took a seat on the edge of the bed and removed the ring from his pocket, then sat listening while he examined its diamond-studded band with his fingertips.

After a time, the humming stopped, and the patter of water fell silent. He tried to stash the ring back in his pocket, but he fumbled it and it disappeared somewhere below. Reece dropped to his knees and searched the floor with his hands. He'd only just recovered it when Amaya stepped around the corner wrapped in a bath towel. "What're you doing down there, silly?"

Reece palmed the ring and slid it into his pocket. "Just dropped my phone." He climbed back onto his feet. "Gonna go brush my teeth. Don't wait up." Amaya pecked him on the cheek and then slapped him on the rear as he passed. It was always hard to tell when she was behaving in earnest and when she was playing. Reece's greatest fear was that she was always playing.

While brushing his teeth, he gave his reflection a dressing down with his eyes. What a thing to fear. To think that after everything they'd shared, she wouldn't jump at the chance to become Mrs. Holloway. But would she do it for the right reasons? Reece spat and rinsed. It was time to stop making excuses. He wanted to see her real smile, that hidden expression he would know as authentic the moment it parted her lips. To find it, he would need to jump feet first into the deep end, come what may. He pulled the ring back out of his pocket and took a moment to admire the way its stones captured and held the brightness. Then he killed the bathroom light and returned to the room.

Amaya was asleep. Reece took a seat on the edge of the bed, smiling at how close he'd come. Perhaps rather than wait for the next brave impulse, he should pick a time and place in advance. He thought back to the night they'd stood together on the sponson, watching the trails of electric blue bioluminescence as the ship parted the water. The more he thought about it, the more ideal it seemed.

He'd do it there some late night underway when they would be alone. Proposing on the ship would demonstrate how unafraid he was of running blindly into the future with her, and it would make a perfect story for her to tell her friends once they were out of the service. He would one day look back and laugh at how foolish his misgivings had been.

Reece placed the ring in the outer pouch of his carry-on bag, then took off his shirt and pants and lay down on his back. As soon as his head hit the pillow, he felt a renewal of the dread which had menaced him on the balcony. He sat back up. The room swam with indistinct forms, and Reece dismissed, as best he could, the feeling that something was watching from among them. *Too much sun and wine is all. Just need some sleep.* He lay back down, his brow cool with sweat. Beside him, Amaya's breathing was so steady it was like a new measure of time, and by the count of six Reece had closed his eyes.

When he opened them again, he felt as though only a moment had passed, but the moonlight streaming in through the window rebuked the notion that he'd been anything but asleep. He tried to roll onto his side, to wrap Amaya up in his arms and embrace her in shadows, but the thought wouldn't translate into action. He tried without luck to move his legs. After that he tried his hands, then a finger—just one damn finger—to prove he wasn't paralyzed.

Nothing. He might as well have been willing the movement of the hairs on his head. He tried to call out to Amaya, to beg her to wake up and shake him from his lucid nightmare, but he was only able to produce the breathy sounds of a dying man. Maybe this was it. The danger he'd sensed on the balcony. The killer climbing the steps. Reece Holloway, dead at twenty-seven. It was then he felt another presence in the room.

It was more than the feeling one gets when they think someone might be watching, although that alone would have been enough to drain the blood from Reece's face. He could sense the visitor's hatred rolling forth in waves like summer heat rising off asphalt. This was no curious spirit. It was malice concentrated, and Reece knew to a moral certainty that if he were to lower his eyes, he would find it standing at the foot of the bed.

He closed them instead. But it didn't take long before he'd castigated himself a coward. There was a threat in the room, and it was his job to identify it. And so he vowed to look on three. *One. Two.* His eyes remained shut. He sucked tremulous breaths through his nose, hoping for a passing moment of courage to latch onto. While he was waiting, he heard the wall-mounted television power on, and his eyelids took on the colors of the screen. Knowing he could no longer hide behind them, he finished the count.

Three. He opened his eyes and gazed toward the foot of the bed. In front of the television stood the black silhouette of a man, cut off at the neck so that it looked like the television was his head. The screen displayed a rapid-fire reel of faces twisted with animus, all male and each appearing only for a fraction of a second, giving the appearance of a single morphing visage. Reece tried to cry out, but it emerged only as a prolonged croak. Then the screen turned to static, and the black figure stepped forward, the shape of his head now visible against the television's snow.

Before Reece could squeeze his eyes shut, the visitor rushed to his side of the bed and began clawing at his face with fingers incapable of rending flesh. He was incorporeal. A living shadow. But even that cold comfort vanished when he reached inside Reece's chest and grabbed onto something as ephemeral as himself. Reece's muscles contracted, and his hips rose off the bed. It was as if he were receiving direct current. Moments from losing consciousness, the visitor let him go, and Reece's body collapsed into a twisted state of paralysis, arms and legs tucked in like the corpse of a poisoned insect.

Time stretched and contracted. At one point Reece thought he was back in Gaeta. Then the room came back into focus, and he found the visitor by the kitchen, pacing in a circle. Something felt different. Reece raised his head off the pillow, lifted his hand, and looked at it as if he couldn't believe it was his again. After a time, the visitor stopped, then he turned his empty face toward Reece, and again the web of paralysis fell upon his nervous system. Reece gave an ill-tempered moan as he went back down, but he went back down nonetheless, and from there he watched the visitor make his way to Amaya's side of the bed.

Reece shouted in his thoughts what he was unable to say with his mouth. *"Stay away from her!"* The visitor showed no response. He moved like both man and ghost, walking as one might expect but leaving the impression that he wasn't really in need of solid ground beneath his feet. His body was such a void that he was more like the absence of man. His fingers were black tornadoes, shifting and lengthening as they searched for land to ravage.

Reece ground his teeth, and saliva spilled from the side of his mouth, collecting beneath his ear. He concentrated his thoughts onto the visitor, who was now leaning over Amaya. *"Look at me, you son of a bitch."* The visitor paused and raised his face. So, he could hear Reece after all. *"Touch her and I'll kill you."*

The visitor's shoulders shook as though he was laughing, but he made no sound. Then he ran his fingers up and down Amaya's body as if to further demonstrate Reece's impotence. Tears poured from Reece's eyes, and at last he managed to produce a noise—the thin whimper of the defeated. Unable to bear another moment, he lowered his gaze to where Amaya lay. Her head was facing his, and her eyes were fixed and vacant like the glass eyes of a doll. Her open mouth drew short, labored breaths, each of them sending a shudder through her body. Reece's inner scream bled into the television's static, and he found mercy at the end of despair as he passed back into a dreamless sleep.

When Reece next awoke, it was to the light of morning. Amaya was absent from her side of the bed, and he nearly panicked until he heard the sound of sizzling coming from the kitchen. He sat up, shaken by how seamlessly hell had morphed into chirping birds and the smell of eggs and toast. He didn't trust it. Not one bit. He felt as though paralysis would fall upon him again the moment he breathed a sigh of relief. But as the minutes passed, he came to accept that it really was over, the episode's absurd conclusion being that it was now time for breakfast.

Reece swung his legs over the side and planted them on the floor. They were a touch shaky, but he managed to struggle to his feet. He made his way around the bed, pausing before the television. His reflection in it was little more than a faceless silhouette. In a flash, he saw how he must have looked in the night, eyes bulging and mouth stretched wide in silent terror. Reece turned his face away. He needed to check on Amaya.

He found her before the single-burner stove, tapping her foot to some internal rhythm. Reece rested his head on the doorframe. She was okay. There was music in her, just like always. He allowed himself a weary smile and to toy with the idea that maybe it had been nothing but a nightmare after all. He continued watching her in silence, not wanting to break from such a comfortable moment. After a time, she took to humming.

She'd been humming the first time he'd met her on an elevator back in Gaeta. Her hair had been shorter then, with spears of gold peeking out from beneath her cuffed beanie. Her air of sophistication had seemed to preclude an attachment to the ship, so he'd assumed her to be a local. Fearful of never seeing her again, he'd rattled off some pidgin about the fineness of the day, and his Italian had been too poor to know that the structure and delivery of her response had been similarly imperfect. He would later learn that despite growing up with an Italian father, she'd spoken very little of it at home and had dedicated her high school years to learning French instead.

Reece took a step forward and the floor creaked. Amaya met him with a grin. "Can't sneak up on me," she said, raising the spatula and flinging bits of egg onto the floor.

"Wouldn't dream of it," Reece said.

She returned to her cooking. "Memories of surprise tickle attacks tell a different story."

"I've evolved since then."

Amaya let out a sardonic laugh. "Since two weeks ago?"

"Yep. You wouldn't happen to have a cup of coffee for a changed man, would you?"

She gestured toward the pot and Reece poured himself a mug, as if all he needed to recover from the night's horrors was a morning jolt. "Breakfast will be ready in a jiff," she said.

Reece set his mug on the table without taking a seat. By all appearances, Amaya was her usual self, but he was having trouble shaking the image of those vacant eyes staring right through him. He placed his hands on her hips and drew his chest against her back. She continued her scraping and stirring, only mildly hindered. "How'd you sleep?"

"Peacefully," she said without hesitation. "How about you?"

Reece wanted to tell her the truth but didn't want to scare her, so he contented himself with knowing that if it had been real, she had no memory of it. "Like the dead," he said. Then he placed a kiss on the back of her head and returned to the table.

The coffee was rich and warm. Just what he needed to take the mysterious chill out of his bones. On the wall across from the table, the seconds ticked by on a clock decorated with a Roman fresco of a coiled snake, its obsidian eye trained upon its watcher.

2
THE CLOSET

As soon as Reece was back in Italy, he threw himself headlong into research about sleep paralysis. He found stories similar to his own on sites ranging from medical forums, where people attributed their experiences to neurological glitches, to those dedicated to the occult, where they blamed their attacks on everything from witchcraft to demon possession. The one thing they all seemed to agree on was that it only happened when they slept on their back.

Reece scrolled down to an artist's rendition of a shadow person standing at the foot of someone's bed, and the air took on a sudden chill. The resemblance to what he'd seen was uncanny. He stared at the image, his eyes going out of focus by measures until finally it was like he was back in Kythira, lying inert under the visitor's potent gaze.

Reece wanted to join the ranks of the incredulous, who even when confronted in their beds by direct evidence of the supernatural, still managed to brush it aside as a curious malfunction of the human machine. Perhaps then he'd be able to cast off this foreboding sense that something had changed between him and Amaya, a change he was beginning to suspect she felt too.

Amaya appeared in the doorway with startling quickness, and with a hurried click Reece switched to another browser tab. "What're you doin', Reecey?"

"Just browsing. Is your soap opera finished?"

"Soap operas are what my mother watches. This is a drama." She said the word with a flourish and a graceful movement of her hand. Her eyes then went to a stack of books teetering on the edge of collapse. "And it's a far sight more interesting than those musty old Greek stories you've always got your nose in."

Reece leaned back in his chair. "Those musty old stories are classics of the western canon. Something tells me the forbidden affair of that handsome young doctor with the permanent five o'clock shadow and his Tuscan winery heiress isn't going to echo through the ages in quite the same way."

Amaya stepped around his chair and draped her arms over his shoulders. "We have a forbidden affair. Are you saying you don't think it's going to echo through the ages?"

"Not saying that at all. Only that if it does, it'll probably be because it better resembles a Greek tragedy."

Amaya withdrew her arms and flicked him in the ear before leaving the room. Reece massaged the sting from his ear and craned his neck into the doorway. "It was a joke!" When she didn't respond, he added a tepid "Sorry." She went about pulling pots and pans from the cupboard. It was clear from the way she was handling them she wasn't the least bit upset. Reece returned his attention to the monitor and cycled back to the previous tab. The room in the painting of the shadow person looked far too much like Reece's own room for his liking.

At once, he felt a strong urge to bring Amaya into the fold, to help her understand why he had so much on his mind and to see how she reacted. These were the risks he needed to take if they were going to commit to each other for the rest of their lives. If the story of the visitor didn't scare her off, they would decide together what to believe, come what may. He would need to do it now while the desire was strong. There was no telling if he'd still have the nerve later.

A banging on the front door nearly startled Reece out his chair, and the impulse to reveal his hidden terrors sank into his feet. He went into the kitchen, where he and Amaya stood watching each other through worried eyes like a couple whose house was full of narcotics and had no idea whether the noise at the door was a sign of friend or foe. Reece made his way down the hall and then latched the chain before peering out through the opening. It was Dan Bennett, his roommate on the ship. "Open the door, Holloway. I need to talk to you."

Reece unlatched the chain and opened the door a bit wider. "You couldn't have called?"

"I did. Several times in fact."

"Sorry, ringer must be off." Reece opened the door a little more and lodged himself within the additional space. "What's this about?"

"It's about Sofia. She's driving me up a wall, man. I need to talk to someone sane."

"Sofia?"

"My girlfriend. You met her a couple weeks ago at that bar with the weird lighting."

"Oh, right," Reece said. "Sorry, I didn't know you were referring to your latest flavor of the month as your 'girlfriend.'"

"Will you cut the crap and let me in?"

"It's not a great time, Bennett. Can't we just talk about it here?"

"In the hallway? Wait. Is that Italian girlfriend of yours in there?" He tried to peek in over Reece's shoulder. "Let me meet her."

"No. I mean, no, she isn't here. It's just not a good time is all."

"Jesus, Reece, don't treat me like I'm some stray cat. It's raining outside, and I want to come in and sit down." Bennett ruffled his hair, releasing a mist of water.

"Fine, alright. Give me a minute to get some pants on." Reece closed the door and found Amaya waiting expectantly in the living room. He lowered his voice to a hush. "Dan Bennett's here, and he's all worked up over some girl. I know it's a pain, but would you mind hanging out in the bedroom with the door closed and keeping quiet for a while? I'll get rid of him as fast as I can."

Amaya had only just nodded her approval when Reece heard the door open. "I'm coming in, Holloway. That old lady in the next unit is giving me the evil eye, and it isn't like I haven't seen you pantsless before."

With Amaya now unable to cross into the bedroom, Reece hurried her toward the living room closet. For a frozen moment they stared at each other, her eyes seeming to ask if he was being serious and his broadcasting an aching remorse that unfortunately he was. If Bennett recognized her from the ship, word could get around. He was a good man, but he liked to talk. With no time left for discussion, Reece guided her in and closed the door behind her.

It wasn't long before Amaya's eyes began to mimic the stolen light, and swirls of patterned waves spilled across her vision. These were the colors she always searched for—the ones which always had a way of calming her when she was in a dark place. Outside the closet, she heard her sister's voice and almost called out to her but stopped herself when she became aware of a second presence. This voice was deeper. After a time, both voices faded into a whisper, and all Amaya could make out was the occasional creak of a bedspring and the rustling of sheets.

She wrapped her arms around her shins and waited. Then their voices grew more distinct, and she heard a boy say he had to get going. The bedroom door opened, then gently shut, and Amaya jabbed the closet door with her finger. It gave a little under the pressure but didn't open. She jostled the door again, and this time she heard footfalls on the carpet and the horizontal bars of light on the door grew dark. Someone pulled from the other side, then unwound the twine around the doorknobs. When the doors flung open, Amaya found Mallory glowering down at her. "You little shit! Are you spying on me?"

Amaya peered up at her through squinted eyes. "Yeah, Mal. I hid in here to spy on you, and I somehow managed to tie twine around the knobs to make sure I couldn't get back out."

Mallory examined the length of twine in her hand, her expression softening. "Mom's on the pills again, isn't she?"

Amaya said nothing and rested her chin between her knees. Mallory extended a hand toward her. "Come on out of there."

Amaya shook her head. "No. If she catches me outside—"

"She won't. Christ sakes, Amaya, she's not even gonna remember she put you in there."

Amaya thought about it for a moment and found her sister's reasoning sound. She offered her hand, and Mallory helped her to her feet. They stood like that for a while in awkward silence. Mallory and Amaya were close enough in years that they had to acknowledge each other's existence, but far enough apart that the workings of the other's mind were always somewhat foreign. Nothing better illustrated this rift than the line of demarcation which ran down the center of their room.

Mallory's black sheets were emblazoned with a cartoon skull, and her wall was a sprawling collage of counterculture fashion and inked young men with electric guitars slung over their shirtless torsos. A small fan scanned the area, its frame creaking with every movement. Plastic threads ripped from an old pom-pom flowed from its guard.

The aesthetic of Amaya's side of the room was one of soft, warm colors and clusters of stuffed animals packed in every conceivable space. A tiny box of a TV stood on a metal cart at the foot of her bed. A stack of tapes, mostly of the sort Mallory had lately taken to calling "insipid," framed it on either side.

On top of the TV, a collection of plastic figurines revealed Amaya's fondness for happy meals.

No longer able to bear the silence, Amaya opened her mouth to speak. She had no idea what she was going to say but figured anything would be an improvement over nothing. But before she could get a word out, their mother's voice sounded down the hall. "Mal! Mal!"

Mallory rushed Amaya back into the closet. Once inside, Amaya heard her wrapping the twine back around the knobs, then the bedroom door flung open and hit the wall where the missing doorstop used to be. "Who's that boy that just left?"

"None of your business," Amaya heard Mallory say, and she covered her mouth with both hands.

"You little tramp. Why can't you be more like your sister?"

Mallory laughed. "Amaya's twelve, Darlene." She'd said her mother's name as though she were spitting out something bitter.

Amaya flinched as the sound of a slap ushered in a silent moment. "I told you not to call me that. I'm your mother. Show me some respect."

"Show yourself some!"

Another period of quiet followed. Amaya knew from experience that this was the pivotal moment when her mother would either fly completely off the handle or back down. "Where is your sister anyway?"

"Probably off somewhere learning to be more like me." The bedroom door slammed shut with enough force to shake the room. After a while, Amaya heard the twine unwinding again, and the closet doors opened. "See? I told you she wouldn't remember." Amaya took a hesitant step out of the closet, examining the room around her as though to rule out any further danger. "Have a seat," Mallory said. Amaya started toward her bed, but Mallory took her by the arm and led her in the other direction. "Not over there. On my bed." Amaya hesitated. Unsavory things had happened there only moments before. But not wanting to turn her nose up at such a rare invitation, she sat down by her sister. "You hear how I just handled Darlene?" Amaya nodded that she had. "That's how you treat people who abuse you. Show them no mercy because they're sure as shit not gonna show you any."

"I understand," Amaya said. "So, who was the boy?"

Mallory took on a look of cynicism that went beyond her usual. "No one. No one at all."

Amaya understood well enough to leave well enough alone. She struggled to think of something else to say. "You're gonna be eighteen soon, Mal. Where you gonna go?"

"I'd like to say I'm going to the other end of the earth. But let's be real. I'm not goin' anywhere."

"I'm not goin' anywhere either," Amaya said. "We sisters need to stick together." She punctuated the sentiment with her best look of cheer, holding for as long as she could her sister's terrifying eyes.

Mallory gave her what Amaya took to be a thoughtful smile. It was if she were seeing her kid sister—really seeing her—for the first time. "Yeah. I guess we do." She reached out and mussed Amaya's hair, then snatched her bag off the bedpost and left the room.

3
MARSEILLE

Italy came and went in an instant. Reece had packed and shipped only the most necessary items, giving away or throwing away the rest. He'd received no further visits from the apparition, an outcome he credited to only sleeping on his side, often with Amaya held close in a protective shell.

But despite their physical closeness, emotionally they'd drifted apart. The closet incident had been a wake-up call for both of them. Amaya had said she understood why he'd done it and that there were no hard feelings, but he knew it had hurt her all the same. Their game had gotten a little too real. It was one thing huddling together in secret with the world outside their door. But once reality had gotten inside and shattered in one unannounced moment their carefully cultivated peace, it had all felt a whole lot less romantic. Even so, Reece kept the faith that things would get better soon. Once his remaining time was up, he would join Amaya's cousin in Milan. There he'd wait out her enlistment, using the time away to transition from naval officer to English teacher. Never again would they need to hide.

The ship's first stop was the French port of Marseille. After a full day of taking in the sights, Reece and two companions set out for an evening of pleasures, stopping first into a seaside bar where they were greeted by an antique diving suit propped up on a wooden frame. Reece examined its aged and oxidized helmet, noting with amusement that his interest was just as much piqued now as it had been earlier when he'd visited the Notre Dame de la Garde Basilica, above which a statue of the Madonna and Child kept watch over the city.

"That's what I'm talkin' about," Dan Bennett said to a chalkboard sign which read *Drink, Food, and Rock and Roll.*

"Looks like my kind of place," Dan Collins agreed. The extra Dan was Reece's coworker. He was a likable enough guy, and although they probably wouldn't have been as friendly under different circumstances, their similar station in life and workplace proximity made them compatible enough.

Moving beyond the entryway, Reece found a pub decorated in a Victorian nautical style. The ceiling was composed of patches of bolted metal, and the bar's brightwork gleamed under salvaged ship lights. All along the walls, ample portholes offered views of the sea painted with the colors of sunset. It was there Reece discovered something unexpected.

Beneath one of the portholes, Amaya was sitting with drink in hand, dispensing charm to her usual collection of acolytes.

"Time to load up," Collins said, heading for the bar.

Reece nodded without looking at him. The people two tables down from Amaya were getting up, and he rushed over, nearly blocking one of them from leaving. They gave him a look, and Reece smiled and took a step back, allowing them to exit. The moment they were gone, he thrust himself into one of the chairs. Amaya still hadn't seen him. Fearful of getting caught watching while sitting alone at a nearby table, Reece turned his attention to his companions at the bar, waving them over as soon as he made eye contact. They joined him soon after, Bennett with a pint in each hand. "Nice work, Holloway. Here, I got you a beer."

"Thanks, Bennett." Reece took the glass and raised it. "To serendipity."

The Dans exchanged amused glances and raised their own glasses. "To serendipity!"

Now that he no longer looked like a lone stalker, Reece felt more comfortable keeping a clandestine eye on Amaya. What a wonderful stroke of luck they'd had, wandering into the same bar. It was almost like being on liberty together. Apparently someone in her merry band of Capulets said something funny because the table erupted in laughter. Amaya smiled wide enough for her canine teeth to show, and Reece wished he was off somewhere with her instead of with the

Dans, who were at present embroiled in some tedious debate about college football. Reece did his best to tune them out, focusing instead on the pleasure of seeing her so carefree.

This was Amaya in the wild, uninfluenced by the observer effect common to all new romances. He longed for her to look at him like that—with joy so pure and unrestrained it would wash his doubts away. And he figured he could make that happen, right there in that bar, by finding a way to pull her aside and introduce her as his girlfriend to Dan Bennett, who he'd been wrong to mistrust. He'd do it too, if it weren't for Collins. Reece was so transported he hadn't noticed the man in question had moved in closer and was hovering just outside his ear.

"She's enlisted," he said in a harsh whisper.

"What? Who?"

"What are we talking about?" asked Bennett, who had his back to Amaya's table.

"Holloway was staring at that DiMartino chick."

"DiMartino?" Bennett looked as though he were about to turn around in his seat.

"Don't turn around!" Collins hissed. "The blonde. You know the one."

"Yeah, I know the one. Just didn't know she had a name."

Collins hooked one arm over the back of his chair. "Probably has a first name too. Something hot like Ashlynn."

"Or Lexie," Bennett said.

Collins chuckled. "Lexie DiMartino. Great porn star name."

Bennett let out his own chuckle before taking on a more thoughtful look. "DiMartino," he repeated. "Where do I know that name?"

Reece took a break from hating Collins to indulge in the fear that Bennett was about to reveal something horrible, something unknown even to him, but Collins swooped in and put an end to the suspense. "Pasta."

Bennett clapped his hands together. "That's it! Damn good pasta that."

Collins made a show of watching Amaya's table out of the side of his eye. "Yeah, she's quite a dish. Only thing she needs is a little—"

"Alright, stop right there," Reece said, holding one hand up like a traffic cop. "We both know what you're going to say next, so how about we just leave the rest to the imagination."

Collins raised an eyebrow. "I thought that's what I was doing."

Reece lowered his voice. "Let's just show the lady the respect of not verbally dragging her through our fantasies while she's sitting ten feet away."

"Holloway, she's not some Grand Duchess. She's a Deck ape. Prettiest one on the ship—hell, maybe even in the fleet—but a Deck ape, nonetheless. You'll find no finishing school graduates there. What's gotten into you anyway? We talk this way about girls all the time."

"Well, maybe we shouldn't. Especially not about this one. You said it yourself—she's enlisted. Talking about her like this is unbecoming of an officer."

Collins threw his head back and laughed so hard tears streamed down his cheeks. His body jostled like a washing machine with an uneven load as he expelled the last of it. "Who are you, and what have you done with Reece Holloway?"

Reece shrugged. "Maybe I'm just growing."

Collins laughed again, but it was the laugh of a man who'd spent all his mirth in one place, and it soon fizzled out. "Bullshit, Holloway."

Bennett planted his elbows on the table. "Now wait a minute. Maybe it's not bullshit. You have to admit, he has been pretty damn good since he started dating that Italian girl no one has ever seen. I, for one, believe him. Although to be perfectly honest, Holloway, I'm not sure I'd fault you for trading in that virtue for a shot at DiMartino, seeing as though you're a short-timer and all. Just let me know if you're planning to make a move so I can get out of here. I'm happy to attend the wedding, but I'd rather not be a witness at the court-martial."

"You guys are a scream, but I wasn't even looking at her. I was just staring off into the distance because you two wouldn't stop talking about football."

"Uh-huh," Bennett said.

"Sure," Collins agreed.

Reece emptied his pint. "Gonna get another beer." He stood and made his way to the bar, and once there, he ordered two more of the same.

While waiting for his drinks, he happened to glance down the bar. Amaya was at the other end, her blue eyes fixed upon his, grinning like a child with a secret. "Love you," she mouthed, and in an instant all his troubles fell away.

Reece glanced about, and seeing no familiar faces, he returned the sentiment. A moment later, the sound of two pints touching down stole his attention, and he paid with cheer, leaving his change behind. Intending to leave Amaya with a wink and a smile, he looked back in her direction, but this time he found her chatting with some rakish man who looked a whole lot like that soap opera doctor she was always drooling over. Reece could tell by the stilted cadence of her speech and the movement of her hands that she was attempting to converse in French, and at once he returned to being miserable. The interloper no doubt found her imperfect French quite charming.

To his relief, it looked like Amaya was seeing her way out of the conversation. After a few moments, she collected her drink and said goodbye with a little wave. Reece lingered on the face of the interloper, who was still leaning on the bar, watching Amaya with hungry eyes as she returned to her table. Gathering a pint in each hand, Reece made his way back through the crowd. He reached his table as she was taking her seat. Their eyes met, and she shot him a brief smile before returning her attention to her friends.

Reece had returned mid-conversation. "Nah, not worth the risk," he heard Bennett say. "Especially when the ship makes stops at places like this."

Reece set a fresh beer next to Bennett's empty glass. "What's not worth the risk?"

"Collins asked me if I'd ever banged an enlisted chick."

Reece groaned. "Fuck's sake, Collins. Are we still on that topic?"

"Afraid so, sport."

Bennett leaned in again. "Thanks for the refill, Holloway." They tapped their glasses together and each took a sip.

Collins held his empty hands out in front of him. "Where's mine?"

"Bennett got my last round," Reece said.

Collins frowned, then polished off the rest of his pint and brought the glass down on the table with a heavy thud. His face had gone pink. "Looks like I'm gonna have to get my own then. But first, we haven't heard your answer to the question, Holloway."

"Don't know what you're talking about," Reece said.

"Oh, yes you do. So how about it? Any enlisted notches on your bedpost? And before you answer, jerking off to that Deck slut doesn't count."

It wasn't Reece's best punch. It was all arm, as sitting punches are given to be, and it was so wide it nearly grazed the tip of Bennett's nose on its arching journey to Collins's chin. But the shock alone knocked Collins out of his chair. It probably didn't help that he'd been in the middle of laughing. He tumbled legs up onto the floor, his empty glass rolling off the table and shattering beside him. Those mingling near the table backed away, setting the stage for them to do whatever the hell came next. The bartender was shouting at Reece in French, but Reece was more worried about the pissed off guy struggling up off the floor.

By the time Collins was on his feet, he was all hands. He gripped Reece's shirt in one fist and rained down crude blows with the other. Reece tucked his chin into his chest and threw a flurry of his own. It wasn't long before their phone booth fight was moving around the bar like a small tornado, prompting a mix of cheers, insults, and indignant yelps as French girls tried to stay clear of its path.

After a minute, each man was leaning on the other's shoulder, sucking deep breaths and pushing with whatever strength he had left. When it was clear neither could continue, Collins collapsed onto a barstool. Reece leaned forward and put his hands on his knees, peering just over his arm in the direction of Amaya's table. She was gone.

Reece straightened up and scanned the bar, ignoring the yelling bartender, who'd discovered a sudden fondness for the word *police*. The rakish man who'd hit on Amaya was nowhere to be found. Without a moment's hesitation, Reece made for the front door and burst out into the open air. To his right, he found only shadows and silence. To his left, a car was disappearing into the night, its crimson taillights fading into the distance like the eyes of a nosferatu sinking into the fog. If ever there was a time to break their no-texting-on-liberty rule, this was it. Reece patted himself down in search of his phone, only to remember he'd left it on the ship.

There would be time for despair later. Right now he needed to put some distance between him and the bar before the cops arrived. The Dans wouldn't be sticking around for much longer either if they knew what was good for them. Soon after he started walking, Reece felt a wetness on his chin and touched it with his hand. Blood. Unsure where it was coming from, he ran his fingers over his lips and checked his teeth with his tongue. His nose wasn't broken, but it was bleeding. Reece reached into his jacket pocket and retrieved the handful of napkins he'd stuffed in there at lunch. He dabbed them around his face and they came back clean. He'd gotten away with nothing more than a nosebleed. With any luck, neither he nor Collins would be marked up enough to prompt any questions.

A row of boats rocked along a multicolored band of light emanating from the shore. Reece crumpled the napkins in his hand and held them to his nose, all the while trying to dismiss the nightmare taking shape in his thoughts. But it wasn't long before memories of a high school beach party took an axe to that closed door. Unbeknownst to him at the time, his first love had wandered into a grove of trees with the captain of the wrestling team while Reece was drinking with friends a stone's throw away. And as the grand finale to his humiliation, once the star athlete had taken his fill, he came and shook Reece's hand. Reece could still see through the haze of memory that boy's smug grin, and now he was powerless not to imagine the same look of self-admiration on the face of the interloper.

After a time, he reached a curve in the road, and wanting to rest, he clambered down onto the moss and rocks which comprised the shore. The adrenaline from the fight had worn off, and he was beginning to feel Collins's punches. Knots of pain appeared across his body, calling to each other like frogs across a swamp. Reece wondered how Collins was faring and felt a pang of regret over having caused the whole ridiculous scene. The man was an asshole, but there was no way he could've known who he'd been insulting.

Reece removed the napkins and found that his nose was no longer bleeding. A thicket of clouds swept away the moonlight, leaving the ocean coal black. Reece stared into that void, not knowing why it demanded his attention. Visions flashed through his mind, and they remained whether he had his eyes open or closed. He saw Amaya in the passenger's seat of the interloper's car. She was reaching across the gearshift and unbuckling his pants. In the next vision, he saw only the interloper's face grinning with pleasure. Each shifting of the gearstick arrived with the sound of violence as they tore their way down the road. *Thunk. Thunk. Thunk.* The interloper's eyes burned with orange fire, and when he licked his lips, it was with the searching tongue of a serpent.

The headlights of an approaching vehicle broke Reece from his trance, and he flattened himself on the rocks until it passed. Again the images flickered across his field of vision. Uninvited, unwanted, but inevitable. Intrusive imagery. Part and parcel with his anxiety, or so he'd been told. But this was somehow different. He rubbed his eyes with both hands, and the images relented long enough to allow him to take stock of his sanity. But it wasn't long before the void resumed its call.

After a time, the ocean began to bubble, and an amber glow grew in strength until the crown of some byzantine device pierced the water's surface. It appeared to be some sort of lantern, a dozen feet tall and half as wide. Water cascaded down its lenses as they rotated at intervals, casting prismatic colors onto Reece's eyes. The lantern expanded and contracted like a lung. Reece hesitated to call it breathing, but he had no doubt it was alive. From its center the primary lens watched, a living eye of polished glass—the eye of night itself—gazing into Reece as he gazed into it. And from within this carnival of light he heard the words *"final home"* whispered like a death sigh.

4

VALLETTA

The sky outside the window of Reece's hotel room looked like it had been drawn with blue and pink pastel chalks. Beneath it was a view of Valletta Harbor, entryway to the fortified city built by the Knights Hospitaller after repelling Ottoman invaders from its shores. Along the edge of the harbor stood an expanse of beige structures, their uniform outline broken in one place by the sharp spire of St. Paul's Cathedral and bulging in another by the rounded dome of the Basilica of Our Lady of Mount Carmel.

Reece picked up his phone and clicked into his email, finding nothing he hadn't already read. Amaya wasn't happy about the way he'd behaved in Marseille, although explaining how he'd only been defending her honor had lowered the temperature a few degrees. Even so, the fight had driven another wedge between them. Naturally, she'd blamed her quick exit on a fear of becoming involved. He hadn't asked about the interloper. There was no point in doing so over email, or perhaps not at all as he sometimes felt in his more thoughtful moments.

He dropped his phone into the armchair and went into the bathroom to prepare for his foray into Valletta's nightlife. Bennett had put a great deal of effort into a peace deal between Reece and Collins, and they were due to seal it with a handshake within the hour. Reece had no real interest in squaring things with Collins, but doing so would go a long way toward showing Amaya that things were going back to normal. On top of that, it meant a lot to Bennett.

The shower's water pressure was on the weak side but it was plenty hot, and before long Reece stood engulfed in a cloud of steam. Water ran in twisting coils down his arms and into the palms of his hands, tracing a path down each finger and dispersing like streams of energy. What had he really seen in Marseille? And what had he heard? He saw again the saltwater passing from the lantern's eye and back into the sea like a flood of tears. "Final home," it had said, and the words had sounded like an invitation. After that, things got hazy. The next thing Reece clearly recalled was standing shirtless in front of his stateroom mirror. Maybe Collins had rung his bell harder than he'd thought.

After the shower, he dried himself with the luxurious hotel towel and changed into a fresh set of clothes. He decided to leave the top two buttons of his shirt undone. Though he had no intention of attracting any local wildlife, it never hurt to look like he could.

Reece headed back into the bedroom, and as he was putting on his watch, he noticed that the indicator on his phone was blinking. As he drew near, the fuzzy letters on the screen took the shape of Amaya's name. A text? What could be so urgent that she would break their rule? Reece fastened the clasp on his watch and picked up the phone.

"I'd rather tell you this in person but it can't wait until we meet again. I went to medical this morning and they said I'm pregnant. What should I do??"

Reece let go of the phone as though it had bit him. He was having trouble stringing thoughts together and wondered if perhaps he'd imagined the contents of the message. He dropped to his knees and read the words again. *Medical. Pregnant.* He could already hear Collins's cutting reproach. "Well, Holloway. You've gone and knocked her up. Anything else you'd care to do to cement your place as the biggest scumbag in the officer's mess, or do you reckon this about covers it?"

Reece clambered onto the bed. The sky outside had grown darker, and the cathedral's spire was now bathed in orange so that it looked like a piece of iron fresh out of a forge. Why should any of this come as a shock? He'd taken no pains to prevent it, and Amaya had always let him do whatever he wanted as long as it aligned with her carefully marked calendar. Even if she'd miscalculated, he couldn't put the blame on her. This was on him for failing to show even a modicum of restraint.

But once he'd gathered his thoughts, a brighter picture emerged. While the news should come as no surprise, neither should it be ill-received. In truth, it was everything he could have hoped for wrapped in a big red bow. As for the delicacy of the matter vis-à-vis their ranks, Amaya would be under no obligation to reveal the father's identity, and in any case, Reece would soon be a civilian. Furthermore, they'd place Amaya on shore duty for the remainder of her enlistment, removing the ever-present threat of charming wolves in exotic locations. With full stock of his blessings taken, Reece chanced a smile. It felt right, like it belonged there. He tapped out a reply.

"Best news ever. Looks like we're going to have to update our plan!"

Amaya replied in seconds with a smiley face and a string of hearts. Not wanting to risk spoiling what was already a perfect moment, Reece slipped the phone into his pocket, snatched his room key off the mini fridge, and made his way to the lobby. If only he could reveal to the Dans after a half dozen drinks that they were actually at his bachelor party and that he would soon be riding off into the sunset with "that DiMartino chick."

It would almost be worth the risk just to see the look on their faces. At the very least, he would have to stay in touch with them once this phase of his life was over. A photo of Reece and Amaya Holloway in front of the Milan Cathedral would make a perfect punch line to their private joke.

When Reece arrived in the lobby, smile lines appeared around the elderly concierge's eyes. "Good evening, Mr. Holloway."

"Good evening," Reece said, matching his cheerful tone.

"Will you be needing a taxi?"

Reece set his room key on the desk. "I'm not sure. I'm meeting some friends on Strait Street."

"About a ten-minute walk that way. And what a lovely evening for a walk it is."

Reece agreed and headed for the glass door. Once outside, he took a moment to breathe the evening air and to allow his nerves to settle. A mild tingling had taken residence in his fingertips, and he gave his hands a good shake while exhaling through pursed lips, then set off toward his destination. Strait Street was the supposed nucleus for those seeking a night of excess in Valletta, and a bit of excess was just what Reece needed. The majority of the ship's crew had no doubt descended upon it the moment the sun had set, if not hours before. Reece wondered what he would do if he found Amaya there with a beer in hand, but he quickly dismissed the notion. She'd never do anything to harm their child.

After a block and half, Reece stopped in the middle of a side street. Or more accurately, he was stopped, but by what he couldn't say. Before him lay as steep a decline as any he'd ever seen paved. At the bottom, it dipped through a bustling cross-street before climbing just as sharply on the other side and continuing into the skyline. Reece recalled from his guidebook that the city's founders had designed its streets with such an uncommon gradient to thwart the advance of enemy soldiers laden with heavy armor. A fine idea in its time, but of little use against an enemy in no need of armor, or even earth beneath its feet. Reece tried to break free of his stasis, to continue in the direction of Strait Street, but his legs wouldn't obey. Suddenly he was burning up, and it became his most urgent task not to collapse in the middle of the road and become a speed bump for the next car which happened to pass by.

Once on the sidewalk, he braced himself against a street sign. Sweat dripped from his forehead and stung his eyes. He squeezed them shut and tried to envision the photo he'd send the Dans. It appeared in sharp detail, a living representation of a life going just as planned. But it soon became corrupted. With a gust of wind the sunlight faded, and Amaya's smile morphed into the satisfied grin of a day-walking dhampir, the grim outline of her victim's skull luminescent behind his gaunt face.

Reece opened his eyes, and the image dissipated like smoke. It was clear he was in no condition to be out in the world. The last thing he wanted to convey to the Dans after what had happened in Marseille was that he was now having a complete mental breakdown. His feet felt like lead, but with effort he made it back to the hotel. The concierge broke from writing in his ledger to welcome Reece back. "Have you changed your mind about going out, Mr. Holloway?"

"Yes," Reece said, placing both hands on the counter. But he withdrew them once he saw how much they were sweating. He wiped the counter with his sleeve as the concierge watched, his true thoughts about this strange man no doubt hidden behind his mask of cordiality. "I'd like six bottles of beer and a bucket of ice, please. Whatever kind you've got."

"I'll have them sent up right away." The concierge handed Reece his key and gestured toward the elevator. Despite the old timer's cheery disposition, Reece still felt as though the ferryman himself had taken him across the river Styx and was now inviting him to bear as he might the consequences of the hereafter. He drifted to his room without taking notice of anything in particular. There was beer on the way. That would take care of his jitters, his fear that something wicked was coming, or perhaps already there.

Reece unlocked the door and entered the room. Once inside, he took a seat at the foot of the bed. It was easy to blame his turmoil on the unexpected news. Far too easy in fact, considering how he now found himself beneath the lantern's gaze whenever he closed his eyes. What did it want?

Why was this happening when everything was going just right? And where were those goddamn beers?

A knock on the door tore him from his contemplations. Reece stood and approached with caution, looking first through the peephole before touching the handle. From the other side, the eye of the lantern watched, cold and unflinching. Reece stumbled backward until he toppled onto the floor. Again the knock resounded. It was gentle—not the sort meant to menace but to show deference. Reece climbed back to his feet and approached a second time, this time skipping the peephole and going straight for the handle. He flung open the door.

Outside, a uniformed attendant cradled a bucket in the crook of his arm. A half dozen bottlenecks peeked out from the ice. Reece bid the man inside, where he placed the delivery on the table, then waited expectantly. "For your trouble," Reece said, handing him a wad of damp bills. Once the man was gone, he shut and latched the door.

Reece popped open a beer and emptied it by a quarter. Then he took several more gulps on his way to the window. Somewhere out there, the Dans were probably musing about how he was late and how it really wouldn't surprise them if he didn't show up at all. "Let them have their laughs," Reece said. He pulled the phone from his pocket and reopened Amaya's last message. It was gone, and something else was in its place.

"I never said it was yours."

Before Reece had a chance to register his horror, the sound of shifting feet prompted him to spin to the rear, but he found only the silent room behind him. At the end of a long breath, a tap on the windowpane sent him whirling back around. Nothing but darkened glass, and beyond it the broken moon, hovering between the spire and the dome. It was many long moments before he was able to swallow again, and it took several more before he mustered the courage to look back at his phone.

When he did, he found only the smile and hearts Amaya had sent him earlier. The cruel message was gone, and Reece struggled without success to even remember what it had been. This must be what it felt like to go insane. To shift the window of experience until anything beyond abject terror seemed like a reprieve, until even madness itself was business as usual.

Reece moved his bucket of beer to the bedside table, then turned on the television and climbed into bed, a bottle held close to his chest like a child with a favorite doll. Some Maltese drama was playing out on the screen. A man in a doctor's coat was laying some heavy news on a distraught woman as he held her by the arms to keep her from collapsing to the floor. Reece was unable to follow the plot, but he was content to experience anything outside the tumult of his inner world. He drank until his fear was nothing more than the distant rumbling of thunder, and once it became clear that another sip would be a profitless burden, he set the final bottle on the table and told himself the timeless lie that he was just going to rest his eyes.

Moments passed, stretching and contracting in the murky waters between waking and sleep. When Reece next opened his eyes, the shade of night outside the window was the same, but the television program had ended. The screen was a solid blue, and a continuous sine wave filled the air. Reece reached for the remote but paused as he heard the hiss of the shower turning on. Before long, Amaya's gentle hum joined the chorus.

Reece's eyes filled with tears. He wasn't sure where he was, either on earth or in the greater span of time. Through his blurred vision, the blue of the TV was an oblong smear. Then the color faded, and Reece blinked his eyes. The screen now depicted Amaya in the shower. She was shampooing her hair while gazing into the camera. The interloper from Marseille stood behind her, grinning with sharp, jagged teeth. His eyes were two blazing coals.

Reece sprung up off the bed and rushed into the bathroom. There was no one in the shower, nor was it even on, but the smell of hot water on flesh still hung heavy. Returning to the room, he found that the image on the TV had changed to a still of his own face, grinning like an idiot— and the sine wave had morphed into the noise of a thousand insects skittering across a forest floor. Reece passed his frozen image, only stopping once he reached the window.

He gazed out toward the line of demarcation between the ocean and sky, and the shades of darkness above and below, which moved like a black veil in the wind. He would need to address the Amaya situation sooner than later. That much was clear. He retrieved his phone from the bedside table and opened a reply.

"I want to see you. Meet me on the aft port sponson at midnight our first night underway."

And then as a second text, he added *"I love you."*

Reece shut off his phone, turned off the television and the lights, and lay down in bed on his back. The room was still and silent, its darkness tinged by nothing more than the golden glow of the harbor. He heard a door open out in the hall. Someone was leaving their room, but that wasn't who Reece was waiting for. The one he was waiting for was already there and had been in the room for some time.

A familiar shadow fell over Reece's nervous system. This time he didn't struggle, nor did he close his eyes. He sensed the visitor moving across the room, first in front of the bed and then along the side. He kept his eyes fixed on the ceiling, even as the visitor crouched beside him and released a slow growl into his ear. But it soon became clear that this too was not the one he was waiting for. The next sound he heard was the plaintive cry of an animal being chased away from its food, and Reece became aware of a second presence in the room.

This time he closed his eyes. He tried to determine by sense alone the second entity's location. Gone was the heat of enmity he'd come to expect from the visitor. In its place he felt the soft pull of longing, of wanting and being wanted in return, and at once he understood that it wasn't standing beside him, or at the foot of the bed. It was hovering right over him.

Even with his eyes shut, Reece saw in flashes. First, he saw the eyes of a spider, up close and shining, eight shimmering globes moving in unison. Next, he saw a procession of neon scales like a snake slithering across his vision, coiling ever tighter around his mind. Finally, he saw the lantern hovering over the deep, its unblinking eye calling him to the infinite waters. It pulsed with light, and all of Reece's dark colors turned to brightness.

The brightness imploded like a dying star, and Reece sat up in bed. The television was on again. After several moments of static, a middle-aged man in round-lensed spectacles appeared. He was wearing a white lab coat, and behind him a wasp was perched upon a caterpillar. The man spoke without introduction, his falsetto Italian-accented voice warbling as though it were passing through the rapidly spinning blades of a fan.

"The parasitoid wasp is one of the most remarkable killers in the natural world. While the adult gets her nutrition from nectar, her offspring subsist on decidedly grimmer fare." He gestured toward the image behind him before continuing. "Take the wasps of the genus *Glyptapanteles*. After identifying her prey, the female injects her fertilized eggs into its body. Therein her larvae grow, feasting upon the host's blood. Once they develop, they gnaw their way through the host's skin while releasing chemical paralytics into its bloodstream." The video showed a close-up of a grub, the tip of its body opening to reveal rows of tiny, saw-like teeth.

The view then shifted to the outside of the caterpillar. Its skin stretched and bulged as the larvae burst from its body. The man continued. "Once they've emerged, the larvae begin the work of building their cocoons. But the unhappy host's ordeal is not over. With the wasps still in charge, the caterpillar blankets the cocoons in its own silk and then acts as a mind-controlled bodyguard for the growing brood."

The video now depicted the caterpillar with its body arched over the silken mound, snapping left and right at approaching enemies. "Once they reach full maturity, the adults emerge from their cocoons and fly away, leaving what's left of their protector in a state of fatal inertia."

All along the walls, faces of men unknown to Reece emerged like Roman death masks. He knew they'd come to bear witness, both to his awakening and to his rejection of the parasite. But most importantly, they'd come to welcome the one who would replace his sore and broken will.

The television now depicted a darkened sea. At its center, a distant light winked at him from the horizon. Reece's limbs shivered, and saliva dripped onto his chin. His final home was waiting. But he would not be welcome there until he showed Amaya to hers.

5

THE SPONSON

Their first night at sea in route to the Greek island of Crete was as black as charred wood, so much so that Reece couldn't see his hand in front of his face as he stood on the sponson waiting for Amaya. Minutes crept by until the breaking of the hatch's seal announced her arrival. His pulse quickened as she appeared in the hatchway, bathed in the red glow of the ship's nocturnal lighting. After some hesitation, she crossed its threshold, and the hatch groaned shut behind her, snuffing out the light. Her faltering voice broke through the hush of wind and churning water. "I'm here," she said, but Reece remained silent. Her fear was palpable, even in the open air. "Shit. Are you even out here?"

Reece opened his mouth, and words he could scarcely call his own emerged like a swarm of locusts. "It's dark tonight."

"Jeez, you scared me. Where are you, Reecey?"

Reece held out his hand. "Come find me."

"Okay," Amaya said after a long pause. Her boots ground against the rough material of the deck as she pivoted in the dark, feeling around for him. Finally, her hand brushed against his, and she rushed into his arms. He held her close, stroking her hair, but before they could exchange another word, Reece saw in a flash the eyes of the spider. It spoke without words, reminding him of his purpose. She belonged beneath the waves, and it was his job to send her there, lest the lantern close its eye on him forever. He ran his hands down her back, searching for the grip best suited to send her over the railing with a simple lift and push.

Correct timing would be essential. Her lungs would need to be empty to ensure a silent fall. Reece focused on the feeling of her breath on his neck, soft and shallow as she searched for his mouth. Once she found it, she placed a kiss on his lower lip and tried to draw his mouth onto hers. Despite its warmth, Reece found within himself no ability to respond in kind, not even for the purpose of drawing from her that crucial sigh. Amaya took in a sharp breath and stepped back, her arms sliding through his upturned hands until he closed them around her wrists, preventing further retreat. "Reece?"

He swallowed hard. "Yes?"

"I'm afraid."

"Afraid of the dark?"

"Of you."

The water dashed against the ship. "Why would you be afraid of me?"

"You seem different."

The ideal moment to act had passed. Reece was going to have to make do with whatever opportunity remained. He tightened his hands around her wrists, and when she tried to free herself, he pulled her back in close, securing her body to his. Rather than resume her struggle, Amaya began sobbing into his chest, and Reece found himself gripped by indecision. He pressed his nose against her hair, breathing in the familiar scent of her shampoo. From somewhere buried deep, a panicked voice shouted for him to wake up.

No more than a hundred feet from the sponson, a patch of water brightened red as if by the light of a flare. Within that space the lantern appeared, hovering over a whirlpool, its downdraft drinking endlessly of the void. A chorus of whispers resounded at overlapping intervals, each finishing another's broken thoughts, often with jarring changes in tone and character.

"Throw her over the side. Like the TRASH she is. Had one just like her myself. Disgusting. PARASITE. Probably not even yours. Rip your goddamn heart out. Right OUT. If you let it. Don't let it. Just toss her. Over the side. Something better. In your final home."

Reece gritted his teeth so hard he thought they might shatter in his mouth, and he squeezed Amaya so tightly she let out a whimper. He placed his lips against her ear. "Is it really mine, Amaya?"

Amaya stopped her sobbing and took to beating against his chest until he loosened his grip. "Of course it's yours, you fucking asshole!" Fearful that the watch might hear them, Reece covered her mouth with his hand. Amaya struggled for a time before giving up and resuming her weeping. Her body shuddered in spasms and warm tears trickled down the back of Reece's fingers as he listened for footsteps on the deck above. After a time, he released the pressure of his hand just enough to see if she would try to scream. When she didn't, he dropped his hand to her shoulder, then let both hands fall to his sides. Though free to escape, she didn't let go. It was as though with darkness all around, she didn't know what else to hold onto.

Reece gazed out at the lantern, and it gazed back without speaking, gently expanding and contracting over the swirling waters. "Why are you doing this to me?" he asked, not even knowing he'd spoken the words aloud.

Amaya raised her face from his chest. "I was about to ask you the same thing."

Reece took her arms and removed them from around his waist, then stepped backward until he hit something solid. He wanted her to run to safety, but she just stood there sniffling and making noises that sounded like tiny hiccups. And through it all he just listened, unable to make himself speak the words needed to save her. Eventually it became clear that she was gearing up to say something, and Reece became terrified because there was no telling what he might say in return, if he was able to say anything at all. "I don't know what's happened to you, Reece. But the baby's yours. I'm yours."

Off on the water, his vision of the lantern had faded. For a moment, he allowed himself to believe that the threat had passed, that all he needed to do to mend their broken ties was to crawl on his hands and knees until he found her boots and then weep and beg for her forgiveness. But instead his body seized, and the image of an electric pyramid, its capstone bejeweled with the jittering eyes of the spider, dominated his field of vision. Then a double helix of neon scales twisted across the canvas of night until all that remained of Reece were lies, and bitterness, and a tongue that was no longer his to control. "I don't want you," he heard himself say. "I don't want anything you have to offer."

Amaya's tears became heaving sobs as the waves crashed against the ship. Reece stumbled toward the bulkhead and located the hatch with his hands, thrust it open, and stepped into the crimson light. He could already feel his memory of the moment leaving him. As he was closing the hatch, the crying stopped. He paused in place, peering out into the final sliver of blackness as he listened. The waves had taken on the sound of rustling leaves, and he even heard the chirping of crickets and the movement of night's creatures as they skittered across the forest floor. Fearful of its secrets, Reece pulled the hatch shut.

The scream of Reece's alarm clock yanked him right through the layer of confusion that usually characterized his return from sleep. He normally awoke to Bennett's alarm and only set his as a backup, so he knew he had no time to waste. He swung his legs over the side of the bunk and hopped down onto the deck, finding Bennett already gone. While shaving and dressing, Reece turned over the events of the previous night in his head. He remembered meeting with Amaya, but he could recall little beyond the faintest details.

On his way back from muster, Reece thought he heard the sound of laughter echoing down the passageway. He stopped and scanned both ways, finding nothing but the occasional shipmate passing through the telescoping expanse of hatches.

Once back in his office, Reece settled in front of his computer. He reached for the power button but froze in place as he noticed the dim reflection of his face in the monitor. Again he heard laughter. Its character was that of a bully celebrating a victim's defeat. Then the darkened reflection shifted, and there in the monitor was Amaya's face, resting under rippling waters. He searched again the fog of memory for what had happened on the sponson, but the more he searched, the thicker the fog became.

It wasn't long before the words "man overboard" sounded over the 1MC, and following the rescue team's return, news quickly spread that Amaya was gone. Minutes bled into hours and hours into days, throughout which Reece felt nothing, as though his body was merely a shell he'd crawled into. The theme of how tragic it was that the girl had died so young pervaded conversations, but no one said a word to Reece they wouldn't have said to anyone else, so he carried on with ghost-like detachment from the pain of those around him until the date of his separation.

On the day, Bennett got emotional and gave him a big hug, but afterward looked disappointed at Reece's response. The Reece he was saying goodbye to wasn't the same one he'd known. After a dozen or so more handshakes and idle promises to keep in touch, Reece found himself on a plane with Italy growing ever smaller behind him, until finally it disappeared under a blanket of clouds. It was as if the weeks had passed in the blink of an eye.

The drink cart stopped alongside Reece's seat, and he ordered a whiskey and coke from the attendant. She poured his drink and then pushed the cart to the next row. Reece raised the shaking cup to his lips, but as soon as he took a swallow the sensation of something being dragged over the back of his tongue caused him to gag, and he nearly vomited on the tray table. The attendant wasn't halfway through her inquiry about how he was feeling when he bolted from his seat and headed for the restroom. By some miracle, it was unoccupied. He latched the door behind him and planted his hands against the wall, then emptied the contents of his stomach into the silver hole at the bottom of the toilet. Once there was nothing left to expel, he rinsed his mouth in the sink. It was then he felt the beginning of a whimper pressing against his chest.

After a month of feeling nothing, he suddenly felt everything all at once. The fog had cleared, and everything which had happened on the sponson was his to see. What had he done to his Amaya, and why had he done it? He searched further back, to Valletta and Marseille. Dim memories like scraps of unburned paper in a pile of charred letters told a partial story of an alien presence that had tried to drive him to murder, and even though he hadn't taken the matter into his own hands, in the end, it had succeeded.

Reece wanted to return to the cabin and pull the latch on the emergency door, sending himself off into white oblivion, but he couldn't abide making anyone else pay for his weakness. If he were going to walk that path, he would walk it alone. The coming days and weeks would reveal if he had the stomach for such a journey.

6

SERENITY

Although his friends and family were happy to have him back, it was no secret that a piece of Reece hadn't survived the trip. He was often sullen and withdrawn, and even those who knew him best hadn't the faintest clue what had happened an ocean away. Not being able to come clean was eating him up inside. A confession booth was not the answer—whether he'd sinned or not was a question that could wait. Nor was a psychiatrist's couch where he needed to be, having already indulged in enough introspection to last a lifetime. What Reece needed was to speak to someone Amaya had cared about, to make himself remember in their presence, and to admit that all excuses aside, he had let her die.

Amaya had sometimes spoken of a sister who worked at a gentlemen's club back in their hometown. He even knew the name of the place, thanks to how often she'd recounted her snap decision to walk into a recruiter's office rather than follow big sis's footsteps through those beaded curtains. And so he'd set off with a couple changes of clothes and a hope that beyond the long, gray miles ahead, he'd find some glimmer of mercy.

Reece had been priming himself for hours, taking expert care to drink enough liquid courage to get him through the door, but not so much that his words would seem suspect once he was inside. He'd chosen vodka for the occasion, as any professional drinker would have done in his shoes.

The phone rang. His taxi was waiting outside. He took the elevator down to the lobby, left his key without a word, and exited into the front lot. Within fifteen minutes, the driver dropped him off on a neon-soaked street, half the worse for wear but ready as he'd ever be.

The doorman glanced at Reece's ID and waved him in. He hadn't been to a place like this in years, and it didn't take him long to remember why. The music was obnoxious, and the lighting was such as to just barely conceal how absurd the whole ritual was. Reece took a seat at a corner table away from the crowd. A waitress who looked like she'd seen better days swooped by about a minute later. "What can I get you, hon?"

"I'm looking for a woman named Mallory DiMartino. I'm told she works here."

The waitress eyed him with suspicion. "Don't know anyone by that name."

Reece suspected she was lying. "Alright. What name do you know her by then?"

The waitress planted one hand on her hip and twisted her mouth. "Keep it up and I'll have you tossed out."

Reece raised his hands from the table in acquiescence. "Sorry. It's just that I've come a long way to speak to her."

"Buy a drink and have a look around. Maybe you'll find what you're looking for."

Reece ordered a beer and did as she asked, taking in the details of each dancer's face one at a time. After a while, a strawberry blonde appeared beside him and asked if he'd like to buy her a drink. He repeated his question to her and got a similar answer. Were they just being cagey, or had Mallory moved on? She had no social media presence, at least not that Reece had been able to find. Maybe she only existed as a figment of his warped memories.

The music stopped, and the DJ dropped his voice to a lower register to announce the next performer. "Alright, everybody. Let's give it up for Serenity." A smattering of applause arose from the crowd, and an alluring rhythm filled the atmosphere. Serenity slinked onto the stage in step with its cadence, then wrapped herself around the pole and twirled to the floor.

Nothing could have prepared Reece for how much she looked like Amaya. Though her dark roots were visible even from a distance, her hair was dyed the same shade of blonde as Amaya's natural color. She had about a half dozen tattoos to Amaya's zero, but their physique and skin tone were near matches. As for her facial features, the two might have been mistaken for twins if not for a few subtle differences.

Mallory went through her routine with bored detachment, but halfway through, their eyes met for a moment, and all Reece could see was Amaya watching him from the end of a seaside bar in what now felt like another life. When the lighting effects kicked on, patches of rippling blue appeared across her body and on the wall behind her, making her look as though she were moving underwater. Reece felt the claws of panic climbing his spine. He struggled against the urge to leave, only holding himself in place by white-knuckling the edges of his chair.

Once her set was over, Mallory made her way down the steps, stopping at the bottom to speak to the strawberry blonde. The girl said something in her ear, and they looked in Reece's direction together. This was it. Either he was about to be thrown out on his ass, or he was going to get what he came for. He wasn't sure which outcome was worse.

Mallory approached and took a seat at his table without asking. She looked him over for a time, and Reece didn't interrupt her. "Who does he owe money to this time?"

"He?" Reece asked.

"Never mind," she said, crossing her legs. "What can I do for you, Mr....?"

"Holloway. Reece. Do either of those names mean anything to you?"

"Nope. Now how about you tell me why my name means something to you."

Reece felt like he wanted to vomit. This was a mistake, but one he had to see through. He drew a napkin from the dispenser and wiped his forehead, then crumpled it in his hand. "I was Amaya's boyfriend."

Mallory raised her eyebrows in the same way Amaya used to. "You mean like in high school?" A look of disgust formed on her face. "If you're sick enough to think that's some kind of in with me—"

"No, no," Reece said. "It's nothing like that. And I don't mean high school." He dropped the balled-up napkin and wiped his hands on his jeans under the table. "I mean at the end."

Her expression didn't change, but it was clear he had her attention. "Buy me a private dance."

"Done," Reece said.

Mallory stood and offered him her hand, then led him to a private room and closed the door behind them. While the main room was lit by shades of purple and pink, the room they were in was bathed in a red which reminded Reece of the ship's nocturnal lighting. Mallory took a seat at the booth. "Sit down, Reece. Tell me why you're here."

Reece sat near her, but not too near. He fidgeted for a time, trying to find a comfortable position, but eventually realized there wasn't one. None of this was supposed to be comfortable after all. "Amaya and I were living together in Italy. We were planning on moving to Milan after the Navy. Your cousin, the one who runs the English language school, was going to give me a job."

"You know about my cousin, huh? Well, I guess you're not completely full of shit. Funny though how Amaya never mentioned you to anyone back home."

Reece struggled under the pressure of her scrutiny. Her eyes were just like Amaya's, but harder. Even her voice was similar. "We had to keep things secret. I was an officer."

Mallory folded her arms and leaned back in her seat. "Mm, it's all coming together now. You saw her down on her hands and knees scrubbing the floor and figured you'd have a piece of that." The rawness of emotion in her voice put the lie to her flippant veneer. "How long did it take you to convince her that you actually cared?"

"That's not at all the way it went. We weren't even in the same department. And believe me, she didn't take much convincing. I was enamored with her from the start."

Mallory gave a dismissive wave and looked away. A shine had come over her eyes. "I suppose I can believe that. Now if you wouldn't mind getting to your point."

Reece rested his elbows on his knees and wrung his hands. When he spoke, he did so without looking at her. "Amaya was pregnant, and I was the father. I said some cruel things to her when she told me. Things I didn't mean. She killed herself that night."

For a while he just listened to the muffled beat of the music outside the door. When he looked back at Mallory, he saw that the whites of her eyes had gone pink. She clutched her arms and leaned in over her bare legs as if she suddenly couldn't stand being quite so naked in front of him. "So, let me get this straight. You stuck your dick in my little sister. Then as soon as you had to deal with the consequences, you bullied her into the ocean and sailed away. Now you've grown a conscience and you're here seeking my blessing to go on living. Am I leaving anything out?"

It amazed Reece how easy it was to get the cold facts correct, yet still miss the warmer truth through poor framing and lack of nuance. "Yeah, you're leaving a few things out. About seven months' worth, to be exact." Reece produced a photograph and handed it to her. In it he and Amaya were embracing at the ruins of Chora Castle overlooking Kapsali's twin bays. "We took this photo while on vacation in Greece. Something attacked us there in our hotel. Something inhuman. Whatever it was, it got into my head and turned me against Amaya. I only remember bits and pieces, except for that last night. That, I can see whenever I want—to watch myself acting like someone else and to forever wonder whether I could've behaved differently if only I'd been stronger."

Mallory finished examining the photo and handed it back to Reece. "If I understand you, you expect me to believe an evil spirit turned you into an asshole?"

Reece shook his head. "I'm not even sure I really believed it up until a moment ago. But it happened. I'm a lot of things, Mallory, but I'm not crazy."

"How about a liar? Is that one of the things you are?"

Reece did his best not to take the bait and to look at her with compassion. "That's for you to decide." He slid the photo back to her. "You can keep this."

She held the photo a second time, and Reece could see she was trying not to cry. "She really does look happy."

"She was," Reece said. "If you take anything away from this conversation, let it be that. Amaya wasn't weak, she wasn't depressed, and she wasn't crazy. She was just unlucky enough to have something evil make her its personal project. And I can tell you from experience that's a hell of a thing to go through."

"Yet she's dead, and here you sit."

"I don't think you'd say that if you knew how little of me there was left. Anyway, I won't take up any more of your time." Reece stood slowly, allowing her the chance to get in a last word. She didn't speak until he was halfway out the door.

"Hey, Reece. You said you were an officer. Does that mean you're out of the service now?"

"Yeah. I separated not long… after everything."

"Did you get an honorable discharge?"

Reece looked down at the floor but then forced himself to meet her eyes. "Yes."

"That's what I thought. Condolences on feeling super sad about losing your pretty girlfriend, but don't come here and tell me you walked away with nothing. In fact, don't ever come here again." Reece acknowledged her wish with a nod and returned to the main room. There he paid his tab, emptying what was left of his checking account into a tip for Mallory. Once outside, he drew a cigarette from his pack and struck the lighter's spark wheel until he was forced to accept that it wasn't going to produce a flame, then he tossed both cigarette and lighter into the gutter.

There wasn't a taxi in sight. Reece pulled out his phone and found that it was on its last sliver of power. He called the taxi service and listened through a series of rings, but the moment a voice appeared on the other end, the line went dead. Reece tightened his hand around the phone to keep from hurling it into the night. He considered going back in and asking to use their phone but remembered his promise, so he opted to just start walking, and to keep going until he either found a cab or walked all the way back to the hotel.

He started down an alley adjacent to the club, following the distant murmur of traffic. After a while, he came upon a bridge and took to its walkway with his hands buried in his pockets and his head held low. The sound of passing cars roared and died to his left, while to his right a river glimmered into the distance. Halfway across the bridge, Reece felt the urge to vomit. He stopped and leaned against the railing but managed to breathe his way through the worst of it. What had he been thinking, driving across states to tell Mallory face-to-face that her sister died as a result of a demonic possession? He was so lost in self-abasement that he failed to notice the sound of the slowing car until it was idling right behind him.

"I thought that might be you." The words had come from a yellow Mustang with a black racing stripe. He crouched and peered inside, finding Mallory's face lit up green by the lights of the dashboard. She was fully dressed in jeans, sneakers, and a t-shirt. "Get in. I'll take you to wherever it is you're going."

Reece briefly considered that she might be planning to kill him but decided he didn't care. It would be an honorable way to go at least. "Nice ride," he said as he climbed into the passenger's seat.

"Paid for by big tippers." Mallory dropped her foot on the gas, and they blasted off down the road. Reece didn't reach for his safety belt, nor did she suggest it. "Thanks, by the way. You didn't have to do that."

Reece looked out the window. "It's nothing compared to what I owe."

"Something got into your head, right? Isn't that the way you said it went?"

"Yeah. But I don't expect you to believe a story like that." Reece rested his head on the glass, soaking in its coolness.

"And maybe I don't. But I can tell you believe it." Then after a time, she added, "That being said, you should probably see a shrink."

"Point taken," Reece said. "And thank you. Really."

They rode in silence the rest of the way, the streetlights washing over them at intervals, casting them into brightness and then back into the dim glow of the dash. When they pulled into the parking lot, Mallory cut the ignition, and they sat for a time while Reece waited for her to say whatever was on her mind. It took her a while, but she finally got it out.

"Amaya was always a bit better than me. Better looking. Better put together. Our folks even gave her the better name. But I could never bring myself to resent her, even when she chose the Navy over the shit job I had waiting for her. I was really proud when she made it through boot camp, and I'm not sure I ever told her that." Mallory turned her face to Reece. Her mascara was starting to run. "Amaya was a better sister than I deserved." She reached across the divide and laid a hand on Reece's shoulder. "And a much better girlfriend than you deserved, Reece."

Reece let out a small but cathartic laugh and then patted her hand. "Thanks for reminding me. Before I go, is there anything you'd like to know about what her life was like out there?"

"Nah." Mallory wiped the area under her eyes with a tissue. "I'm just happy knowing it was wonderful while it lasted."

With nothing more to say, Reece wished her a good life and reached for the door handle but paused as a car entered the lot behind them, blocking them in. Its brights flashed on, filling the Mustang with blinding light. A door opened soon after, then slammed shut. Mallory tilted her head toward the window and examined the reflection in her side mirror. "Great. Just what I needed."

"Who is it?"

"My boyfriend. He was supposed to be out of town."

"But we haven't done anything," Reece said.

"Yeah, good luck with that argument." She then got out of the car and made her way to its rear.

An angry male voice cut through the silence. "Did you have enough time to get your stories straight?" Reece rested his forehead in his hand as he listened to Mallory attempt to explain herself. Under such heavy questioning, even what he knew to be the truth sounded like lies. "Just shut up," he said after a time, and a few moments later he appeared at Reece's window. "Get out."

Reece opened the door and stepped out into the lot. "Look, she was just giving me a ride."

"Yeah, I bet she was." The man's greasy hair hung to his shoulders, and a pair of ropy arms extended from the sleeves of a skintight black t-shirt. While Reece couldn't quite make out the prison tattoo on the back of his hand, he was pretty sure it wasn't the word *mercy*. "So, how long have you been bangin' my girl?"

"Like I said, she was just giving me a ride. I was close with her sister."

"Oh, I see. You had one sister and now you gotta have the other. Is that how this works?" Reece was getting a headache just trying to speak to this idiot, but he was clearly dangerous, so he made sure to govern his tongue accordingly. The man turned his attention to Mallory. "I'm gonna ask you one more time, Mal. What were you doin' with this guy?"

She flapped her hands out and then let them fall back to her sides. "What do you want me to say, Marco? I already told you the truth." She pulled the photo of Reece and Amaya out of her back pocket and handed it to him. "It's like I said, he was dating Amaya when she died."

Marco squinted at the photo, then tore it up and gave the pieces to the wind. Reece made a fist and planted his feet, but Mallory begged him with her eyes not to make things worse. Reece relaxed his fist and tried to let his anger cool, but all the while he was swearing an oath in his thoughts. *If he hits her, I'm going to kill him.*

Mallory frowned at Marco. "That was pretty fucked up."

Marco made a threatening move in her direction, causing her to flinch, and Reece put a hand on his shoulder. Within half a second he had Reece up against the back of the mustang, a knife held to his throat. With the headlights at his back, he appeared as little more than a silhouette. "Touch me again," he said. "Go on. Do it."

Reece raised his hands in surrender. Mallory was crying and begging him to let Reece go. By the front door of the hotel, a drunken couple was stumbling around and making a high-spirited racket. It wasn't clear whether they'd noticed the commotion, but the movement of Marco's eyes suggested they'd caught his attention. He closed the knife with one hand and then readjusted the collar of Reece's shirt.

"Here's what's gonna happen. You're gonna go inside while I finish talkin' to my girl. Then we're gonna leave, and you're never gonna see her again. If I find out that you have seen her again—I don't care if it's in person or on the goddamn TV—I'm gonna open you up like a zipper." He traced the butt of his folded knife from the center of Reece's collarbone down to his navel.

Behind him, Mallory looked like she'd shrunk several inches. "Please, Reece. Just go."

Reece looked back at Marco. "Happy to oblige her if you'll get out of my way." Marco gave him a crooked grin and stepped aside. Without wasting another word, Reece passed back into the hotel, only stopping once he was in his room. Leaving the lights off, he punched in the safe code and retrieved his pistol, then moved to the window and peered through the curtains. Outside in the parking lot, it looked like Mallory and Marco's row was coming to a close. Again he repeated his oath. Soon after, they both got into their cars and took off in the same direction.

Reece tossed his gun on the bed and splashed some vodka in a glass. He gulped it down and then filled it again. With drink in hand, he returned to his little view of a city still hours from waking. It was quiet outside now. Beyond the parking lot in the building across the street, a single floor was illuminated—an unfurnished and unoccupied office, a symbol of empty potential calling out into the void. Reece raised the glass again but set it down before the liquid could pass his lips. He'd had enough. Enough food and drink. Enough pleasure and pain and everything in between. Enough of every ephemeral promise the world had to offer.

He took a seat on the edge of the bed. Across from him, the fitted sheet he'd draped over the TV hung like a death shroud. Reece picked up the gun and placed it against his temple, flirting by measures with wrapping his finger around the trigger. Once he did, he found it wasn't as frightening as he'd thought it would be. He applied a bit of pressure, depressing the trigger's safety, and soon after felt the soft resistance of the trigger itself. It would be so easy to go all the way. It would all be over in a second.

But he couldn't do it. The will to act was there, but his finger wouldn't respond. From behind closed eyes he heard Mallory's voice again. *"Better than you deserve, Reece."* The voice didn't sound like a memory. It sounded like it was coming from somewhere in the room. He opened his eyes and glanced about, all the while keeping the pistol's barrel pressed against his temple as though he were holding himself hostage. A woman was standing against the far wall, the pale of her naked skin just visible enough to reveal her shape.

"Mallory? How did you get in here?"

"I came in through the open door." Reece couldn't tell where the words were coming from. They seemed to be everywhere at once. He looked to the door, finding it closed just as he'd left it. "Not that door," she said. "The one you left open for me. The one you'll never close." She stepped forward from the shadows and into the dark blue beginnings of twilight. Reece's heart pounded in his chest. Her tattoos were missing.

"Amaya?" His hand shook violently, but he kept the pistol to his head. When she reached the bed, she placed one hand over the gun and his arm went numb and fell to his side. Then she straddled his legs and settled her weight onto his lap. Even through his jeans her flesh felt cold. When she spoke, she did so without moving her lips.

"You haven't yet earned the right to die."

Reece's entire body shook, save for his right arm, which still hung limp by his side like a vestigial organ. Amaya's face was close enough that he could smell the seawater on her breath. Her eyes were like those in a photo Reece had once seen of a Columbian girl who'd been crushed beneath volcanic debris—eyes once bright and full of life now swimming with blood, dark to the point of blackness, and accusing all who dared to look of failing to do anything more. Reece struggled to string his words into a coherent thought. "What is it you want me to do?"

A cool hand touched down upon his left cheek, and then another followed on his right. Then the blackness retreated from her eyes and the blue he knew so well came to the fore. Her eyes spun backward in their sockets, alternating watery blue and meaty red with strobe light precision. Reece convulsed in terror, but his face stayed anchored between her hands. He saw in flashes images of their past together, ending with a view of Kapsali Beach as seen from the water.

It was still and empty, and the cold light of morning lay upon the sand. A crop of hair floated just below the water's surface, its wet locks moving like fingers with the tide. Then the surface broke, and Amaya rose from beneath it, water pouring down her shivering body. It looked at first as though she was suffering from the cold, but the fury written upon her features bespoke another cause, and when her mouth formed words they emerged not as a plea, but as a command, playing in an echoed loop until they were all Reece could hear.

"Come find me."

7
SEMPREVIVA

Selling his car and gun had been easy. Getting rid of his other stuff had taken a bit more patience. Reece briefly considered pawning the engagement ring he'd never given Amaya but decided against it. It was hers, and he had no right to sell it. After two weeks, he had more than enough money for his trip to Kythira anyway, and fearful of angering her further, he handed out the rest of his belongings to random passersby in front of his apartment building. He did this with cheer, feeling all the while as if he were leaving what he cherished most to a group of dear friends. These were the good ones, the ones who held no debts to vengeful ghosts and who would keep the world turning after he was gone.

He couldn't leave anything to his real friends, of course. If he did, he would need to tell them why, and they'd probably respond by dragging him kicking and screaming to the nearest psyche ward. And maybe they'd be right to do so, but to Reece it no longer mattered. After everything he'd gone through, if he was insane, he didn't want to get better. Because then he'd know for sure that the vile words which had driven Amaya to suicide had come from him after all.

Once on the island, forgotten impressions returned in painful waves, but Reece carried on from an emotional distance like a detective trying not to get too close to a case. He'd made sure to reserve the same hotel room he and Amaya had stayed in in the hopes that some sort of psychic memory lingered there. After he checked in, he spent the afternoon retracing the steps they'd taken together, first visiting the ruins of Chora Castle and standing before its unparalleled view of the bays. Next, he walked the streets of the nearby town, searching for signs of Amaya within the sherbet-colored windows of each whitewashed building, but found nothing more than tourists and friendly locals selling their wares.

Reece came upon a booth selling wreaths of a native flower which the Kythirans say never dies. Amaya had returned from their vacation with one just like it and had taped it to the wall of her rack on the ship. Reece held the wreath in his hands. Maybe such a totem was just what he needed. He paid the old woman, and her weathered face became creased with smile lines.

With wreath in hand, Reece made his way down to Kapsali Beach. There he walked the warm sand, surrounded by others but alone, looking out past the breaking waves and to the end of the shoreline where the quaint white lighthouse stood atop the marina. Doubt gnawed at his stomach. What if Amaya wasn't there at all? What if his vision had been nothing more than a nervous breakdown triggered by meeting Mallory? Reece cycled the flowers of the wreath through his fingers like the beads of a rosary. He needed to decompress. He'd been walking in the sun for hours, and it was a lot for him to ask of himself to do everything all at once.

Reece made his way up to the beachfront and took a seat in the patio section of the least crowded restaurant he could find. Despite not being particularly hungry, he ordered more food than he could possibly eat, along with a beer which he would be far more likely to finish.

He picked at his food but ate enough to feel full. With the beer he exceeded expectations, emptying three bottles of *Mythos* as he watched the late afternoon turn into early evening. Reece brought out the wreath again and gazed at his window to the sea, framed between a cluster of trees and a thatch-roofed cabana. A pair of small boats coasted about on the waters. The moment he laid eyes on them, he heard in his thoughts the noise of skittering insects, and despite how unpleasant the sensation, he knew he'd found the answer. Amaya didn't want him to relive their best moments together. She wanted him to meet her where she'd experienced her worst.

He called over the waiter and asked where he might rent one of those boats. The man gave him directions to a place nearby and Reece paid, leaving a tip several times the price of the meal. Then he set off along the shore for the bay beyond the lighthouse.

The boat rental was in a small hotel nestled away above the main road. The owner was happy to rent him a boat but warned that since it was so late in the day, Reece would have to return it in less than an hour. Reece said that was fine, and after a cash exchange and a brief lesson on the craft's mechanics, he climbed aboard the five-meter runabout and set out onto the waters.

He began his drive with a leisurely back and forth, and once the owner saw that he could handle himself, he gave Reece a wave and headed back inside. The moment he was out of sight, Reece started off toward the horizon. After some distance, he cast a glance back at the shoreline. The world he'd known was growing smaller by the moment, and it occurred to him that it had always been smaller than he'd imagined. But the ocean was forever, and the further he got from the island, the better he understood just how little hope he had of returning. The version of Amaya who'd visited him in the small hours of the morning had not been one who wished him well. She would want to take whatever he had left. He just hoped it was enough to wipe the slate clean.

Once the island was far enough in his wake, Reece cut the engine and the boat coasted to a stop. The sea had nearly swallowed the sun, and a sky of oranges and reds followed as the night assumed its watch. Reece cast a wary eye back toward the island, scanning the expanse for signs of boats in pursuit. He removed the wreath from his jacket pocket and threaded the string through Amaya's ring. With reverent movements, he knelt at the edge of the boat and set it adrift on the water. It danced for a time through rippling shards of moonlight before finally disappearing.

Nothing. Reece waited a few more moments before making his presence known. "I'm here," he said, and his thoughts returned to that night on the sponson when his world had been the smallest it had ever been. "That's what you said to me, isn't it? You said, 'I'm here,' and I just stood there in the dark, watching you. Is that what you're doing now? Watching me?" A gust of wind caused the water to swell, and Reece grasped the railing as the boat followed. Once the waters calmed, he continued speaking. "It was a hell of a thing I did to you, Amaya. You deserved a whole lot better. Whatever price you think is fair, I'll pay it. But I want you to know that I never meant for it to end that way. Something took hold of me, something that wanted nothing more than to ruin what we had. I don't know if I could've stopped it, but I'd do anything for another chance to try."

Another strong breeze rolled over the water, prompting Reece to fumble with the buttons of his olive-drab Army jacket. Halfway through, it occurred to him that not only was he trying to strike up a conversation with a dead woman—he was doing so while wearing the standard issue uniform of the unhinged. At once he felt more lucid than he had in a long time. Yes, it was possible that she was out there somewhere, watching in silence and relishing every moment of his surrender. But it was more likely she had no interest in the world she'd left behind and that his true task out on the water was to come to grips with the reality that, in a manner of speaking, he'd been the visitor all along.

The only remaining question was whether or not he was going to end it. Back in the direction of the island, a pinpoint of white light had appeared. They were looking for him. For all he knew there was a GPS tracker somewhere on the boat and they already knew where he was. He could wait for them to arrive and drag him back to his little gray world, or he could make sure he'd never hurt anyone again by giving himself to the sea. His friends and family would hear that he had died while on an adventure, and although they might always wonder, Mallory alone would know just how dark things had gotten.

A splash drew Reece's attention to the port side. He listened for further disturbances but heard only the sound of the water lapping against the boat. He stood with care, knees slightly bent, and peered over the edge. A flash of bioluminescence lit up the area surrounding the boat like lightning distant enough to be beyond the sound of thunder. He settled back onto his knees and planted his hands on the gunwale. After a time, a glimmer of white took shape within the murk, and Reece's breath froze in his chest as a pale smudge emerged. Another flash of bioluminescence followed, brightening Amaya's grinning face, and Reece let go of the gunwale, shrinking back into the boat.

He told himself it was just more madness, that she was just another hallucination, but he no longer felt so confident about weathering even such a storm. It was easy to say a hallucination wasn't real, but those who said such things have clearly never seen one looking back at them with the enigma of being in their eyes.

Reece placed his hands back on the gunwale and peered over the side. Amaya was still there, disappointment written upon her face. "What do you want from me?" he asked. A smile crept back onto her lips, and she drew her hands toward her in swift motions. So that was it. The truth was as mundane as he'd expected—he was to join her in wherever it was that suicides go. He was going to do it too, and not for some high-minded notion of protecting others from himself, but because the thing in the water demanded it as the penalty for his failure. He could only hope there would be some recompense for paying it willingly.

Off in the distance, the white light had grown larger. If he allowed them to catch him and bring him back to shore, she'd never let him forget it. Reece rose and placed one foot on the gunwale. The water lit up in a long streak of electric blue, and beneath it Amaya grinned, revealing a mouth full of teeth blackened by the deep. Her hands called him forth with greater urgency. It was time to act. Reece raised his face to the starry sky, taking one last look at the heavens before dropping into the water.

Icy cold filled his ears, and the world fell silent. The rush of water brought with it a jolt of mental clarity. This was a mistake, but it wasn't too late to turn back. He needed only return to the surface and grab ahold of the boat, his last link to the solid world. But before he could act, a cold body pressed against his back, and a pair of arms wrapped around his torso like a lover seeking warmth in the night. Reece kicked with his feet, struggling in panic to breach the surface, but something powerful coiled around his legs and squeezed, causing the insides of his knees to smack together. Reece's cry of pain escaped in a roiling torrent of bubbles. Water roared in his ears as he thrashed, and as his consciousness began to fade, the darkness of the water gave way to a crackling blue light. In his final moment of awareness, he saw before him what looked like a shimmering portal.

The brightness faded from his eyes, and the rushing in his ears morphed into the sound of trickling water. Reece was in the courtyard of his hotel, kneeling on throbbing knees before its rugged stone fountain. He searched his memory for how he might have arrived there but found little perch in time or space.

The face of the Aphrodite statue standing by the fountain was not as he remembered it. It was now Amaya standing upon the scallop shell, clutching a hand to her breast and shielding her most sacred parts from view. Moonlight lay like a pale sheet over the land, but beyond it the ocean was black as midnight, save for a faint white light no bigger than a pinpoint. To his left along the mountain ridge, tongues of fire reached up into the sky like the condemned reaching up to a heaven which had long since closed its gates.

Reece shuddered as leaden footsteps resounded across the courtyard. Something large was moving through the hotel's halls. Every so often a door would slam, and then the footsteps would continue on—*thoomp, thoomp, thoomp, thoomp*. It wouldn't be long before it found Amaya. Reece had to protect her.

He rose from his knees and faced the hotel. There were only ten rooms, and the footsteps seemed to be coming from all of them at once. He climbed up onto the stone wall, then clambered the rest of the way up onto the balcony of his room. The glass door was already open, and upon entering, he caught the scent of hot water. He ran to the bathroom. The shower was on, but no one was inside. He searched the rest of the room but came up empty. Amaya must have run when she heard the nemesis approaching. But where would she have gone?

Reece made his way to the front door and peered through the peephole. The hall was dark and the footsteps loud and steady, as if the nemesis was walking an endless path and would appear whenever and wherever Reece showed his face. He opened the door a few inches, then a few inches more until he was able to poke his head out into the hall. Much like the statue in the courtyard, the hotel's interior was not as he remembered it. Widely spaced wall sconces cast dim illumination down an endless corridor, and the Victorian-style wallpaper and mahogany trim put the lie to the notion that Reece was still in the same building.

At once the footsteps grew louder, and a man larger than Reece had thought possible emerged from the shadows. He was wearing a double-breasted suit, and he moved with an unhurried cadence as if catching his prey was not a matter of if but when. Reece tried to slam the door shut, but the behemoth thrust his hand in and ripped a chunk of the frame from the wall as though he were tearing through papier-mâché. Reece darted back to the balcony and scrambled back down the way he came, landing in the gravel of the courtyard with a crunch.

Some distance above, the bell of the old church was ringing. The nemesis was looking in the wrong place. Amaya had escaped the hotel, and she was risking everything to call Reece to her. He sprinted up the path, his heart beating its way out of his chest. He had no way of knowing if the nemesis was behind him, and he didn't dare look back. The pinpoint of light out on the water had grown larger and was now flashing in bright pulses. The bell fell silent just as Reece reached the door.

He threw open the door and stepped into a chamber crawling with the light of a hundred candles. In the center of the room, the nemesis was on his knees. His massive back, gnarled with ropy scars, was facing Reece. A woman hidden in front of him was stroking his neck and hair with a pair of porcelain hands, drawing forth with each caress a sound like that of a primordial horror awakening from an eons-long slumber. After a time, she drew herself up and peered at Reece over his shoulder. It was Amaya, her blue eyes twinkling at him in the candlelight.

An incalculable weight landed in Reece's stomach. Without thinking, he stumbled back through the door, not daring to stop until he was a safe distance away. The doorway took on an orange glow, and soon Reece heard the unmistakable crackling of flames. Within minutes the church stood engulfed, and he staggered back down the path as a man mortally wounded. The white light on the water was now flashing brightly enough to hurt his eyes, and he shielded them with his hand as he made his way back to the courtyard.

The hotel was silent. All Reece could hear was the now distant sound of fire and the gentle trickling of water coming from the fountain. He returned with defeated steps to where he'd started and fell back to his knees. The face of the statue had changed again. It now depicted a woman he didn't recognize, carved in stone yet animated in flesh. She turned toward Reece and offered him a smile, then removed her hands from her body, abandoning all modesty, and reached out to him with welcoming arms.

8
ANOTHER WORLD

"Hey. Get up. What are you doing in the water?" Reece found himself being pulled to his feet and led out of the surf onto dry sand. "Are you alright?"

He blinked the water out of his eyes, and a young woman came into focus. She was leading him up a moonlit beach. Once they stopped, Reece bent forward and placed his hands on his knees. "I think so," he managed to say between breaths.

The young woman laughed. "What were you doing in the water with all your clothes on?" The upper half of her face was hidden behind a black lace masquerade veil. Below it, she wore a matching choker and a top of delicate white fabric. Beneath her black layered skirt, he found a set of legs bare to the knees, where a pair of French heel boots took over.

"You're not exactly dressed for the beach yourself," he said.

"We were on our way to a party." She gestured toward a man standing further up the shore. "I saw you thrashing around in the water and pulled you out."

"Thank you." Reece hoped he sounded sufficiently grateful, but his mind kept wandering off to examine the empty chasm between his final moments on the runabout and his odd new surroundings. "Where are we?"

"My, you are quite a mystery man. A handsome mystery man spat out by the sea. It's like something out of a fairytale. Well, mystery man, to answer your question, we are in Kapsali."

Reece scanned the coast from left to right. On the bluff, where the ruins of Chora Castle should have been, stood a gothic mansion. Ahead was the Kapsali beachfront, but the stores and restaurants were gone—only the pine forest where he and Amaya had once spent a day camping remained. When Reece looked to his right, he nearly became dizzy. In place of the modestly sized Kapsali Lighthouse was a massive stone tower. "This is Kythira?"

"Yes. You have washed ashore in Kythira. How lucky for you."

"It's different," Reece said, not sure how else to express his shock.

The young woman looked at him quizzically. "Different from what?"

With answers only giving rise to more questions, Reece decided that for the time being he would focus on giving his rescuer her due attention. "Never mind," he said with his eyes downcast. "I'm sorry you had to get your boots dirty pulling me out of the water."

"Oh, it's nothing. The sand will dry and fall right off."

Reece nodded. "Look, I don't mean to put you out, but I'm afraid I'm a little lost. Do you live here?"

"Yes. Kythira is my home."

"I see. Your English is quite good."

"Yes, it is. Now come with me. We'll skip right past the pleasantries and enjoy ourselves." The young woman took his hand and led him up the beach as though they were a couple returning from a swim. "I'm going to take you to a lovely party. You'll have lots of fun and forget all your troubles."

At the mention of troubles Reece's mind drifted back to Amaya, and he let his hand slip free as politely as possible. "I came here looking for someone."

"Ah, so you have a purpose here after all. I like how the mystery is deepening as we go. So, who is it you're looking for?"

"Her name's Amaya."

"Never heard of her," she said without a pause. "But maybe she'll be at the party. All of Kythira's finest specimens will be there."

Reece thought he detected a hint of animus in her voice. "Yeah, maybe she will be."

At the top of the shore, they stopped alongside a 1930s art deco convertible. It was in rough shape—the headlights were missing, and the paint was dull and worn off in spots, but Reece could tell that it had once been magnificent. "Nice ride. My name's Reece by the way."

The young woman leaned against the car and looked him up and down, running her tongue over her teeth. "You look like a Reece."

He wondered what looking like a Reece entailed exactly. "I'm glad you think so," he said, assuming the best. "And how well does your name fit you?"

"Quite well." She stepped away from the car, and her companion opened the door and lowered the seat for her. "Maybe later I'll tell you what it is, and you can decide whether or not you agree."

"Alright then."

She climbed into the back seat, and her companion, who by now Reece had surmised must be her valet, shut the door behind her just as Reece was stepping forward. The young woman threw her head back and laughed. "Don't mind him. He's easily offended by rivals."

Reece considered revising his theory, at least in part. He opened the door and climbed in, taking a friendly tone as he addressed the valet. "And what's your name?"

"Ignore him," the young woman said. "He doesn't speak English. Do you, garcon?" The man made no sign that he understood. "See, no English. Or French, for that matter." The car stuttered as the valet turned the key, and once it roared to life, they began their moonlit drive. A break in conversation gave Reece enough time to take stock of the evening's horrors. The frightening notion that he'd drowned and was now in some strange hereafter kept bobbing to the surface, but every time it did, a growing dullness of memory swept it away. It was as if he'd awoken from a dream, and despite his efforts to hold onto its details, he could only watch as they slipped through his fingers like dry sand.

When they reached the end of the beachfront, the road became tree-lined on both sides until it merged with a major artery. Reece was struck by the fact that there wasn't another car in sight. If it hadn't been for the yellow rectangles burning against a darkened building some hundred yards from the road, he would have thought this bizarre facsimile of Kythira uninhabited, save for present company.

After crossing a stone bridge, the young woman tapped her valet on the shoulder and said something to him in Greek. The car came to a halt, and the valet exited and opened the door for her. She stepped out into the road and Reece followed her lead. "Why have we stopped?" he asked.

"The moon is bright tonight, and I want to show you something." The valet got back in the car and continued up the hill. "Don't worry. He'll be waiting for us on the other side. Now come, follow me." She led Reece into a narrow walking path flanked by what appeared to be small townhouses sized for one or two people.

Thick brown vines climbed the walls, branching out like veins across a manicured canopy of grape leaves. Innumerable spots of moonlight peppered the path before them, moving like glitter in a snow globe as the leaves conformed to the breeze. While the vines were well-maintained, the houses themselves were in a deep state of disrepair. Chunks were missing from the walls, and the wood of the doors and windows was split through. The young woman held out her hands, and the spots danced across her palms. With a swift motion, she tried to snatch one out of the air and then placed the top of her fist against her mouth and blew at Reece with the theatrics of a magician. Despite his lingering unease, her playful grin drew one from him in kind. After a silent moment, she raised her face to the flittering canopy. "We love our wine here in Kythira."

"I wouldn't turn down a drink," Reece said.

"Soon you'll have all the drinks you want." The young woman drifted a few steps ahead, and Reece maintained the distance, watching her as she walked. Her arms, legs, and hips were in a harmonious state of perpetual motion, elbows just far enough in and wrists just far enough out to allow her backside to swing hypnotically as she placed one boot in front of the other.

They stopped at a set of steps leading back up into the open air. Facing each other, they passed another wordless moment. This time Reece broke the silence. "I appreciate everything you're doing for me. I'm still pretty dazed, but I'd be a lot worse off if you hadn't been there."

"I'm sure it will all make sense soon. Just give your thoughts a rest and follow the tide. It's taken you this far." She offered him her arm. "Now help a lady in heels up these steps."

Reece obliged, locking his arm in hers. Once they reached the top, they found the valet waiting as she'd promised. After they'd repeated their ritual of deference, he started the car again and they continued their climb up the winding road. "What sort of party are we going to anyway?" Reece braced himself against the door through a sharp turn.

The young woman took some time before answering. "The sort I'd have no interest in if I'd been invited."

"Ah, so we're crashing."

"We wild ones go where we please. Are you a wild one, Reece?"

Her eyes pierced the darkness beneath her veil, and Reece swallowed hard before answering. "I've had my moments."

She twisted her mouth in disapproval. "You either are or you aren't."

"Okay then. I am."

"Good," she said, her expression softening. "Then we will go where we please together." The moment she finished speaking, the car swerved off the road and came to a stop. From this vantage point Reece could see all the way back down to the beach. Beyond it, columns of brightened windows climbed the dark face of the tower, which Reece now recognized as a lighthouse, its lantern casting a beam of light out over the ocean.

"Come," the young woman said, taking Reece by the hand. She led him out of the car and together they dashed off into the dirt and brush toward a nearby cluster of buildings, discernible in the dark as a craggy outline of rooftops set against a magenta glow. Some distance ahead, the edifice of the mansion loomed over a treacherous cliff.

As they drew nearer the buildings, a chain link fence came into view. It was torn in several places, and the posts were bent in various directions. The valet rushed ahead, finding an opening and peeling the fencing back so that the young woman could pass through. "Thanks," Reece said as he passed through behind her. The man looked away. Either he hadn't heard, or he was pretending he hadn't. Once on the other side, they entered a gravel lot ringed with shabby, white-walled tenements. Not a light was burning behind their metal mesh window coverings, but from the sides of the buildings, florescent tubes of assorted shades of pink and purple emanated a sustained buzz into the otherwise silent space.

"I guess we're early," Reece said.

"We have a little further to go." The young woman pointed to a narrow cobblestone path, which veered off sharply enough that Reece couldn't see what was around the bend. His suspicion that the path terminated at a set of steps leading up to the mansion filled him with both excitement and dread.

9
THE PARTY

A winding trail of stone steps led Reece and his companions to the front gate, beyond which stood the mansion, severe as a headmaster, daring the uninvited to approach. It was four stories high and hedged with wispy trees, its face hidden behind dark ivy. Gothic dormer windows peered from beneath the leaves, and iron cresting ran along the roof's edge. A pair of stone turrets flanked the entryway, rising into sharp pyramid spires, piercing the night. A chorus of clinking glasses issued from within, and silhouettes of people conversing with drink in hand were visible all along the ground floor's windows.

The young woman led the way to the side of the house, where they moved at a crouch along its foundation. After a time, she stopped and raised a finger to her lips, then lowered herself to one knee and examined the masonry. "There it is," she said to no one in particular. The valet retrieved a long metal hook from beneath his frock coat and fed it into a broken space where one of the stones didn't fit quite flush. Positioning his feet on either side, he shifted his weight rearward and pulled until his arms trembled. The young woman watched with glee as he struggled, silently cheering him on until the stone slipped free and fell to the earth with a thump. She once again raised a finger to her lips, mostly it seemed to stop herself from laughing, as her valet had landed flat on his back. Reece offered the man his hand, which he accepted reluctantly after a time. The young woman brushed the dirt from the back of his frock coat and peeled it off him without asking. "Here, wear this."

"I'm not taking his coat," Reece said.

"You can't go in there dressed like that."

She had a point. The coat, in addition to his black jeans and boots, would at least have him looking somewhat the part. Reece removed his jacket and stashed it in a bush. Then he donned and buttoned the frock coat and thanked its owner, who again looked away without reply. One at a time, they slipped into the hole in the foundation and made their way down a gently sloping tunnel, dropping into a pitch-black room at its end. The young woman landed first, followed by Reece, who despite his sudden panic managed to stay quiet until the third and final set of feet touched down on the floor. "Where are we?"

"Wine cellar," she said, taking Reece's hand and leading him through the darkness as if she knew the room's layout by heart. "Careful, there's a step coming up." They slowed almost to a stop, giving Reece time to feel for the step with his foot. Once he found it, they resumed their pace, moving upward in a spiral until they reached the top. A vertical thread of light appeared as she pushed on the door, and she took a moment to peek through before opening it the rest of the way and emerging into a private library with Reece in tow. When she looked back, Reece was able to make out in the candlelight a pair of stone-gray eyes under her veil. A feeling came over him like he was a willing captive, and it persisted even after she let go of his hand. The secret door through which they'd entered went back to being a bookcase as her valet pushed it shut.

"How did you know about this entrance?"

"I've done this before," she said, not quite answering the question.

"Is there some reason you can't use the front door?"

"Let's just say I'm no longer in the host's good graces." The young woman looked Reece over, then licked the palm of her hand and ran it through his hair. "With the coat you look like a proper man of mystery. Just don't let the help take it from you."

Their exit from the library was far less subdued than their entrance had been, and by the time they were in the grand foyer they were engaged in lively chatter. The trio stopped before an enormous statue of a muscle-bound hero wrestling with what appeared to be a sea serpent, which served as the centerpiece connecting a pair of identical winding staircases leading to the second floor.

"Oh my," she said, fanning her neck with her hand. "What a specimen he is. What do you think, darling?"

Enjoying the performance, Reece committed himself fully to his part. "I didn't know you liked them quite so robust, my dear."

"Oh, you never can have too much man," she said. "But don't worry. You're more than enough for me." The young woman hooked her arm around Reece's waist, and he responded by putting his arm around her shoulders. The valet appeared to be ignoring their banter and seemed more interested in his ongoing examination of their surroundings.

"Come, darling," she said. "Let's return to the other guests. I simply have to catch up on all the latest gossip." Reece looked away from the servant stationed at the front door as they passed through the gallery and into the billiard room, where several guests were mingling at a mahogany bar.

At last, he was in his element. "May I get you a drink, my dear?"

"He'll get the drinks," she said, indicating her valet with a movement of her chin. She gave him her order and then told Reece to do the same.

"Dealer's choice," Reece said. The woman translated, and the valet headed off to the bar.

"Come. He'll bring them to us." She led Reece through another door and into a larger space, where a greater number of guests had congregated. Recalling his charge, Reece scanned the room for signs of Amaya, though it was madness to think he would find her there. While the details of his journey were yet lost in the fog, the one thing he recalled clearly was how her face had looked in the water, every feature upon it touched by death. For all its oddities, this otherworld he'd landed in was by all appearances the realm of the living. Yet this is where he'd ended up, and he had to wonder if that might not have been an accident.

Reece examined the women in the room one by one, picturing Amaya in each of their places. A delicate woman in a sheer blouse stood by the window smoking from a silver telescopic cigarette holder, her face divided into equal parts of white and black makeup. Another wore a corset and a layered open front dress. The men all looked similarly dashing in their vests and tailcoats. Although Amaya had always shown an interest in fashion, it was hard to imagine her at home in such an ostentatious crowd. But perhaps it was unfair of him to predict who she might have become had she not died so young.

Right on the heels of Reece's melancholy, the valet arrived with a drink in each hand. Reece took one and thanked him.

The young woman took the other without a word and then clinked her glass against his before swallowing its contents all at once. "Mm, I like that." She returned the glass to her valet and looked at Reece expectantly. "Drink, Reece, drink. Fate has left you like an infant swaddled on our doorstep. So you must do as we do and seize life's joys wherever you find them." Reece raised his glass to both his companions in turn and then drained it to the last drop. The moment it was empty, the valet took it from his hand and disappeared back into the billiard room.

In the hopes of avoiding another round of painful introspection, Reece resolved to turn his attention outward, starting with getting better acquainted with the woman behind the veil. "Do you know anyone here?"

"I've seen a few familiar faces. But I don't think anyone's recognized me yet." She led Reece to a sofa on the far side of the room, and they took a moment to make themselves comfortable.

"Who are all these people anyway? Some sort of noble class?"

The young woman laughed. "Hardly. They're just tenement dwellers trying to impress the host into thinking they're something more."

"I see. They certainly appear well dressed."

She gave a dismissive wave. "So they got their hands on one nice outfit. It's not like it will do them any good. He's not the type to be impressed by costumes." Apparently sensing Reece's puzzlement, the young woman let out a sigh. "Please don't think me overly judgmental. I just find myself vexed by people who put on airs."

"Aren't we putting on airs?"

"Yes, but not in earnest. These people actually hope to be taken seriously as a result of this playacting. It's appalling."

Reece figured there must be more to the situation than he was able to understand at present. "Your vexation is really quite charming, you know."

The young woman shot him a beguiled grin. "So, what about... I'm sorry, what was her name?"

"Amaya," Reece said. The spell of the moment had been broken. "She isn't here."

"You sound very sure for a man who hasn't visited the great hall."

"The great hall? Is that where the host is?"

"Of course. It's the beating heart of this soiree."

Reece was struck by a mixture of disappointment and shame—disappointment at learning that his search was ongoing, and shame over finding that disappointing. "I suppose I should go up there and look for her then."

"By all means. I can entertain myself."

"You and your valet should come with me. Or are you afraid the host might recognize you?"

Again she captured him in her eyes, and once more Reece felt the intoxicating thrill of being ensnared. "That sounds like a challenge," she said. "I accept."

"Glad to hear it. But before we go, tell me something. What's your name?"

"I'll tell you if we make it out of here." The valet returned with their drinks, and the young woman raised hers in a toast. "To finding your lost Amaya."

Reece raised his drink and emptied it. Then they set their glasses on an end table and returned to the gallery. As they passed the front door, they captured the attention of the servant, and Reece thought he saw the man's eyes narrow. Placing his hand on the young woman's back, he hurried her up the stairs as quickly as her boots would carry her. Once at the top they paused, facing the great hall. It was far larger than the room they'd come from and featured many times the number of guests. Reece offered the young woman his arm and they entered together.

The room was two floors high, and at its far end, a semicircular recess housed five floor-level windows. Above them, a single rose window offered a glimpse of a starry sky through its geometrically patterned grilles. In the center of the room hung a menacing chandelier. Thorns of iron ran the underside of its arms like the spines of a hydra, and from its crown-shaped candle cups, yellow light spilled out over the gathering.

The floor was composed of rich dark wood, and large mirrors framed in gold stood along the right wall. On the opposite side, elevated upon a dais, a man sat on a throne between two flaming sconces. He was huge to the point of being beyond belief—even the structure of his bones was intimidating—and his throne was of such proportions that anyone other than him would have looked like a child despot in it. His black hair was slicked back against his skull, and it was long enough that the tips nearly brushed the jacket of his double-breasted suit. He might have been handsome if not for the fact that his features were exaggerated to the point of distortion. A set of gloved hands which looked like they could crush boulders gripped twin lion heads carved into the arms of his throne, and he watched the guests through eyes that flickered in the trembling light. Reece felt like he'd seen the man before, but the idea that he could've forgotten someone of such enormous proportions struck the notion from his thoughts. "I take it that's our host."

The young woman plucked a flute of champagne off a passing tray. "Mm-hm."

"Well, I suppose I should take a lap through the crowd. You'd better stay here." He was suddenly feeling less cavalier about having her flaunt her impropriety before the host.

"I'll be waiting."

Gazing out over the assembly, his eyes settled on a blonde about Amaya's size. She wore a dark cocktail dress with a matching shawl over her shoulders, and her hair was pinned back under a peacock feather headpiece. Reece's pulse quickened as she turned in his direction and her blue eyes met his. It wasn't quite Amaya, but she bore a remarkable resemblance to Mallory. However, there was nothing in her expression to indicate that she saw Reece as anything more than just another man in the crowd, and it made no sense that Mallory would be there anyway, so he looked away and kept moving. Along the right side of the room, several guests were standing before the mirrors looking pleased with their reflections. It seemed the young woman had been right. This really was a collection of the lowborn playing at being upper class.

Reece made ever briefer examinations of the faces in the crowd as he drew nearer the music emanating from the end of the room. Once he emerged on the other side, he found a quartet of musicians performing by one of the windows. Reece approached the middle window and looked out over the island. To the right was nothing but ocean. A gully of white light lay between the moon and the shore, separating two coal black expanses. Directly ahead, the shorelines of the bays formed the lowercase Greek letter omega, with the lighthouse towering at its center.

Facing the crowd again, Reece repeated his survey and readied himself for a second pass. While doing so, the servant who'd been standing by the front door stepped up onto the dais and said something into the host's ear. At first the host registered no reaction, but then he turned his head toward the front of the room where the young woman was waiting. The servant then spoke into his ear a second time, and the colossus turned his head the other way until he was looking directly at Reece. The music in Reece's ears was replaced in measures by a severe ringing until only the ringing remained, and the gaze that pinned him against the window carved away in strips the pretense with which he'd entered the room.

Once Reece was able to move, he shot into the crowd, no longer caring if Amaya was mingling somewhere among them. Halfway through, he caught a glimpse of his reflection in one of the mirrors and barely recognized the man he saw. Gaunt, ghoulish, and shrouded in shame, he looked in the valet's frock coat like a nosferatu who'd just suffered the indignity of an evening dining on rats. Within a moment he'd passed the mirror, and he put the image out of his mind, focusing instead on the urgent need to escape. Once on the other side, Reece found the young woman leaning against a wall, sipping champagne. He grabbed her by the arm. "We have to go. The host knows we're here."

Reece led his companions out onto the landing where they found a man stationed at the bottom of each staircase, daggers exposed. "You weren't kidding about having fallen from the host's good graces," he said. He took the young woman by the hand and led her across the mezzanine and through a bedroom to a hallway on the other side. From there they burst out onto the balcony overlooking the front steps but found the escape route unsound, as several of the help had congregated in the courtyard. "Back inside," Reece said, and they returned to the hallway, but they froze in place as leaden footsteps grew in intensity from somewhere around the corner. *Thoomp, thoomp, thoomp, thoomp.* The elevator at the far end of the hall would no doubt deliver them right into the hands of their pursuers, so Reece made the snap decision to run toward the sound, hoping they could cut off its author before entering the right wing of the mansion. They edged their way into the adjoining hall just as the host appeared around the corner and then kept running past door after door, never daring to stop until they had no other choice. Reece jiggled the handle of the final door. It was locked.

The host hadn't once quickened his pace. He just continued forward, entombing them more completely with each booming step. Without warning, the valet launched himself down the hall in a full sprint, but a sledgehammer fist cut his charge short, sending him careening through the wall. Having hardly broken his stride, the host resumed his march through a cloud of plaster. Reece guided the young woman behind him and then moved forward with trembling steps, his hands held out in supplication. "Okay, you've caught us. But I assure you we didn't mean any harm." With one fluid movement, the host snatched Reece by his frock coat and lifted him until his back was flat against the ceiling. Reece looked down at the coarse face in terror, at its shining eyes with gold-rimmed pupils and its teeth, large and blunt like those of an ogre.

"I know you," the host said in a voice that sounded like it was coming from the mouth of a crocodile.

Reece was reasonably certain that the valet who came crawling out of the hole in the wall was not the same one who'd gone crashing into it, but he was in no position to be picky about the company he kept. Once on his feet, the valet closed the distance and began working over the host's back. The first couple punches had little effect, but after a half dozen or so, the larger man began to wince, and with a look of irritation he let Reece fall to the floor and turned to face his attacker. Reece brushed aside the young woman, who looked oddly delighted by all the action taking place, and with a lunge, he slammed his foot into the door, repeating the motion until the lock gave way. Together they rushed through the open door into what appeared to be a study and then slammed it shut behind them.

The young woman went to work trying to tip over a bookcase. "Give me a hand here."

"What about your valet?"

"You really need to stop worrying about him. Now help me."

Reece pulled from the other side, and after a short struggle, the bookcase came crashing down in front of the door. "The desk," Reece said, and as though of one mind, they each grabbed an end and aimed it like a torpedo at the full-length window at the front of the room. The door rocked violently, causing books to shoot from the toppled bookcase and onto the floor. When it didn't give, the host concussed it with a more forceful blow, warping its hinges. Then the handle snapped off, and a pair of massive fingers crawled through the hole like the legs of a tarantula, tapping and feeling their way to a solid grip. Once they found their purchase, the door buckled outward, cracking and splintering as he pulled it inch-by-inch through its frame.

Moments from being cornered again, they drove the desk across the floor, and with a final push, they sent it crashing through the window and onto the lawn. Once it settled, the young woman hopped down onto the desk and then onto the ground, making space for Reece to follow. "Come on! Jump!"

With a crunch the door split open, and as the host entered the room, Reece leaped down onto the desk, landing with less grace than his companion had. His momentum sent him rolling into the yard, peppering his frock coat with shards of broken glass. When he looked back up at the window, the towering form of the host was gazing down at them.

The young woman ripped off her veil and threw it to the ground. "I hope you enjoy the renovation of your study." Her face was beaming, but her voice betrayed an inner fury. "Do let me know if any of the other rooms in your house could use a woman's touch."

"We really don't have time for gloating," Reece said, crawling to his feet and tugging at her arm. The rising din of voices inside the house suggested word was getting around, and the help would soon be flooding back out into the yard. The young woman gave Reece her hand, and they ran until they were beyond the light of the mansion, passing at last through the open gate.

Once they'd made it down the steps, they stopped in the lot, resting with their hands on their knees. The young woman glistened under the pink florescent light, her perspiration crystalline upon her skin. She was watching the path behind them with wild anticipation, as if she were hoping the host might come tearing his way down and begin the chase anew. "What's your name?" Reece asked.

The young woman looked at Reece with excitement in her eyes, sharing a victorious grin. "My name's Mia."

10
THE EYE OF NIGHT

Despite now being one person short, Mia insisted they had every reason to celebrate. It seemed to Reece inadvisable to revel so near their enemy's mansion, but she assured him that they would be as safe as anyone should care to be. This assurance was of course coming from a woman who'd just shrugged off the likely death of her valet, so Reece was hesitant to follow her blindly lest he meet the same fate. But at the moment he was feeling good, and he hadn't felt good in a long time. For now he would do as she said—he would follow the tide.

As they passed from quiet moonwashed houses into the tinsel of the bar district, Reece was struck by how many people were packed into such a small area. "Is there some sort of special event going on?"

Mia shook her head. "Not unless you consider the sun going down special."

"You mean it's like this every night?"

"Pretty much. We really know how to enjoy ourselves here."

Reece's thoughts took a mischievous turn as he recalled the conversation they'd had in the mansion. "Isn't that what all those 'appalling' people at the party were doing? Enjoying themselves?"

Mia made a playful show of recognizing the provocation. "My, my, mystery man. What a sharp tongue you have."

"I just call them like I see them. No mercy, even for the beautiful."

"Ah, sharp and silver. But you're right, of course. I am intolerant of those who seek their pleasures there. But it's only because I know that while an evening of enjoyment might be their purpose, it certainly isn't the purpose of their host, and I have little patience for those who struggle to see that."

"Fair enough. What is his purpose then? And does this monster have a name?"

"Never mind his name. Better that you don't speak it and bring trouble down upon your head. As for his purpose, only the Devil knows. Nothing good, I'm sure. What I do know is that he has a habit of inviting select guests to stay the night. After that, they're changed. Some are never heard from again. And yet people keep lining up at his gate, invitations in hand, when everything they could possible want is right here."

Right here consisted of twin rows of bars, emblazoned with signs etched in luminous colored chalk. A sea of faces alight with mirth flowed toward them and parted like water before vanishing from Reece's field of vision. Off in an alley, the pale of a man's flesh stood stark against the shadows as he thrust his hips between the legs of someone reclining on a stack of crates. A group of young girls, their faces made up into skulls in the style of the Mexican Day of the Dead celebration and wearing little more than glowing body paint, passed by without a glance. Reece returned his attention to Mia. "I see what you mean. But if you have everything you want here, why sneak into his parties?"

Mia smirked. "To cause trouble, of course." She then bounced her finger at him significantly. "You know, it's a good thing I brought you along. If I hadn't, one day you probably would have received an invitation of your own and been taken in by all that pageantry, poor unsuspecting foreigner that you are."

Reece laughed. "Do I really seem that naive?"

"Maybe. Or maybe I just feel responsible for you since I saved your life, and now I'm taking a bit of pleasure in ensuring your well-being. You'll forgive me for that small indulgence, won't you?" She locked her arm in his and cozied up against his shoulder.

"Yes," Reece said. "I'll forgive you. And I'm grateful, of course." And he was grateful—grateful to her for pulling him out of the water and grateful to her for bringing him along for the ride—but he couldn't help but regard his encounter with the host as anything but fortunate. Whatever fate had befallen Mia's shape-shifting valet, the monster wouldn't stop there, not after what they'd done to his house. For as long as Reece remained on the island, he would have a powerful and terrifying adversary. Seeming to sense his disquiet, Mia grabbed his arm and draped it around her neck like a fur stole. The warmth of her body against his had an immediate calming effect.

After a time, she slipped back out from under his arm and withdrew into a crowd gathered along the side of the road where vendors tossed and scraped food on grills powered by portable gas tanks. When Reece arrived behind her, he found her poring over a menu. "We missed the dinner part of the party, and I'm famished."

"I could eat," Reece said. Then he remembered he only had a wallet full of damp euros and had no idea what sort of currency they traded in a place like this. He peeled a bill from the top of his stack. "Do they take these?"

"Do they take money? Yes, Reece. They take money." Grinning, Mia passed the bill to the vendor and ordered for the both of them. Within minutes they had their food, and they continued their walk, chatting between bites.

A pale young woman with two diamonds like harlequin tears tattooed beneath her eyes approached Mia on unsteady legs. "The queen has arrived," she said, performing a drunken curtsey. Her words were accented in German, and Reece took comfort in knowing he wasn't the only foreigner around. "Mia," she continued. "It's so nice to..." Her voice trailed off and she swayed, looking Mia over with admiration.

When it was clear she wasn't going to finish her sentence, Mia reached out and took her by the hands, steadying her. "The feeling is mutual, my dear. It is indeed always nice to."

Apparently unaware that she was the butt of a joke, the woman beamed. She then called out to her companion who was speaking to someone along the side of the road. "Come 'ere! This is Mia!" When she looked back, her eyes passed over Reece, then swung back in his direction but overcorrected before finally settling on his face. Once she'd achieved a measure of focus, she leveled her finger at him. "It is your great privilege to belong to her."

"I'm sure it is," Reece said, smiling with the good humor of someone who'd been in her sorry state plenty of times.

A short man with a wide, flat head appeared from behind the woman and wrapped his arm around her hips. His eyes were swimming in the same uncertain manner. "This is Mia," she repeated.

"I see," the man said nervously. "Very pretty." When he had finished speaking, his jaw snapped shut, which seemed to cause him some discomfort.

Mia looked them over with a crooked grin. "Just what sort of party favors have you two gotten into?"

The man dug his free hand into his hip pocket and produced several chalky tablets. "Just a little something I cooked up. W-want some?"

Mia looked at Reece with her eyebrows raised, and he responded by moving his head steadily back and forth. "I guess we're good," she said.

"Suit yourself. I've taken three, and I'm c-c-crawlin'."

"That's nice," Mia said. "We're going to keep crawling in that direction. You two enjoy yourselves."

"Oh, we will," the woman said, and her companion nodded in vociferous agreement.

Mia placed her hand on the woman's arm and stroked it with her thumb. "Come see me sometime."

"Oh, I will," the woman said, performing another curtsey.

The man's cheeks twitched as he drew them back into a grin. "I'll make sure she does."

Reece's eyes were on Mia as she watched them stumble away. Whoever Mia was, it was clear she wasn't just another face in the crowd. "I didn't think I was so hungry," he said, tossing his empty box atop an overflowing trashcan. Beyond it, a side road led up to a dome-shaped building with a glass roof. The sign outside read *The Eye of Night*. "How about we get a drink?"

"Or three," Mia said. Reece placed his arm around her again. This time it felt more natural, like it belonged there.

The centerpiece of The Eye of Night was an ovoid bar under a glass ceiling of the same shape, surrounded by a stylized replica of the town. Behind the buildings, a painted sky of eternal night glimmered under a soft backlight. A bartender with neon threads in her hair was attending several customers on the far end. Reece took a seat at the end nearest the door and peeled a couple more bills from his stack. Mia called out their orders, and when the bartender brought them their drinks, Reece found himself being stared at by a fluorescent eyeball painted onto her lips. He peeled off another bill and dropped it into the tip jar. The bartender smiled, splitting the eye in two and revealing a row of teeth which glowed under the bar's blacklights.

Reece swirled the liquor in his glass. "Everything's so strange here."

"Is it? I hadn't noticed."

Reece looked at Mia for several seconds before setting his glass on the bar. He'd gone along with everything since his arrival because he'd felt so out of his element, but it now seemed as though time and alcohol had brought him to the moment for questions. "Where are we, Mia?"

"The Eye of Night."

"No, I mean where *is this*?" He waved his hand around in the air, indicating everything in every direction.

"Kythira?"

Reece struggled against a rising sense of frustration. Either Mia didn't know she lived in a madhouse version of reality, or she was pretending not to know. "What is beyond Kythira?"

She tilted her face away and looked at Reece askance, a bemused smile forming upon her lips. Then she swept her arms out theatrically and said, "The entire world."

Reece lingered in her eyes, trying to judge her sincerity. But the longer he lingered the less he was sure of and the more he kept falling back into her and into the notion that he was exactly where he was supposed to be. It was like in a dream, where one placidly accepts whatever's happening around them, no matter how unusual. "Sorry. I didn't mean to get philosophical on you." Reece finished his drink and slapped another bill on the bar.

"It's fine. You've been through a lot tonight, but you're safe with me now." She laid a hand on his knee.

"Thanks. I'm going to go check out the town model. Maybe that'll give me a better idea of where I am in the world." Mia said nothing but raised her glass in toast to his plan.

Reece started on the right side, taking in every minutia of the build. Tiny figures populated the streets, traversing the scenery like clockwork along a series of tracks. Never before had he seen such detailed workmanship. He peered through the glass dome of the replica of The Eye of Night and found an ovoid bar just like the one he was in, complete with a miniature copy of the town model. Behind the bar, a woman tended to a series of figures on stools.

At the focal point of the display was a remarkable likeness of the mansion. Although Reece suspected that beyond its windows he would find an impressively intricate environment, it was one he had little interest in revisiting, so he moved on to an examination of the shoreline. A layer of sand had been combed over a hand-painted ocean. To its left stood the lighthouse, its windows illuminated by a bulb within its lantern room.

On his way back around, something caught his eye as he passed the model of the mansion. An icy rigor seized him. The glass in the window of the study was missing. Reece moved in closer, examining the window through panicked eyes. He had nearly managed to persuade himself that it was just a coincidence when the front door of the mansion sprung open, and a figure which looked like the host's servant made its way down the track, stopping just beyond the gate.

The clinking of ice cubes next to his ear broke Reece from his trance. When he turned, he found Mia offering him a fresh drink, and without delay he took it and drained it by half. He considered showing her his discovery, but something told him she'd only respond with more bemusement, so he remained silent. "Drink," she said, lifting the bottom of his glass with the tip of her finger. He obeyed, inviting the liquid fire to burn away his fear. Mia pulled a silk handkerchief from her blouse and dabbed his forehead. "Something's got you all worked up. I told you, you're safe with me now. Don't you believe me?" Reece's gaze kept drifting toward the bar's entrance in expectation of the servant's arrival. Mia took his chin between her thumb and forefinger and turned his face back toward hers. "Reece?"

"Yes, I believe you." He flashed a nervous smile and then gave a hard swallow. "I think I could use a bit of air."

"Of course." She led him out the back door and into a lot where a small crowd had gathered to loiter and smoke. A single lamp hung over the doorway, casting a faint light over an area of shattered pavement. A series of dimly lit figures sat perched like crows along a crumbling half-wall. Off to the side, a woman and two men were embroiled in some sort of controversy.

Hoping to calm his nerves, Reece approached the men on the half-wall in search of a cigarette. "Bum a smoke off one of you guys?" None answered—it wasn't clear whether any of them even spoke English—but after a few moments, the man nearest Reece handed him one. While he was giving Reece a light, the nearby quarrel became more animated.

"Shut up. Just shut up." The woman was jabbing her finger into the chest of the scrawnier of the two men. The other stood by with his arms crossed, laughing in unruly bursts. "Your mouth has run its full course tonight," she continued.

"I'm just sayin' it seems wrong," the scrawny man said, slurring his words. "Didn't it feel wrong?"

The other man guffawed. "It's none of your business, quarter brain."

"Exactly," the woman said. "Keep this shit up and see what happens."

Mia placed her hand on Reece's elbow. "Let's take a walk. There's nothing to see here."

Reece took a pull from his cigarette and looked out toward the road. It wasn't quite visible from his present position, but the murmur of voices suggested that the streets were still quite crowded. If the town model was any indication, somewhere within that throng, the servant was on the prowl. Reece took another drag. "Just going to finish this." Mia nodded, but her discomfort over the drama unfolding before them was evident. It was the first of its kind he'd seen in her, and he couldn't help but be curious as to why.

The scrawny man lowered his eyes to the pavement. His face bore the crestfallen expression of the bullied. "It just seems wrong is all."

The woman threw her hands up, her fingers curled into tense claws. "What did I just say? Not another word from you!" Anger flashed across the scrawny man's face, and he took in air as if preparing for a retort, but when he opened his mouth his chest heaved, and he sprayed vomit all over the side of the dumpster. The woman clucked her tongue. "Well, at least that's an improvement over what was coming out of your mouth a moment ago." She turned her attention to the second man. "So, you man enough to finish me off tonight while numbnuts here watches from the doghouse?"

He ran his fingers through his greasy hair. "More than man enough."

Mia groaned. "As I said—nothing to see."

When the scrawny man had finished vomiting, he lapsed into what appeared to be a state of morose contemplation. "I'm tired. Sick and tired of it all." He looked up from the dumpster, flecks of vomit in his goatee. "There's no light in this world!"

The woman threw her head back and cackled into the sky. "Here we go. Back into the abyss!"

"Don't be an idiot," the other man said. "The light will be here in a few hours."

The scrawny man wiped his mouth on his sleeve. "That's not what I meant."

The other took on a look of annoyance. "You want light?" He produced a pocket flashlight and set it on strobe mode. "I'll give you light." The ensuing staccato flashes revealed frame by frame the anguish of the tormented as he sought to shield his eyes, and Reece discovered a portion of pity on the far side of his disgust.

Mia tugged on his hand again, this time with greater force. Reece managed to tear himself away from the drama for long enough to meet her eyes, which reflected from the dimness a measure of the flickering light. "Sorry," he said. He spared one last glance at the ongoing clash. "I guess some people should learn to enjoy themselves a little less, eh?"

"He'll be fine," Mia said. "They all will. Everyone makes it through the night here." She punctuated her strange statement with a look sweet enough to evoke his trust, and once again Reece felt like he was sinking into her like quicksand.

"I'm sure you're right." Reece ground his cigarette into the pavement. "I'm ready to go. Got any place special in mind for our next stop?"

"My place is pretty special."

A kaleidoscope of anticipatory pleasure erupted in Reece's brain. He would have to risk the road, but it would be well worth the danger. "I'd like that," he said, and when she drew him forward again, he moved like a straw on water.

On their way out of the lot, Reece caught a glimpse of something on the wall of the building next to the bar. It was a chalk drawing of a tree, and it was only visible within a single flash of light. But to speak of it would risk breaking the moment, so he abandoned it to memory and cleaved to the one thing he understood.

They headed back down the hill and passed into the crowd, the sounds of bickering and laughter fading behind them. The road was the same they'd taken to the bar, the one which led to the mansion. But Reece's fear of running into the servant had given way to more pleasant expectations. He needed only follow Mia, his north star through the unknown. His path to year zero. Clinging to that notion, Reece discovered a cheer diminished only by the pangs of impatience. "I'm guessing you don't have a spare key to the car, which means we're walking."

"I'm afraid so," Mia said, clearly unbothered.

"How far is it to your place?"

They emerged at the edge of town, and the road back down to the beach came into view. Mia flung her finger out toward some vague spot in the distance as if she were casting a fishing rod. "That far."

"That's pretty far."

"About forty-five minutes by foot. But don't worry. It'll be worth your while." Mia turned on her toes and kissed him, then withdrew.

Not keen on letting her get away with such a modest show of affection, Reece pulled her back in and secured her lips to his. Their mouths moved in slow cycles of engagement and retreat, and the next time she pulled away, Reece was satisfied enough to resist pursuit. "I have no doubt it'll be worth my while," he said. "I just don't know how you're going to make it all the way there in those boots."

Mia laughed, then hooked her fingers in his and set off down the road. "You can carry me the rest of the way if I fall out."

"Oh no. If you fall out, I'm leaving you where you lay."

She withdrew her hand in mock indignation. "And where will you go then, pray tell? Back into the ocean?"

Reece laughed in return. "Good point. It could be that I haven't thought this through." To his right, the eyes of the mansion watched, and his smile was tempered. "Do you have any roommates?"

"You could say that. But don't worry, there's plenty of space. We'll be quite alone."

While Reece was processing what that meant, the feeling of being followed came over him. He glanced over each shoulder, seeing no one but finding that to be of little comfort. The speed at which dead quiet had descended upon them was unsettling. Only the sound of the wind in the leaves stood as evidence that all the world had not been condemned to silence. He tried to refocus his mind on what was to come, but it wasn't long before the intuition became too strong to ignore, and with it came an involuntary rebuke of the passions which were carrying him down the winding road. Uncertainty appeared like a rush of bile in the back of his throat, bitter and inescapable. He slowed his pace, resisting the pull of Mia's hand until the tension became so great that she gave up and shot back into his arms. She kissed him again and then held him in her eyes. "Stay here with me, Reece."

"I'm here," he said, but his attention was everywhere else—on the rustling trees and on every shadow the moon produced along the road. Speaking those words had carried him back to his final moments on the boat, and he recalled more clearly than ever the pale figure in the water which had beckoned him below. Was she watching him again now? Perhaps this entire night was nothing more than a test to see how badly he'd mishandle the chance to make things right and then punish him for it.

The silhouette of a man stepped out from behind a tree along the side of the road behind them. Reece took Mia by the arm and pointed in its direction.

Mia sighed. "The servant."

Reece experienced again the horror he'd felt in the bar. "Why is he following us? To find out where we're going?"

"Oh, I'm sure he knows where we're going. It's more likely he's taken on the role of assassin. You won't let him hurt me, will you, Reece?" Mia clutched his arm with both hands.

"No, I won't let him."

She moved closer to his ear, and the next words arrived on the warmth of her breath. "Then go tell him so."

Reece freed himself from her grasp and walked to the edge of the pavement. The servant stepped out from the shadows, and the two men stood in silence for a time, eyeing each other from opposite sides of the bend. The man was dressed more casually than he had been at the party. Reece fortified his posture and addressed him. "You're quite the dedicated servant, doing this in your off hours."

"A dedicated servant has no off hours."

"What happened to our companion?"

"He took flight. Heaven knows where."

Reece felt a surge of relief but maintained a stern expression. "Let me put this to you simply—what happened in your master's mansion was unfortunate, but it's over now. If you insist on pursuing a vendetta against Mia, you won't like the outcome."

The servant's demeanor remained unchanged. "I see. And what outcome might I expect?"

Reece swallowed hard, hesitating before speaking. It was doubtful he could take the man in a fight. From the looks of him, he was no stranger to lifting heavy things. "I'll kill you," Reece finally said. Once the threat had passed his lips, another followed with greater ease. "If you so much as touch her, I swear I'll kill you with my own hands."

The clouds shifted, spilling moonlight over the road and brightening the servant's face. The expression he wore was one of pity. "You're going the wrong way."

Reece wasn't sure how to respond to such a mild comment after all his bluster. He had no real desire to kill anyone. He only wanted this fool to leave him alone so he could continue on his way to a new life with Mia. "Where I go is none of your concern," he said. A silent moment followed with each man acknowledging the other's final position. Then the servant gave a subtle bow and began his walk back up the road.

The sound of Mia's heels on the pavement signaled her approach from behind. She wrapped her arms around his midsection and again he felt the warmth of her words against his ear. "Great rewards await you."

Reece turned and held her in kind. "I can't wait," he said, sinking back into dreamlike nescience. She pulled gently away, leading him by the hands the same way she'd led him out of the water back on the beach, then turned and guided him forward. Every few steps, she looked back as if to confirm he was still with her, her face projecting quiet joy every time she found it so.

When they approached the next bend in the road, Reece was struck again by the feeling of being followed. Angry at having his will so deliberately undermined, he spun to face the servant but found him already some distance away. By all available evidence, they were alone. Yet the sensation of being beneath the eyes of an observer continued rising within him, and this time it was clear that Mia felt it too. It was like the boom of thunder rattling his chest cavity, but sustained and without sound—a silent storm, conscious and full of wrath. Reece stopped in place, again ignoring the tug of Mia's hand.

When he looked to the sky, he felt as though something impossibly large was passing overhead. Mia was sweating. Her calm and capable demeanor had scattered like birds from a shotgun's report. "We have to go," she said.

Reece glanced about, his gaze falling upon nothing in particular. "Something's out there."

Mia took on a forced smile. "It's nothing. Come."

This time he followed. After a few steps she began to jog, and soon after that, her jog became a run, leading Reece around the bend and down a steep section of road. The entrance to the vineyard lay ahead. "What's out there, Mia? What's coming for us?" Reece's voice was breaking, and he was no longer trying to hide his fear. An invisible hand as vast as the ocean was nearly upon them, and its wielder was furious.

"Quick, Reece. Into the vineyard. Hurry!"

Reece skidded to a halt at the top of the steps. They were chipped and cracked, each one fainter than the last as they descended into the darkness. An unseen force was closing in on them, and yet the path ahead filled him with an equal portion of dread. Mia had one leg on the steps and one on the road. She was pulling Reece with both hands, her nails digging into his forearm. "Come on!" she said, her voice filled with panic and anger. Reece felt like a small animal before the headlights of an approaching car, knowing neither what was bearing down on him nor how to respond to it. With a final tug, Mia's hands slipped free. For a moment Reece witnessed the beginning of her fall, and the look on her face was one of profound disappointment.

Once she hit the first step, time resumed its normal pace. She tumbled downward, her head and limbs smacking against the steps until she lay near the bottom, her hair matted with blood. Reece stared in disbelief at his broken lover, his breath coming in quickened fits and starts. He wanted to run to her, to lift her in his arms and retreat further into the vineyard, but the magnetic call to stillness kept him disengaged. After a time, Mia began to move again, slowly at first, then with a disquieting suddenness as she scrambled to her feet and disappeared below.

11

A WORD WITH THE BARKEEP

Prevented from moving forward by a barrier of fear, Reece found that he was only able to retrace his steps. The walk back up seemed far longer than the one he'd taken to the vineyard. It was more than the fact that the road back was all uphill. It was mostly because he was alone—not merely in the sense of having no one to share the road with, but rather of being entirely on his own in the world, and he continued putting one foot in front of the other for no better reason than that he didn't know what else to do with them.

Reece returned to the spot where they'd parked and found that the car was still there. It seemed virtually assured that Mia's valet would have driven it home had he actually taken flight as the servant reported. For all Reece knew, with a little help he'd taken flight off the side of the cliff and was now lying dead below. Having nowhere else to go, Reece climbed inside and lay down in the backseat. The stars above were the same ones he'd seen from the runabout on the waters, but everything below was a world apart. And yet as different as this world was, he'd carried into it all his old faults—weaknesses that had once again allowed tragedy to befall someone he cared for. Reece draped one arm over his eyes, snuffing out the starlight. If Amaya was watching now, it was with a deep sense of self-satisfaction.

When Reece next opened his eyes, the darkness had grown pale with early morning. He sat up and searched his surroundings, finding only stillness. It was now beyond certainty that the valet was dead. Either that or the host had captured him, and he was now wishing he was. The gravel crunched beneath Reece's feet as he climbed out of the car. In the pre-dawn light, the landscape looked even more consumed by entropy than it had in the dark, and a reminder of how this was not the Kythira he knew played again in his thoughts. No matter how many times it had to claw its way up from the chasm, it bore repeating that none of this was normal. And yet he would no doubt soon forget it again as the memory of the world he knew slipped further out of reach.

Reece headed into town and found the streets deserted. It was as if the rising of the sun had sent everyone into hiding all at once. He trudged along the slender paths, finding not a shutter open or a shade undrawn. There were no eyes upon him but those which watched from beyond the sky.

As he arrived in front of The Eye of Night, he heard what sounded like the lowering of a metal shutter. Enlivened by a sign of a nearby human presence, he ascended the incline and onto the property for a second time. There he found the bartender standing in front of the shutter rooting through her backpack, apparently unaware of Reece's presence. Reece was mindful not to startle her, but finding no way of avoiding it, he settled for announcing himself as mildly as possible. "Excuse me."

The bartender looked up from her bag and seemed to recognize him at once. She looked far more conventional in the light of day than she had in the bar, something Reece often found to be the case. Aside from being plain in the face, she was as gangly as a teenager, although she was probably approaching thirty. "Ah, hello. You have come back already. But I am afraid we are closed."

"I know. And I'm sorry to bother you. It's just..." Reece rubbed the back of his neck as he tried to decide how much to tell her, or if he should tell her anything at all.

"Did you get separated from your lady friend?"

"Yes."

"And now you are lost, yes?"

"Yes," Reece said more quietly.

"Hmm. It is quite a thing to be lost in an unfamiliar place. Come with me. I will take you home."

"Home?" Reece felt a tugging in his heart just saying the word, despite not having a clear picture of just where or what in the world home was.

"Yes. I am going home, and I am taking you with me."

Reece felt confounded nearly to the point of suspicion. "Are you sure?"

The bartender flung her bag over her shoulder and started around to the back lot. After a moment of hesitation, Reece followed. "You are not the first stray I have found around here. I do what I can," she said, shrugging.

"Th-thank you," Reece said, trying to dampen the emotion in his voice. "My name's Reece by the way."

The bartender stopped and offered him a hand of bony fingers. "I am Alessa." After they shook, she led him down an alley on the far side of the lot, barely wide enough to ride a bicycle through. The walls were covered in grime, and thick coils of blackened wires were anchored by metal boxes precariously fastened to the pavement. At the alley's end, they ducked beneath a line of drying clothes, and then Alessa took a turn up a set of rusted stairs. Stopping at the top, she rooted through her backpack again. Reece glanced about, supposing this is what Mia had meant by tenement dwellers. The windows of the building across the street were either broken or smeared to the point of being opaque. Plastic crates were stacked everywhere, as if deliveries had been made and no one had ever thought to collect them.

Alessa popped open the plywood door and bid Reece inside. A musty odor greeted him at first, but it was soon tempered by the scent of flowers and herbs. "It gets stuffy in here," she said. "I will open a window." Alessa peeled her shoes off with her feet and left them in the small vestibule by the door before disappearing around the corner. Following suit, Reece knelt and unlaced his boots. Alessa poked her head around the corner. "Will you have tea?"

"That sounds nice." Reece stood and stepped up onto the softwood floor. Beneath a framed sketch of a cottage stood an accent table displaying an assortment of items: a ceramic coin bank shaped like an owl; a jagged amethyst cluster; a wooden king chess piece carved in an ancient Greek style; and an antique kerosene lantern. Alessa's tastes were either highly eclectic or entirely undiscriminating.

He found her in the kitchen boiling water on a two-burner stove. She had several jars of loose leaves open and was taking pinches from each and sprinkling them into tea infusers, one shaped like a submarine and the other like a man in an old-timey diving suit. "No eye of newt for me, please," Reece said. Alessa looked back at him with confusion and then returned to her task. By the time the water came to a boil, the meaning of the joke had dawned on her.

"Ah! You think I am a witch."

"No. God, no. I'm sorry. It's been a long night."

"It is quite all right. Perhaps I am a witch, and I am planning to cast a spell on you." She poured the boiled water into two glass mugs and dropped the infusers in, letting their chains dangle over the sides. Tea-infused water poured out of the submarine's port holes, releasing a golden cloud into the liquid. Alessa leaned against the counter, somewhat coquettishly, Reece thought.

"If I may ask, why do you paint your lips that way?"

She raised her fingers to her lips as though she'd forgotten there was an eyeball painted on them. "Oh, I do that for work. It is my gimmick. Honestly, I have done it for so long that the customers would be disappointed if I stopped."

"Seems like a lot of trouble to go to."

"Not so much. I have gotten very good at it." A silent minute passed as Alessa watched the second hand on the wall clock. Then she removed the infusers from the mugs and gave each a final shake before dropping them into the sink. She handed a mug to Reece. "Make yourself at home. I am going to go wash up." Alessa disappeared through the doorway and Reece was left standing alone in the kitchen. He raised the mug to his mouth and blew on the hot liquid, but as he was about to hazard a sip, he saw Alessa's mug on the counter and switched it for his. After bringing that one to an appropriate temperature, he took a taste. The drink was earthy but not unpleasant, and he found himself inclined to drink more. As he did, he examined his surroundings.

What a difference this was from the first house he'd visited. While the kitchen was clean, the items in it seemed as randomly selected as the items in the hall. Along the counter were several elegant bottles of flavored oils, infused with garlic, lemon, rosemary, and other things he couldn't identify. Next to them, a dish drainer was stacked with scratched and faded plastic plates. The bottles filled with spirals of different colored beans certainly brought an aesthetic charm to the place, but they were a far cry from the hardwood and black marble of the mansion.

Outside the kitchen window, several other apartment buildings framed a view of a mountain range. Reece listened for signs that he wasn't alone, for the sound of a dog barking or a child at play, but all he heard was the groan of the pipes as Alessa turned on the shower and the water sputtered into a steady hiss. He passed into the living room, which apparently doubled as her bedroom. A simple wooden-legged sofa like one might find in the waiting room of a doctor's office abutted the wall. In front of it was a small wooden table. On it sat a lamp with a stained glass shade, along with a collection of well-worn books, mostly in Greek. Against the adjacent wall was a twin bed, above which hung an engraving of a tree.

When the hiss of the shower fell silent, Reece took a seat on the sofa, wanting to appear comfortable when Alessa found him. The patting of bare feet on the floor first signaled her move into the kitchen, and shortly after, she returned to Reece with a mug in hand, wearing an oversized t-shirt that covered the upper half of her thighs. The neon threads of yarn were missing from her hair, which now lay twisted and damp over one shoulder. "How is the tea?"

"Very good." Reece fidgeted in his seat. He was no stranger to going home with women he met at bars, but he was hard-pressed to know what to do in this situation.

Alessa took a seat on the edge of the bed, tucking one leg under her and keeping the other on the floor. "The tea should help you relax. It is my own special blend."

Reece's hand shook a little as he placed the mug on the table in front of him. "I could definitely stand to relax," he said, rubbing the palms of his hands against his jeans. Alessa seemed to be assessing him, but for what he couldn't tell. He only knew that he'd felt safe while she was in the shower and now felt uneasy in her presence.

"What happened between you and your lovely lady friend?" Her eyes took on a shade of gold as she turned her face toward the muted light coming in through the window.

"It's hard to explain." Reece picked up his mug again, emptied it, and then sat it back down harder than he'd intended to. "We were attacked, I suppose. By something unseen, but it was definitely there." Alessa gave no reply, and there was nothing in her expression to indicate that she understood. "She's hurt," Reece said, his voice cracking. "She's hurt, and I don't know if she's going to be okay."

"It sounds like you have had a very difficult morning." After she'd spoken, a whistling issued from the kitchen. "The water has finished boiling. I will go make us some more tea."

"Okay," Reece said in place of the refusal in his thoughts.

"I want you to sit here, not as though you are a guest, but as though you are in the home of a dear friend." She went back into the kitchen and after a few minutes returned with two mugs, then handed him one. "A stronger blend," she said, reclaiming her seat on the bed.

Reece held the drink under his nose and whisked the steam away with a breath before taking a sip. It was sweeter than before, and he was glad to have it. Alessa sipped along with him. "Where did you meet your lovely lady friend who is now hurt?"

"We met on Kapsali Beach. She took me to a party at the mansion overlooking the bays."

"Ah. I have been to such parties."

"The owner doesn't much like my friend, and now he doesn't much like me either."

"Have you given him reason not to like you?"

"Yes," Reece said. "I suppose I have." The sounds of sipping again filled the silence. "What sort of man is he anyway?"

"A very large one," Alessa said, and they shared a smile. "In more ways than one, really," she said with more seriousness. "Some people find themselves drawn to his gatherings. He shows them things."

Reece recalled what he'd seen in the mirror in the mansion's great hall. "What sort of things?"

Alessa held her mug in both hands and leaned forward like she was telling a story around a campfire. "He looks at you. Then when you look in his mirror, you see yourself as he sees you."

Reece felt a knot form in his throat. "And that's something people seek out?"

"If one is truly seeking, it is unlikely they will be troubled by what he sees."

"Did you see something in his mirror?"

"Yes." She offered no further explanation, and Reece chose not to pry. "Can I make you some breakfast?"

"You're very kind, Alessa. But I really can't stay much longer."

"Ah. You are eager to find Mia."

"Yes. Wait, you know her?"

Alessa blew gently into her mug. "Of course. Everyone knows her. She is a prominent woman."

Reece felt his pulse rise, and he straightened in his seat. "Then you know how to find her?"

Alessa tilted her head so that the sunlight was shining on only one eye. Dust motes danced in the air between her face and the window. "At this hour I expect you might find her at home."

"And where is that? I only know that she lives in Kapsali."

"The lighthouse."

"She lives in the lighthouse?"

"Yes," Alessa said. "It is hers."

Reece was baffled. His mysterious provocateur was a lighthouse keeper? "Are you sure?" he asked, a mania growing within him.

"Quite." Alessa drew her other leg onto the bed. Reece sat back against the sofa, staring absently into the tiny golden universe of dust motes in the center of the room. At once everything seemed possible again. "I have told you where to find her because you asked, but I do not think you should go there."

"Why is that?"

"I do not want you to become lost."

"I can't imagine that happening," Reece said. "The lighthouse can be seen from miles away."

Alessa bit down on her lower lip and gazed into her mug before replying. "Remain here in town, just until you are not so much a stranger to this place. You can stay with me, and I will help you find your way. Mia comes to town frequently. You will certainly see her again."

An offer of a place to stay was more than Reece could have hoped for, and he was tempted to accept. But visions of Mia consumed his thoughts, and he found within himself no power to overcome them, not even for the gift of shelter. "I'm honored by your hospitality, Alessa. But my heart won't be at ease until I know she's safe. I hope you understand."

Alessa took on the same expression of pity he'd seen on the servant by the vineyard, but soon after, she conjured a smile and nodded with sympathy. "Of course. Just know that you have a friend here."

Reece raised his glass and drank to the sentiment, then set it down on the table. But when he tried to rise, a weakness in his legs brought him back down to the sofa. "You weren't kidding when you said this tea would relax me."

"A fine reason for you to stay a while longer."

"Maybe just for a few minutes." Reece sank back into the sofa. The room faded and returned in slow pulses as if he were awakening from a dream. But instead of opening his eyes, he found them closing, and in the haze which followed, he felt his mouth being drawn into a kiss. He was floating in an infinite black expanse, and the kiss seemed to come from the darkness itself. Then it released him, and by measures he blinked the bleariness from his eyes until he was back in the room. Alessa was watching him from her bed. "Sorry, I must've dozed off." Reece sat back up in his seat and wiped the sleep from his eyes. "I think I was dreaming about her."

"Were you?"

"It's hard to say." Reece massaged his forehead with his fingertips. "In any case, I'd better get going." This time when Reece rose, he was on steadier legs. Alessa stood with him and then led him back into the hall.

"One last thing," she said. Alessa disappeared into the kitchen, and when she returned, she was carrying a small bundle wrapped in a cloth napkin. "It is amygdalota, a tasty Greek food."

"I really can't—"

Ignoring his protest, she pushed the bundle into his hands. "Eat. You have a long walk ahead of you, and you must retain your strength." Reece thanked her again, and following wishes of meeting again under better circumstances, he passed back into the bright light of morning.

12

THE LIGHTHOUSE

Reece took his amygdalota in nervous bites, not knowing what to expect when he reached the vineyard. To his relief, the journey there was absent the sensation of being shadowed, and once he stood at its entrance, he found that the invisible barrier which had previously restrained him was gone as well. He stepped forward and peered down into the network of vines. Given the speed at which Mia had moved following her startling recovery, it was unlikely she'd used the vineyard as anything more than a thoroughfare to get back home. Even so, he called out her name in case she was lying injured within. Receiving no reply, he removed his foot from the top step and backed up onto the road. There may have been nothing standing in his way, but neither was there anything for him to gain by revisiting that place.

He continued along the road, and in time he set foot upon the sand of the beach where Mia had pulled him from the water. At the far end loomed the lighthouse, looking even more imposing in the light of day. It stood halfway between two mounds on a massive stone fortification. The quaint white lighthouse and the old church across from it were both gone. Reece recalled an artist's rendition he'd seen of the Lighthouse of Alexandria, one of the Seven Wonders of the Ancient World. According to Alessa, this marvel belonged to Mia. If true, Mia was something of a queen, and he would no doubt find her on her throne, her injuries only minor and her face full of joy at the sight of her mystery man from the sea. She would forgive him for not following her into the vineyard. After all, she'd felt as acutely as he had the oppressive force which had come between them. It was only natural that one should find himself inert with terror in such a moment. But once the moment had passed, his heart had urged him to seek her, and for that she would take him back into her arms. She would forgive him, and all would be as it was. Reece quickened his pace.

At the end of the beach, he climbed a set of zigzagging steps and then passed through the open gate into the courtyard. The main structure of the building consisted of eight rows of windows, above which stood a separate level bordered by windows as tall as those he'd seen in the mansion's great hall. Atop that stood a smaller tower supporting the lantern room. At the dome's apex, a statue much like the one Reece had seen in Marseille surveyed both land and water, though this Madonna was without child.

Reece searched the windows for a face he might meet with a look of cheer but found only one of granite, that of a woman, watching from the center of the stone molding through smooth and featureless eyes. He was struck by the same sense of familiarity he'd felt upon seeing the host, and although nothing substantial emerged from the fog of memory, this time the feeling was decidedly positive. When he passed under her eyes, a click issued from within the door. Reece gave it a push. It opened with more of a hush than the groan one might expect from a door that size. Once inside, he shut the door behind him.

Not in his wildest imaginings could Reece have conceived of an odder lighthouse. Gold shimmered from wall to ceiling under the light of a massive chandelier. A pair of curved staircases identical to those in the mansion led to a second-floor landing. Between them, a full-length mirror, black and shining like polished onyx, stood affixed to the wall. On the left side of the landing, an enclosed staircase snaked its way up the perimeter of the room and disappeared into the ceiling.

"Hello?" Reece's voice resonated throughout the chamber but drew no reply. Unsure what to do next, he examined the illuminated niches which lined the walls. Some contained esoteric artifacts he wasn't able to place within any known civilization. Others displayed busts from the Greek pantheon.

After exploring both sides, he returned to the center and investigated the mirror. Although it gave off the appearance of black liquid, it was solid to the touch.

Reece took an initial step back, then continued until he was back at the bottom of the stairs. The banister was smooth and shone like gold in an oil painting. He called up the steps. "Is anyone there?" Finding only bright silence, he ascended, and at the top found a French door. The detailing of its frosted glass, divided into two mirror images, was an art deco design of a goddess rising out of the water from within crashing waves. A soft light gleamed from behind the glass, and Reece took in a sharp breath as he spotted a figure drifting within it. Thin and wispy, it moved like a ghost across the room. Then as if suddenly made corporeal, it gained fullness and approached the door, taking the shape of a woman on the other side. His pulse quickened as he reached for the doorknob, but his fingers curled into a fist before he could touch it.

Who could he credit these confounding misgivings to but Amaya? What exquisite torture it was to have the object of his desire dangled before him, only to be filled with an irrational dread of possessing it. He reached for the doorknob again, but his hand snapped shut, and he took a step back. The figure behind the glass tilted her head as though puzzled. Something was off. An ill-defined voice in the back of his mind urged him to escape this uncanny valley. Breaking into a clammy sweat,

Reece retreated down the stairs, the room's fine trappings swimming before him as he rushed toward the entrance. An arm's length away, another click issued from within the door. He struggled against the handle. It was locked.

Reece stood facing the door, his hands blanched by their grip on its handle. Alessa had been right. He shouldn't have come. Now he was trapped inside this place with God knows what. He felt a set of eyes upon his back and turned to meet them, then flattened himself against the door in fright. Mia was standing within the black mirror, her form ghostly pale against the void. She called him forward with a movement of her fingers, and Reece found within himself no power to resist. This is what he'd come for, and she wasn't going to allow him to forgo it. He approached with careful steps until he was standing only inches from her. She placed her hand flat against the other side of the mirror, and Reece discovered that despite his terror, he still wanted to be with her. He placed his hand against hers, and at once both Mia and the barrier disappeared, revealing a set of steps leading to the level below.

This time he would follow her all the way down. After the first difficult step, each one became easier, revealing in pieces the bright and sterile corridor ahead. At its end, he arrived in a hallway with an identical view to both his left and right. Vaults in stacks of three covered the wall, shining like the steel doors of a mortuary refrigerator. Centered upon each was a screen displaying a holographic image of a man's smiling face, each of them unique but wearing the same placid grin. He approached the screen in front of him, searching the subject's eyes for some spark of awareness, but found only the fixed expression of a man who'd looked upon a Gorgon with pleasure.

Choosing to go left, Reece moved with quiet steps until he reached the hall's end. He peered around the corner, finding another hall just like the last. Somewhere within this fallow abyss Mia was waiting. He crept onward, scanning the faces until he came upon one he recognized—a middle-aged man wearing round-lensed spectacles. He couldn't quite place the man's face, but the image of a wasp on a caterpillar burrowed into his thoughts. The impulse to run was powerful, but with nowhere to run to, he continued on and turned another corner. Halfway down the third hall, he came upon an adjoining passage. It was now clear that had he initially gone right, he would have ended up in the same place, having only passed a different collection of faces along the way. Ahead a final gauntlet waited, and beyond it, a door. Whatever Mia wanted to show him, it was in that room. Reece took a step forward and the screens flickered, replacing the faces of the imprisoned with that of their keeper. "Welcome home, Reece."

While the reasons were yet unclear, Reece understood that he'd reached the visitor's endgame. "My final home," he said.

"As promised. Your destiny awaits you just beyond that door." Reece made his way forward, Mia's eyes following him from every screen. He stopped in front of the door and pushed it open. The room was dark but alive with blinking lights. At its center stood a pyramid with its capstone removed. It was waist high and covered in leaden circuitry, through which an electric blue light ran like a rat through a maze. Above it, a man hovered with his back to Reece, his legs crossed as though in meditation. "You wondered what happened to my valet. Well, there he is. Or more accurately, there they are."

The valet's flesh and hair morphed like a face viewed in a mirror at the peak of an acid trip. "Which one of these men stood at the foot of my bed in the hotel?"

"All of them. They were all there watching. Discovering you. For me."

Reece's blood ran cold. "There must be a hundred of them."

"Ninety-nine to be exact. You have the honor of occupying the final white room, of being the final pound of flesh taken from the world for my beautiful composite man. Along with the others, you'll walk with the one who came first, the one who built this tower. And wherever you walk, you'll go there for the love of me."

To Reece's left, one of the vault doors stood slightly ajar. White light shone from the open space. Its screen was blank. Reece tried to make a sound of derision, but it came out in a quiver. "You don't really expect me to lie down in there, do you?" He was holding back tears, ready to take his final stand whatever form it took. The valet still had his back to him. It was unclear whether or not he was aware of Reece's presence.

"Not now, no. You must come see me first. They all came to see me first, and after seeing all of me they wanted nothing more. No one resisted until you came along. Perhaps it's because I didn't take you straight home from the beach. Perhaps in my arrogance I allowed you to become corrupted by my old friend and his servant. They are full of tricks those two, and I regret flaunting you before them. But never mind that. You must come see me. It's time we finished what we started."

"Why… why would I submit to being kept here?"

"Because it means being kept by me. Look at them, Reece. Never in your life have you been as happy as they are now." The screens flickered again, bringing back the grinning faces of Mia's captives. Her voice continued disembodied. "Their rooms may look small from where you stand, but I assure you they are vast."

Reece studied the faces one by one, his gaze finally falling back upon the room which was to be his. Sickened, he turned away and stepped forward through the door, then circled the pyramid until the valet's face came into view. His eyes were open slightly and trained upon a life-sized statue of a woman sitting on a throne, gripping a staff in her left hand. Her hair cascaded in delicate waves, framing a face both regal and sinister. It was the same face he'd seen over the front door. From above, a crescent of television screens bathed her in flashing colors. Images flickered across the screens almost too briefly to identify: lipstick applied to a vermillion smile; flesh moving against flesh; a delicate hand caressing silken sheets. The form of the valet changed every few seconds, cycling through the identities of the men in the vaults, each receiving equal time in physical worship before the idol.

The light of the screens blinked away, and when it returned, Mia's face appeared across them. "Are you ready to join us, Reece?"

Tears rolled down his cheeks. "What is it you want me to do?"

"No more than what you were going to do before you were led astray. My body awaits you on the second floor. Do open the door this time."

With that, the screens flickered again, and the images returned. Reece felt like someone had hollowed him out and discarded his contents. So this was his final home, to be one of many and each a slave. He faltered back out into the hall, falling to one knee by the door which was to bear his image. He tried to look in, to see for himself the inside of his shiny coffin, but he couldn't bring himself to open it. Mia said her inmates were happy, and Reece couldn't deny that it appeared so on the surface. But each of them had arrived with their own tale of misery, perhaps now forgotten, but nonetheless etched into the record of their lives. Their stories had each begun with a late-night visit from a stranger and had ended here in this living morgue. They smiled, but it was the empty smile of the hollow, of bodies sick with dead pleasures.

And then there was Amaya, an innocent bystander driven to her death for no apparent reason but the pure joy of evil. Reece struggled to his feet, his jaw clenched and cheek twitching. Never before had he hated someone so much. Provocateur, monarch, slaver. Bewitcher and destroyer of lives. He had come to the lighthouse seeking Mia, and it was high time he found her.

On his way back to the ground floor, Reece felt like one of Alessa's figurines moving forward on a predetermined track. He didn't know what he planned to do, only that he couldn't stop until he looked the devil in the eye. He found the French door closed, with no sign of movement beyond its glass. This time when he reached for the doorknob, he found no resistance.

The room's decor was much like that of the grand foyer—an array of deep reds and lustrous shades of gold. On the right, a spiral staircase disappeared into the ceiling. Against the wall to his left, he found a vanity set and mirror. At center was vanity itself in the form of an opulent bed under an oil painting of its owner. Sitting on the front edge of the bed with her legs crossed was Mia, dressed in a gold silk camisole, leering from beneath thick black lashes. Her arms and legs were speckled with bruises.

Reece held his fists by his sides, the muscles of his arms and shoulders tense. With effort he relaxed his jaw enough to speak. "The whole way to the lighthouse all I could think about was making things right with you. Can you believe I was actually going to beg for your forgiveness?"

"Imagine that," Mia said.

"Yes, imagine that."

"But you don't need my forgiveness, Reece. You need only remain in my good graces. And for that, you need only do what comes naturally." Mia uncrossed her legs and leaned back on her hands. "You were on the right track last night, until you got derailed by that servant." She clucked her tongue and gave her head a dour shake. "Imagine following a servant when you could follow a queen."

"Imagine that," Reece said. Mia held him in her eyes, and Reece fought against the sensation, well known to him by now, of falling into her.

"He has some impressive tricks," she said. "Even I don't know how he pulled that stunt by the vineyard. But he's not the little birdie who's been whispering in your ear, is he?"

"I don't know what you mean."

"I'm talking about that ugly bartender, Reece. She put an influence spell on you and apparently didn't think I'd notice." Mia scrutinized her nails. "What an amateur."

"Enough! I'm not here to discuss your petty rivalries."

Mia leaned forward with her hands on the edge of the bed. "So what are you here for then?"

"Same as I told you on the beach before you got into my head and made me forget. I'm here to find Amaya."

Mia smirked. "Would that make you happy?"

An exasperated laugh escaped Reece's mouth. "To hell with happiness. Especially if it comes from the likes of you."

"Don't be ridiculous. Happiness is happiness, no matter the source. It's only chemicals, after all." Mia clucked her tongue again. "And you accuse me of being petty. If only you understood what I was offering."

"I've seen what you're offering."

Mia gave a dismissive wave. "You've seen nothing."

"I've seen enough to know I don't want it."

"You don't know what you want," she said, taking on a fierce expression.

"Oh, but I do." Reece took a step forward. "I want you to suffer for what you did to us."

Mia ran her manicured fingers over the silken sheets, watching absently as the wrinkles disappeared under her hand, and then peered at him again from underneath her lashes. "Very well then. If hatred is all you have, then take me with that. Beat me and take me bloody and battered. But you must take me. The Rite of Assent must be performed."

Reece rushed forward, wrapping his hands around her throat and pinning her to the bed. "I'll take you! I'll take you straight to hell!" Saliva dripped from his mouth and onto her face as he squeezed, and the muscles of his forearms bulged. Mia's eyes grew glassy, and a series of tiny noises escaped her lips. After a time, she managed to free her legs from beneath his, and she drew her knees to her chest and then kicked him so hard he flew back off the bed and landed on the floor.

Mia sat back up in bed, gasping for air, but with a look of intense exhilaration on her face. Before Reece could climb back to his feet, the section of floor he was sitting on sprung open beneath him, and he fell into darkness.

13
DOWN IN A HOLE

The trapdoor had been hidden beneath the plush rug at the foot of Mia's bed, and now Reece could only watch helplessly as it snapped shut above him with the rug still attached, stealing the remaining light from his eyes.

He rolled onto his elbows and crawled up off the dirt floor. Darkness surrounded him, and the only sound was that of his own breaths. He broke into a cold sweat as a single word entered his thoughts: oubliette—a dungeon with only one entrance and no exit. It wasn't a place for prisoners but for people to be discarded and forgotten. Darkness itself was the weapon. His thirst and hunger were the torture devices that would bring about his slow demise.

Staying close to the floor, Reece felt around with his hands, hoping and praying he didn't find the bones of the last poor soul who'd dared to turn his back on Mia's silken altar. The first thing he touched was the frame of a bed. On it, there was a mattress with sheets, and thankfully no body. He stumbled in the dark a bit longer until he came up against a wall. The wallpaper was peeling and felt quite old. He continued until he bumped into a piece of furniture. A chair. A desk. A mirror. The vanity set he'd seen in Mia's room. Reece was in some sort of replica of the space above. If that were true, there must be some analog to the French door. He kept feeling his way around to the wall across from the foot of the bed, but instead of a door he found an alcove, and at its end what felt like the black mirror he'd touched in the grand foyer. He rapped on it with his knuckles. The material was solid, more like obsidian than glass. It would take some doing if he meant to break it, but if he succeeded, he would no doubt find the grand foyer on the other side.

A static charge prompted Reece to take a step back. Scan lines rolled down the surface of the mirror like a bad TV, and Reece continued backward until he fell into a seated position on the bed. An image had emerged—a solitary glow in a sea of black, and for a moment Reece was back on the sponson, Amaya weeping an arm's distance away, the mustiness of Mia's dungeon replaced by the salty ocean air. Staring from the black mirror were the eyes of the spider, shimmering like soap bubbles and surrounded by coarse red hairs, demarking with fierce intensity the leathery flesh around them. There was no message. Just the glistening eyes watching him like an insect bound in silk to be fed upon later. Perhaps that was the message after all. *You are simply waiting to die.*

It was a full minute before Reece was able to consider a course of action. He had to try to speak to it, lest he sit there in silence until he died of thirst. Odds were it understood English. Odds were it understood every language. "What do you want from me?" he asked. Reece's watcher remained silent. "What are you…?" He swallowed hard, working to get the feared question whose answer he couldn't do without past his lips. "What are you going to do to me?" Eight lustrous spheres hung before him without reply.

In the room above, someone was pacing the floor. The footsteps carried from one end to the other, causing the trapdoor to creak with each pass. At once it became clear. The spider wasn't toying with him—it was awaiting instructions. Reece's fear of the unknown gave rise to a sudden and satisfying renewal of his belligerence, and he grinned like a madman in the dark. "She hasn't decided what to do with me yet, has she? And all a lackey like you can do is watch and wait for permission." The creature's eyes vibrated subtly. Reece was getting through. "Well, I'm here to tell you that you're not even allowed to do that." Though his legs were unsteady, he rose from the bed. If he was going to mock death, better he do it on his feet. It wasn't long before what was left of his anesthetized fear burst into flames of wrath. "Do you hear me, you son of a bitch? You don't get to just sit there and stare!"

The moment Reece started shouting, the footsteps above came to a stop. *Good. Now I have everyone's attention.* He gripped the bedpost nearest him, and then using his foot as leverage, he pulled until the rotted wood splintered and broke. Then Reece spun to face his watcher. With weapon in hand, it was time to give his rage a proper showing. "I'll have no more of your fucking eyes!" Reece charged the mirror, but before he could attack, the spider flicked its jaws out, revealing a set of fangs which protruded beyond the mirror's surface. Reece dropped his weapon and threw his hands up to block the attack. With a hiss, the spider ejected a stream of liquid into Reece's face, causing him to stumble backward, and when his head smacked against the bedframe, the room fell back into darkness.

The morning sun lay in repose over rolling green hills in a land outside of time. All around, birds were intoning their songs of love, and Reece knew that somewhere within the idyllic hamlet below, Amaya was tending the fire as she awaited his return from war. He could almost smell the hot meal that would be waiting for him upon the one table in the world where he was a king. Reece closed his eyes and took in the spring air. He pictured her at her bedroom vanity set, brushing her golden hair. His desire to see her again grew ever stronger as he watched her in his mind's eye, until finally he broke himself from his fantasy and resumed his trek down the cobblestone path into the village.

Reece stole a glance through the open window of a flint rock house with a thatched roof. A man was sitting in a chair with a child on each knee. His wife was setting the table and smiling broadly at something he'd said. "That will be us one day, God willing." Reece picked up his pace. Passing another house, he spied a similar scene. A woman with flowing red locks was laying out her family's breakfast. From the looks of it, they were having homemade bread and a variety of fruits, cheeses, and sliced meats. "Looks delicious," Reece said, swinging his arms with increasing fervor as he continued down the path. Next, he passed the town chocolatier, who could be seen through his window detailing a tray of sweet delights. The man looked up and waved, smiling warmly as he passed. Reece waved back and then let out a cheerful laugh. "Ye Gods, every fine fare imaginable are on display today. I can't wait to see what Amaya has prepared." Onward he continued past house after house, finally arriving at the other side of town. There was only one house remaining between him and the procession of hills that marched into the distance. "That's funny." Reece looked back the way he came. "Has it really been so long? I can't remember for the life of me which house is mine." It was then he noticed the birds were no longer singing.

At the edge of the flowerbed to his right, a wild rabbit thumped its foot with its ears directed toward the hills. The wind had picked up, and the grass bowed in one direction and then in another as it shifted. Then it died down, and from beyond the hilltop a dusky figure in black came stomping into the hamlet, his eyes bright red and full of violence. He stopped before the final cottage, fists tight by his sides, knees bent, and back hunched as if struggling under the weight of his fury. Across his forehead, six additional eyes burned forth from his flesh like flaming coals, while two sets of spider's legs ripped their way out of his back. Once the transformation was complete, the creature spoke. "What are you going to do?" he asked, and Reece's only reply was a look of shocked horror. The monster took another step forward. "You don't get to just stand there and stare!"

Reece stumbled backward, nearly losing his footing. "Stay back!"

"I'll tell you what I'm going to do," the monster continued, his fist quavering in front of him. "I am going to possess you—forever!" He punctuated the final word by bringing his fist down upon the mailbox, shattering it to splinters.

Reece fumbled for his dagger before whipping it from its sheath. "I said stay back!" Ignoring the threat, the monster closed the distance in a few bounding steps. Reece swung the dagger, parting flesh and sending a stream of blood across the cobblestones and into the flowerbed, sprinkling the flowers with crimson dew. A second slash across the monster's face caused one of his eyes to dislodge. It dangled by a thread of pink tissue, tumbling back and forth across his face as they fought. Blood poured out of the wound, staining his gnashing teeth, but if he felt any pain, he gave no sign.

"I will possess you forever!" A crushing blow landed on Reece's ribs, and in the shock of pain his hand opened halfway, leaving the dagger balanced between his thumb and forefinger. The monster slapped it away, and it went twirling into the flowerbed, and then he gripped Reece by the collar. Reece tried to free himself by applying forward pressure with his hand, but the fiend bit into his flesh, his eyes flashing as he tasted blood. Reece let out a wail and yanked his hand free, leaving a chunk of meat behind. He tried to turn and run, but the monster twisted the collar of his shirt with both hands, binding him ever tighter and forcing him to the ground. His blood dripped onto Reece's face, and his errant eye swung like a pendulum as his arachnoid limbs lashed out like vipers. After opening a series of cuts, they drew back and the upper limbs lowered in unison, slowly converging over Reece's face. The black barbs upon their tips scratched hungrily at the air. When the monster spoke again there was a mocking joy in his voice. "I'll have no more of your fucking eyes." Reece cocked his head back, pawing impotently as he tried to hold his attacker at bay.

On the road behind him, standing no more than a dozen feet away, Amaya was watching with a look of detachment. She was wearing her nightgown and brushing her hair with long, slow strokes. Reece took in a panicked gasp and emptied his lungs. "Run, Amaya!"

At once the sunlight faded, casting a shadow across the land. Bits of the village, stones, and pieces of thatched roofs broke free and rose into the overcast sky. Even the monster was lifted up and devoured by the heavens. All the while Amaya kept brushing her hair with an expression of indifference, and as everything around them floated upward, Reece felt himself falling.

14
THE RITE OF ASSENT

Reece blinked his eyes open when he heard the sound of Mia's voice. He raised his throbbing head from the floor, finding himself at the foot of the bed. The room, now lit by candlelight, was just as he'd expected—identical to the one he'd fallen from except more timeworn. While the one above matched the luxuriousness of Mia's grand foyer, this version looked more like the rest of the island.

Mia was sitting at the vanity set, brushing her hair with long, slow strokes. A white nightgown extended to her ankles, and her feet were bare. The mirror in the alcove had gone dark. "It's funny, isn't it? No matter how deep an abyss you're in, there's always something below it." Reece took a moment to absorb what he was seeing before pawing at the painful spot on the back of his head. He winced as his fingers passed over a sticky cut. Mia peered at him from the reflection in the cracked mirror. "A strange place to take a nap considering there's a bed right behind you. But I suppose you know best."

Reece sat up the rest of the way and rubbed his eyes with his forearm, unsure of whether or not he was still dreaming. "It's probably in my best interest to apologize for trying to kill you, but I'm not sorry at all, so I guess we're both out of luck."

"I expect I'll get over it. Besides, it's going to take much bigger hands than yours to kill me, Reece." Mia laid the brush on the vanity set and took one last look at herself in the mirror before turning to face him. She looked almost innocent without makeup, which was terrifying considering how guilty she was.

"Why can't you just leave me the hell alone?"

The light from the candles danced in her eyes. "Get that notion out of your head. It's time you came to terms with the fact that you will never be rid of me. That might scare you now, but there will soon come a time when the idea of being separated from me will be the only thing you fear." She stood and moved toward him, her nightgown whispering with every step.

Persuaded that he was in fact awake, Reece scrambled up onto the bed. By the time his back hit the headboard, Mia was standing at its foot, watching him with what looked like satisfaction. She drew open the nightgown's bow and let it fall over one shoulder. "I know what you want." She paused, seeming to gauge his response, then let the gown pass over her other shoulder and onto the floor.

Reece looked away. "You can't possibly think I'd want this. I'd finish the job I started upstairs if you weren't my only hope of getting out of this room."

"Your only hope of getting out of this room is right here in this bed. So what do you say? Are you going to invite me in?"

"No. I don't want this."

"Yes, you do. You think you tried to kill me because you suddenly realized I'm evil? Wrong. You tried to kill me because you thought I was all yours, and when that illusion shattered, you broke right with it. But what you don't understand is that I belong to all of you just as much as you belong to me. You are all carefully chosen, and I make sure to personally call each of you into the water."

Reece lowered his eyes. "She never came back, did she? It was you who visited me. The image of Amaya was just bait."

"And what wild game you turned out to be. But now I've got you, and it's time at last to bring you into this eternal fold. You need only give yourself to me. But I warn you, this will be your last chance. You've denied me twice already. I won't suffer another insult."

There was no way out. Reece tried to project strength, but between the violence of the dream he'd endured and the weight of Mia's presence in its aftermath, he didn't have much fight left in him. When he spoke, his voice sounded shot through with defeat. "Does it have to be here? Does it have to be...like this?"

Mia's face darkened, and she released a slow hiss through her teeth. "Yes, Reece. It does. You could have had me any way you wanted, but those doors are now closed. So you're going to take me as I am, right here in this fetid pit." She leaned forward, and the light from the sconces brightened her features. "What's it going to be? Will you love me, or would you rather find out what it's like inside my pyramid?"

Reece pulled his shirt off and tossed it aside, and a faint smile crept across her lips. Once he was fully undressed, she placed her hands on the edge of the bed and crawled toward him, then reached forward and touched his thigh. He didn't flinch. Her touch was inevitable, and all that mattered now was that it was a gentle one. She dipped down low, curving her back and gliding up to meet his lips in one fluid movement. Reece went through the motions as if they were the same people they'd been in the bar the night before. Once Mia withdrew her kiss, she placed her hand on his chest and pushed him back against the headboard, then moved in the rest of the way and straddled his lap. She gathered her hair into her hands and tied it back into a messy double knot, revealing the finger-shaped bruises around her neck.

Reece ran his fingers over the injury and closed his eyes. When Mia guided him inside of her, he found himself floating on the surface of an endless sea. All that existed beyond him was the rise and fall of the waves and the salty breeze which carried a lover's words to his ears.

At the end of an indefinite expanse of time, Reece lay awake, entangled in Mia's limbs. Although she was still and silent, he somehow knew she wasn't sleeping. "Was that it? Was that the Rite of Assent?"

Mia gently stirred. "Mm-hm."

"Are you sure it took? I don't feel any different. I still hate you for instance."

"And you love me."

"I fear you. Something tells me you're more than old enough to have learned the difference between love and fear by now."

"Fear is the beginning of love for a man such as you, Reece. Now that you've surrendered your will, you're finally free to love. Your intellect will rebel at the notion, but if you search your heart, you'll find that what I say is true."

"Then I'm free to hate you as well."

"Yes." Mia rolled Reece onto his back and positioned her body atop his, curling her fingers into his hair. "But you won't want to. The ritual has bound you to me. From now on if you stray, you'll wilt like a flower in darkness. When you leave here and go out into the world, you will find it exactly so. In fact, it's of vital importance to me that you do. Once you're in my keep, I can't have you wondering what it would be like to be free again. I need you to know what it's like, and I need you to hate it."

"And my hatred of you?"

"Will die a natural death."

"Why not just treat me with kindness so that I'd never feel the need to stray?"

"You're being obtuse, Reece. And I suspect it's deliberate." Mia tugged at his hair, and a look of controlled madness came over her as if she were weighing whether she wanted to start ripping it out by the handful. "There's only one way this works, and it has nothing to do with kindness." Mia let out something like a purr as she took his lower lip in between her teeth, nibbling gently for a time before snapping her head back and drawing blood.

"Ow! What the hell was that for?"

Mia flopped onto her back and stretched her arms out over her head. "As if I need a reason."

Reece smeared the blood away with the back of his hand. "How am I ever supposed to trust you if I have to live in constant fear of being attacked?"

"The Rite of Assent is complete. I no longer require your trust."

"Even so, you didn't have to bite me."

Mia sat back up with alarming speed. "Do you really want to compare wounds?"

He looked away. "No. I don't suppose I do." Mia crawled back onto his lap and gripped the back of his neck. When she moved to put her mouth against his, he flinched, and she waited in place until the muscles of his neck relaxed, then took his lip into her mouth and sucked on it gently. Reece didn't dare move for fear of what she might do next, but as the seconds passed the rhythmic pull of her mouth set him at ease, and eventually, despite himself, he placed his hands around her waist. Mia had a real talent for inflicting fear and pain and then contrasting her affections against it, making an unexpected gift out of every tender touch. When the bleeding stopped, she released his lip. "What happens next between us?" he asked.

"You're going to leave me for the last time. I want you to spend a night as far away from me as you can get. By the time the sun rises, you'll know where you belong."

"You mean in my very own tomb in your basement."

"Tombs are for the dead, Reece. There is a room waiting for you below, but it's not a place of darkness. It's one of light."

A horror Reece could scarcely fathom gripped his heart. "I'm scared. I don't want to be kept inside one of those rooms. Can't I just serve you like this?"

"I'm afraid not. But don't give a moment's worry to how you'll feel. I want you all to enjoy every moment in this wonderful world."

Reece let his head fall to her shoulder. He desperately wanted to believe her. "If there's any mercy in you, please give me your word. Give me a real promise I can hold onto." For a time, he heard only the cry of his inner anguish, then she spoke.

"I promise, Reecey." Reece knew the voice well. He lifted his head from her shoulder as if trapped in slow motion, and as he drew back, Amaya's breast came into view, detailed down to the faintest freckle. He flung her aside and leaped to his feet, hiding his face behind outstretched hands. Roiling panic rampaged through his body, and it was some time before he dared to hazard a peek through his fingers. When he did, he found Mia reclining on her back, propped up on her elbows and wearing an amused expression. "Just look at you. Talk about an overreaction."

Reece lowered his hands from his face. "That was a cruel trick."

"I thought it might please you."

"If that's true, you have the emotional intelligence of a snake."

Mia laughed. "Such fire. You really are a wild one, Reece." She lifted her legs from the bed and rubbed them together slowly. "Honestly, I'm glad to see it. Some of you are no fun at all."

Reece was nearly breathless with exasperation. "Do whatever you want with me—just leave Amaya buried, okay?"

"By 'buried' I'm assuming you mean 'picked apart by fish,' because that's what happened."

"Whatever you want to call it. You know, after all of your explanations there's still one thing I don't understand. You say you want me to enjoy every moment in this world, but you don't seem to have any idea what I want or any misgivings about tormenting me on the slightest whim."

Mia sat up. "You're right, you don't understand. You seem to think that once you're down below, I'm going to keep you satisfied by doing things for you. That's not how it works. I keep my people satisfied by doing things for me. It is my pleasure that feeds the white rooms. There it is processed and sent back to me all at once from the nervous systems of a hundred bodies uncorrupted by death. Then the heightened signal is sent back to the rooms, and the cycle continues until we're all gratified beyond want." Mia rose from the bed and approached Reece. She wove her fingers behind his neck, her eyes wild with passion. "Imagine being a part of such a machine. That's what awaits you upon your return. And once the Rite of Merging is complete, you'll look back in wonder at how foolishly you obsessed over how I treated you, as if kindness could have ever bound you to me."

Whether or not any of what she was saying was true didn't matter. She was offering him an open door. Only time would tell if he would walk back through it all on his own. "Okay, I'll do as you ask. I'll go as far away as I can, and if what you say is true, I'll come back at dawn."

Mia raised herself on her toes and kissed him once more. "The path down to your room will be left open for you." She headed toward the mirror in the alcove as Reece dressed. With a wave of her hand, it blinked to life. The shimmering orbs which had been the spider's eyes coalesced in neat columns and rows at its center, forming an eight-digit keypad. Mia entered a code, and the eyes broke off in pairs to the edges of the screen, revealing what looked like a ceremonial chamber on the other side, with flickering candles and esoteric symbols carved into a stone floor. After casting one last glance at Reece, she stepped through, and the screen went dark behind her. Then it flashed electric blue, and the surface of the mirror vanished, revealing an open door back into the grand foyer.

15
THE PYRAMID

The silence Mia left behind was bittersweet. On the one hand, the weight of fear of her next caprice was gone. But on the other, Reece now had to wonder when he would begin to feel the pangs of her absence, a state of mind he could hardly imagine and one that if realized would be something akin to madness. It was a strange feeling, imagining one's sanity slipping away like sand through an hourglass, not knowing the hour yet knowing it was at least as near as the next sunrise.

He passed through the open door and into the grand foyer, another round of electric blue flashing behind him. When he turned, he found the path down to the white rooms open as before, just as she had promised. His vault was waiting—cold, bright, and eternal. But forever would have to wait. For now, his task was to run and to keep running until he understood at last that there was nowhere to run to at all.

Inconceivable as it was, Mia's prediction rang true. She wouldn't be sending him on this fool's errand if its outcome wasn't foreordained upon every vault door. But maybe there was a chance, however small, for Reece's story to end differently. After all, the others hadn't seen her wicked side, hadn't tasted the stale air of the pit or stood before the nightmare face within her black mirror. Perhaps these differences were enough to break the thread of fate. They'd certainly been enough to make her promise of paradise ring hollow.

Reece paced the room while throwing glances toward the front door, certain only that if he crossed its threshold, he'd be turning his back on those who'd tried to help him. However, if he failed to follow Mia's instructions, she would consign him to her pyramid, whatever that meant. Lost in what might be his final inner dialog as a free-thinking man, he walked the perimeter of the chamber, passing before the eyes of forgotten gods and relics of lost ages, until he came upon an artifact within a glass dome display case. At first, it looked like a piece of a withered branch, but upon closer inspection, Reece recognized the two black barbs at its tip. It was the same appendage the monster in his dream had tried to take his eyes out with, and Mia was keeping it here as a trophy. Her words rang in his thoughts. *"You'll walk with the one who came first, the one who built this tower."* So, he was the core of her composite man of shadows, the infernal heart beating beneath the human bones and sinew. Reece had given himself to Mia, but it was the spider he was to be joined with in the Rite of Merging.

At once, Reece felt several times larger than his frame. He marched back along the procession of gods, stopping at the end just long enough to wrestle the bust of Artemis off its pedestal, and then made his way down the steps and back into the basement with the goddess of the hunt tucked under his arm. Halfway down the hall, the displays on the doors began to flicker, and the face of Mia again replaced those of her captives. "You're back early. And with your arm around another woman. *Tsk, tsk, tsk.*" Reece rounded the corner into the center hall. Twin rows of Mia's lay before him. "What are you planning to do with that? Kill my valet? A bold move, but I'm afraid it won't work. There are far too many of them. Snuff out one, and another will instantly take his place." Reece peered at the screen to his right, at the face of the woman he'd adored only hours before.

"You really are a difficult one, Reece. But that's what makes you special. And you'll have a special place here, above the others. We wild ones have to stick together." She granted Reece a silent moment to consider her proposal. He responded by swinging the statue back like a battering ram and slamming it headfirst into the screen. Then he continued his march to the pyramid room, the shattered screen spitting sparks as Mia's voice followed him down the hall. "I really do have great affection for you, Reece. But don't go thinking that's going to save you."

Inside the room, the crescent of monitors was playing a frenetic feed of violent imagery. Grainy clips of hammers smashing into skulls and gangs of men surrounding and stomping pleading victims flashed across the screens. The valet remained above the pyramid with his eyes half open, but his muscles were tense, and his limbs twitched in spasms coinciding with the sounds of battered flesh emanating from the video feed.

Reece lifted the bust and balanced it on one shoulder, preparing to launch it into the valet's skull and granting those imprisoned the deliverance they were too far gone to seek themselves. But at the last moment, he hesitated. Not for any lack of will on his part, but because he knew that what Mia had said in the hall was true. His plan wouldn't work. He'd seen proof of it with his own eyes back at the mansion when the host had demolished one man only to have another materialize unharmed.

Beneath the valet, an electric blue light raced through the pyramid's circuitry. There was power in this device. It was perhaps itself the source of the valet's abilities. Reece lifted the bust above his head and brought it crashing down upon the pyramid's face. Fiery sparks shot forth, hissing like an enraged snake and rising to consume the valet, who fell shrieking from his perch and onto the floor, his flesh crackling under the flames.

By the time the fire died, the pyramid's light had faded. The face of Artemis watched triumphantly from within its smoking wreckage. The sounds of mayhem from the video feed went silent, and Mia's image appeared on the screens. Her eyes were as cold as stone in winter. "It's going to be a long, painful road back into my arms, Reece Holloway."

"That isn't a road I'll be taking," Reece said. A moan drew his attention to the floor, where the scorched valet was stirring. Apparently, Reece had been right. Destroying the pyramid had been enough to keep him from changing form. Judging by his grotesque appearance, he'd been stopped mid-transition. His hair consisted of black bristles poking through his scalp in patches. His face was a mass of melted flesh, and his mouth a mere slit as if opened by a surgeon's knife.

Reece backed up until he hit the door and then took off in a run down the hall past the faces on the white rooms. Each now wore their own expression, some of fear and some of anguish, but most of them twisted in snarling rage. He turned the corner and raced up the steps but froze in place halfway. The door was closed, and the black mirror once again projected the face of the spider, twitching like a broken hologram and brandishing its fangs in shuddering pulses.

The sinking feeling in Reece's stomach threatened to spill its contents onto the floor. There was no way out. He would have to return to the pyramid room in the hope of finding a way to disable the mirror. Otherwise, he'd be trapped between what was left of the valet and the spider's dripping fangs, already primed to send him back to a nightmare from which he may never return. Reece rushed back down the hall but stopped short again as he turned the corner. The valet was limping toward him at speed, his furious eyes trained upon Reece from within dark hollows.

Reece headed back down the hall and turned the other corner, rushing down the opposite way toward the pyramid room. Once he reached the adjoining corridor, the valet appeared on the other side, and both men stopped in place, waiting for the other to make the first move. Reece broke the stalemate, racing toward the final hall and heading off the valet by no more than an arm's length for a final sprint toward the door. He slammed it shut, throwing the latch without a moment to spare. The door rocked and shuddered as the valet threw his body against it, roaring in outrage. Reece stepped back, watching with caution. He was under no illusion that the valet would give up anytime soon, but it looked like the door would hold for now.

There was no obvious control module for the room's equipment, only a screen like a large computer monitor mounted between two towers of blinking lights. Reece ran his fingers along its bottom and sides, searching for a power button, but found nothing. He pressed his hand against its surface, becoming ever more frustrated as the hammering on the door grew louder. This might be the end for him, entombed between Mia's broken pyramid and the bronze queen on her throne, there to bear cold witness to his demise.

Reece approached the statue and searched it with his hands. Behind him, the door bucked on its hinges, and he remembered his encounter with the host. But this time he was alone. If there was a way out of the room, it was up to him to find it. He moved around to the back of the statue and found an identical throne but no queen. He took a seat, and it lowered a few inches. Then it rotated a hundred eighty degrees, and as the door burst open and the valet rushed into the room, the throne sank into the floor.

The ceiling closed above him, and Reece found himself rumbling down into the abyss. The throne's armrests became slick with sweat as he pondered whether he was escaping or merely delivering himself to the very fate Mia had promised as the price of disobedience. For a time, there were only the bare rock walls illuminated at measured intervals and the din of the gears driving the platform lower. Then the wall ahead opened into a subterranean chamber, and the platform slowed as it finished its descent, coming at last to a booming halt.

He stood and stepped out from within the wall's recess. On either side of him, stone reliefs more than a dozen feet tall and depicting the valet's arachnidian form knelt in supplication. On the other side of the chamber, twin statues portraying the woman on the throne stood silent watch over a steel vault. Along the walls, slivers of light shone from the masonry, crawling over the rippling waters of a pool carved into the center of the floor and casting a pattern like television snow onto the ceiling. The room was a veritable festival of lights yet still quite dark, as none of them aspired to anything beyond a glimmer. Reece made his way down a ramp and approached the pool. The movement of the water suggested an entrance to the sea somewhere beneath its surface. As Reece neared its edge, he was able to make out the black shape of a tunnel some distance below. He knelt and dipped his finger in the water, then tasted it. Saltwater. So, the front door wasn't the only way in and out. But what sort of creature might make use of such a passage?

He continued along the edge of the pool to the vault on the other side. As he drew near, a screen half his height and several feet wide came into focus. No sooner had Reece made sense of what he was looking at than it powered on, revealing Mia's scowling face. Reece leaped back, and her scowl became a crooked grin. "Looks like you're between a wolf and a precipice, Reece."

Reece took two more steps to the rear. "What's in the vault, Mia? What are you hiding?"

"Only my curse." A metallic clink issued from within the screen, and it separated from the vault, hovering in a cerulean aura. When it advanced, it sounded like the drone of a vacuum cleaner running at quarter speed, and Reece gave ground with cautious steps, not knowing whether it had the power to attack. After some distance it circled right, revealing the window it had concealed. Behind it, a humanoid creature rested within an amber fluid. As with the host, she was a picture of beauty distorted, with sharp but feminine features and a thin line of a mouth extending to the back of her jaw. Where her eyes should have been, there were only empty sockets.

Mia spoke again from the screen, her voice dripping with venom. "I offered you the gift of forever and you spat in my hand, as if nothing could be worse than an eternity with me. Oh Reece, if only you knew." Laughter erupted from the screen, and the vacuum cleaner sound mingled with that of the amber fluid draining from the vault, creating a noise like surgical equipment slurping up mangled viscera.

"I know one thing, Mia. Your inmates might smile, but your paradise is just another form of hell. I submitted to it mostly out of fear of something worse, although I will admit there might've been some part of me that actually wanted to be undone by you, just like that and for all the wrong reasons. But if it was ever there, it's dead now."

Mia raised an eyebrow. "Dead like the people of this island, or dead like Amaya? They're two very different things, you know."

"Dead and gone," Reece said. "And I won't be terrorized into submitting to you again."

"Dead like Amaya then. And on the contrary, you will be terrorized into submitting to me again. And a lot sooner than you think. A change in stimuli can do wonders for a person's outlook."

"It'll make no difference," Reece said, shaking his head. "I reject you now, and I'll reject you in an hour. And the others will reject you too once they find out what you are." A fire was roaring within him. He nearly believed his pronouncements.

"Many have rejected me. They now reside within my pyramid."

Reece made a show of laughing scornfully. "You mean the one I just destroyed?"

"You destroyed nothing. But you did create a splitting headache for its chief engineer, and for that I'll have to give him last crack at you."

Reece busied his mind on crafting a plan of resistance. Inside the vault, the level of fluid was just above the creature's eye sockets. The exposed portion of her skin shone iridescent under the lights like the scales of a Boelen's python.

"It didn't have to be like this, Reece. You could have taken your place in my machine, and in time I would've revealed myself to you in just the right way—not with anger, but with love. Drunk on pleasure, you wouldn't have cared what I looked like, and following in the footsteps of wiser men, you would have renewed your pledge to me and entered the circle of my most trusted servants." A cowl of shadows fell over her image. "Or perhaps you would've been like the others, loving only hollow beauty, and upon seeing me you would've woken up screaming in your vault, our bond forever broken." Mia's features twisted into a pantomime of terror, and she let out a piercing scream. His nerves shredded, Reece turned away and dropped his gaze to the floor.

"What a disappointment that would've been for me," she continued. "And in my disappointment, I would've likely given you a whole lot more to scream about. But such chagrin can't compare to what I feel over you not even deigning to step foot into my white and glistening world. You've traded a lover for a vivisector, and for zero gain, making you my greatest fool. And through your foolish lips you declare that you reject me, as if my offer was still on the table, as if you weren't already falling into your final endless night."

In the aftermath of her speech, Reece stood listening to the amber fluid draining from the vault, his eyes still lowered to the floor. "Look at me, Reece." After some hesitation, he raised his eyes to her ashen hologram. "Not at the screen, Reece. Look at *me*!"

Cringing, he turned his attention to the vault. The fluid level was just below the creature's nose. At first her shoulders merely shifted, as if she were just stirring from the deepest layers of sleep. Then she raised her hands and pressed them against the empty sockets. When she lowered them, she was gazing at him through eyes like great black pearls. Reece looked back at the screen. "You're nothing but a monster role-playing as a human being. And who is this unlucky woman whose body you've been wearing like a dress? I assume you have others like her in your closet."

"A lovely piece, isn't she? The finest in my collection. Remind me to tell you where I get them before I send you on your way."

"I don't understand. If you have them, why ever reveal your true face?"

"Because to love a mask and not its wearer is to not love at all."

Reece made a sound of disgust. "And what does a thing like you want with love anyway?"

For an instant, her expression softened. He'd doubted it possible, but he'd stung her. Then her expression hardened again, and the smirk returned. "All will be revealed soon. I'll make everything you want to know into a lullaby and sing it to you as we're taking you apart."

Reece looked back at the vault and judged his liquid hourglass about two-thirds full. The level of the fluid was now at her shoulders, and her mouth had opened into a saw-toothed grin.

Reece swallowed hard and steadied his resolve. "Will you also be showing me the rest of your white rooms? The ones where you keep the living, breathing women you call masks? I know you have Amaya there."

"There are no other white rooms." Behind the glass the creature's mouth was moving in tandem with the words emanating from the hologram. "There's nothing in my masks which could experience such a thing."

"Enough lies, Mia, or whatever the hell your name is. Just bring me to Amaya. Show her to me one last time, if only so you can see how much it pains me to say goodbye."

"Sounds like a blast. But as I've already said, Amaya's fish food." The screen spun on its axis, casting the pale holograms of a dozen young women standing as if propped up dead, their eyes nothing more than vacant blue voids. Reece searched their faces as they circled him but found no sign of Amaya. Then they flickered back into nonbeing as the rotating screen slowed, and Mia's face reemerged from within its midnight canvas. "Satisfied?"

The panel advanced, following Reece as he retraced his steps around the pool's edge. Tears welled in his eyes. "You're lying. I've seen you take her form."

"Parlor tricks, nothing more. But enough talk. You and my valet have unfinished business." A metallic thump resonated throughout the chamber, signaling the throne's upward return. Mia erupted in laughter. "He's on his way, Reece. And oh, does he have a bone to pick with you."

Reece made one last search for anything he might use as a weapon but came up empty. Out of options and short on time, he returned his attention to the pool of saltwater and the black smudge rippling beneath its surface. Repositioning his feet by the pool's edge, he started filling his lungs, then purging them. Before long, the sound of the gears reversed, indicating that the throne was on its way back down. Mia wore an expectant look, as though she feared she might have gone too far and given Reece over to an easy demise. "You'll never make it."

"I think I'll give it a try if it's all the same to you," he said between gasps.

Reece filled his lungs a final time and dove into the water, kicking his way toward the tunnel. Once inside, he found only more of the same impenetrable murk, but it was too late to turn back, so he swam blindly forward. After what seemed like an eternity, the darkness took on a paler form, and he experienced a surge of hope. But his confidence waned as he felt the last of the oxygen leave his body. He cleared his lungs a little at a time, his strokes becoming ever more frantic. Twice his hand scraped against the rocky wall, shredding the skin of his knuckles. The paleness ahead was growing larger, but too slowly, and he had no idea how far he would find himself from the water's surface once he emerged. Mia had been right. He wasn't going to make it. He kicked as hard as he could, the last of his air escaping in a stream of bubbles.

Still conscious beyond his expected limit, Reece passed through the tunnel's mouth and into the expanse of the sea. He couldn't tell how much further he had to go, and his vision was going dark, so he fought with all he had left to propel himself upward toward the rippling sun.

16
DREAM HOUSE

When Reece came to, he found himself face down on a beach of small rocks, the surf rolling over his back. He pushed himself up onto his elbows and surveyed the shore. A gaggle of seabirds had gathered nearby and were watching him from a curious distance. "I'm not food for you just yet," he said, pushing himself up the rest of the way onto his knees. Mia's lighthouse loomed to his left. If they were pursuing him, they wouldn't be far behind.

He scanned the beachfront. No sign of Mia or her valet, but she was no doubt aware that he had made it, contrary to her prediction. A maniacal laugh worked its way up from within Reece's chest, and it continued until tears rolled down his cheeks. A trailing chuckle filled his next moments, until through the blur of tears he spotted a figure standing further up the shore. It was a woman with blonde hair, wearing a pink sundress that clung to her body in the breeze. Amaya had worn one just like it the first day of their vacation, and a local had been kind enough to take a picture of them in the light of the setting sun. Reece cleared his tears with the back of his arm. She flashed him a smile, then turned and started up the hill toward the mountain ridge.

Reece scrambled to his feet and staggered forward like a man who'd seen a desert mirage. Perhaps that was just what this was—a mad wish. He had taken in too much saltwater, and now he was hallucinating. But he didn't care. Real or not, he needed to speak with her.

Once she reached the foot of the mountain, she continued up a winding path, with Reece following not far behind. But every time it seemed like he was closing in on her, she appeared in the blink of an eye some distance ahead. It was clear he wasn't going to catch her, so he contented himself with matching her pace. After a time, she crested the ridge, then disappeared over the other side. When Reece reached the top, he found her a great length ahead. Suddenly very tired, he fell to his knees. Maybe it was time to give up, to die right there with the ocean wind at his back, doing just what he'd agreed to do—look for Amaya. At this point no one could say he hadn't given it his best, not even her. And on top of that, he'd made one hell of a stand against the one who was responsible for it all.

Ahead his guide had stopped. She was looking back over her shoulder and seemed unwilling to go on without him. *All right then*. Reece climbed back up from the dirt and rocks and continued moving forward, and his guide did the same.

The shadows streaking across the barren earth grew longer, and the brightness beneath his feet dimmed. Still his aching feet trudged through the dirt as if they were carrying him all on their own. His body had become a machine of perpetual motion that if stopped might never start again. It was unclear how far he walked, but when he looked back up, he found before him a single two-story house. It had a flat overhang supported by posts carved in the style of ionic columns. A series of withered bushes dotted its perimeter, and nearby a garden lay untended. By all appearances, it had once been the kind of house he and Amaya had dreamed of, but like so much of the island, it had fallen into disrepair. Beyond it loomed a wall of lush pine forest, its surface crawling in the wind. Reece tried to call out to Amaya, but his throat was so parched he had trouble making a sound. Maybe he'd find some water inside.

The front steps creaked and groaned, and at one point a cracking sound caused him to have to shift his weight and find new footing. Ahead the screen door tapped gently against its frame. Somewhere in the overhang, a small animal was chattering, but it fell silent the moment Reece raised his eyes. He drew the screen door open and turned the doorknob. It was unlocked. With a sudden gust of wind, the knob slipped from his hand and the door slammed into the wall of the vestibule, causing Reece's shoulders to jump up next to his ears.

The entryway was marked by framed photographs hung askance, and a fog of dust danced within the spears of light that passed through the open door. The screen door fell shut behind him, then began tapping again as if to urge him forward. Directly at the end of the hall to the right of a set of stairs, he found a living room. A crochet blanket lay over the back of a worn sofa, and atop it a procession of stuffed animals, some with missing eyes and wounds bleeding tufts of bright white cotton, sat with frozen smiles.

At the other end of the hall past the stairs was the kitchen. Reece threw himself at the sink and turned the knob. The pipes groaned for a time, then the nozzle started sputtering water, and he cupped his hands and drank of it greedily. Once he'd had his fill, he opened the refrigerator just enough to smell why he needn't open it any further. Next, he rooted through the drawers, pushing aside spent lighters, assorted nails, and corroded batteries before finally uncovering his prize. It was a flashlight small enough to fit in the palm of his hand. Reece flipped its switch and the bulb sparked to life, casting a respectable beam across the room. Not wanting to waste its charge, he killed the light and clipped it to his hip pocket. It was then he noticed what sounded like someone dragging a sharp object along the outer wall.

It started on the far side of the house outside the master bedroom and then worked its way around to the rear. Reece grabbed a kitchen knife out of the block and gripped it, knuckles white. Before long, the sound appeared outside the kitchen wall. Then it paused for an instant as a shadow passed the blinds before continuing around to the front of the house.

Reece crept back into the hall and peered around the corner, holding the knife close to his chest. The sun was setting, and the sky was streaked with colors so vivid and indiscriminate that only a mad artist in the height of derangement could have put them to canvas. The screen door cycled through several taps before falling still, and for a moment all was silent. Then a creaking issued from the front steps, and soon after that, a dark head bobbed into view. A new piece of the figure emerged with each step until the black silhouette of a man stood on the other side of the screen, the unmistakable shape of a blade extending from his hand.

Reece withdrew his head and flattened himself against the wall, rationing out his breaths as he fought to stay calm. Slipping into the stairway, he snuck to the second floor. The screen door downstairs creaked open, then banged shut, and footsteps fell along the hall. Passing into the room ahead, Reece lifted the latch on the window and pushed it open. If he dropped from the edge of the overhang, it would only be a short run to the woods. He swung one leg over the windowsill and climbed out. All seemed well at first, until a series of cracks gave short notice that it wasn't, and with a violent crunch he fell through the overhang and onto the porch, landing in a pile of splintered wood and broken shingles.

No sooner had he landed than the sound of thumping boots came barreling down the vestibule. Still on his back, Reece extended his leg, pinning the screen door shut, but for naught as the visitor's blade tore through the screen. He stepped through the frame, and Reece snatched the kitchen knife from the debris and scrambled to his feet just in time to receive a kick to the face, sending him tumbling down the steps and onto the lawn. The fading light cast in red the disfigured face of the valet as he made his way down the steps, tossing his knife from hand to hand.

Reece clambered to his feet, his own blade at the ready. The two men circled each other, Reece with blood trickling from his nose and the valet with his slit of a mouth pushing forth an airy malevolent laugh. While Reece was eyeing his opponent's blade, he got a good look at the tattoo which had been illegible in the early morning darkness a few weeks before. Now in the light of sunset, he could see lovingly rendered in sprawling ink the name *Mallory*.

"Marco." So, it had been Mallory Reece saw the night before. Perhaps it had even been her he'd followed to the house, thinking she was Amaya. "What did you do to Mallory? Why is she here?"

"This ain't about her. It's about Mia. She's ours, and you ain't fit to share her with us." Having only scarcely finished his sentence, Marco feinted high, causing Reece to reflexively raise his hands, then followed up with a lunging stab below. Reece sucked in his belly and took a clumsy step back before checking Marco's knife hand and moving to the outside. Before Marco could recover, Reece closed the distance and buried his blade. Marco froze in place, his arm still extended from his failed attack. The odor of decay rushed forth from his mouth as his lungs emptied into a sigh. Reece twisted the blade as he removed it, rending flesh and dumping blood onto the soil.

The knife slipped from Marco's fingers, and he fell to one knee, gripping his wound with a blood-slicked hand. Reece kicked the weapon a safe distance away and then gave the downed man some space. The blood pooling around Marco's knees mixed with the dirt until he was kneeling in a puddle of mud, and he gazed about the clearing, a look of confusion in his eyes as if he were unsure of where he was. Reece tightened his grip around the kitchen knife. "What did you do to her, Marco?" The dying man's eyes followed Reece's voice as if suddenly reminded that he wasn't alone. Although his face was a gnarled mass of unfinished flesh, his eyes were sufficient to convey the sense of resignation which had come over him.

"I did what I had to. That morning when I got her home, I knocked her around pretty good. A little too good, because after a while she stopped crawling back up off the floor. By the time I was finished, she was breathing real shallow, and I knew she didn't have much time left. But what was I supposed to do? Carry her into the hospital beaten nearly to death, my own knuckles bruised and bloody? Uh-uh. No way I was goin' back inside."

"I'm glad to see you're giving me no cause to regret killing you, Marco."

A parody of a smile broke across the dying man's face, and he swayed as if he were about to fall over, but with effort he managed to steady himself. "I wrapped her in a sheet and put her in the trunk of my car. It's funny. All a sudden I was treating her real gentle, as if all she needed was to rest awhile and she'd be okay again. We drove pretty much all day. I didn't know where we were goin', but I knew which direction I was supposed to go in. Knew it without a doubt, like a bird flying south.

"Around evening we arrived at the beach. I parked facing the water and watched the sun go down, just like me and Mal had done back in better times. I knew she was already dead, but it didn't matter. Her soul was linked to mine. That much I was sure of." Marco sputtered blood onto his chin. His breathing was growing more labored.

"Once it got dark, I took Mal out of the trunk and carried her to the sand. Then I laid her down and unwrapped the bloody bundle. She was so pale, and her skin was cool to the touch. It was then I saw her ghost out on the water, calling me to come join her. I can't even tell you how happy I was. I kissed her lips, then stood up and waded out into the ocean. Next thing I remember I woke up here on the beach."

"Wait. You mean you weren't visited in bed?"

"No. She only visits the ones she truly wants. But after that, she can touch anyone they make a connection with. It's like a virus that spreads in clusters, forming sticky threads between people. I've seen these threads myself, seen them with my own eyes, white and glistening. And nothing forms a stickier, more tangled web than murder. You want to know why Mal's here? She's here because I am." Marco leveled a trembling finger at Reece. "And I'm here because of you. Everyone on this island, every ghost in every hollow copy of a human body, is here because someone real got a visit in the night. Some of the visited are alive—hell, more than alive— in the white rooms. Others, the heretics, are as dead as you can get, lost forever in the forgotten place."

"The pyramid." Again the frightful word oubliette entered Reece's thoughts. "And where will you end up now that I've killed you, Marco?"

"You've killed nothing but a projection, as fake as any of the bodies the ghosts of this island are walkin' around in. Once this copy dies, I'll wake back up in my white room. Normally the next guy in the chain would take my place, and so it would go forever, but when you trashed the pyramid, some important connections got broken. Until those are fixed, there'll be no next man in line. And that's rotten news for you, Reece. News I'm happy to spend my final breaths delivering. Once I'm gone, you're gonna have to deal directly with the man at the core of this body. And while he's ripping you open, I'll be back in paradise enjoying my reward." Marco appeared to be in his final moments. His eyes had become unfocused, as though he were speaking to someone off in the distance. "So yeah, Reece, you beat me. Congratulations on that. But I… still… win."

The sun had finished setting, and the moon's pale light lay upon the clearing. Marco's eyes were still open, but his breathing had gone quiet. Beyond the stillness near the tree line, a flurry of movement caught Reece's eye. It was Amaya, moving along the clearing's edge. Then at once she was absorbed into the dark.

Reece retrieved the valet's knife and sheath and fastened it to his belt, and then with his kitchen knife in hand, he sprinted for the woods. Once he reached the edge, he pulled the flashlight from his pocket and shone its beam into the trees. Reece listened for her voice but heard only the ancient harmonies of night's creatures. He took a step forward but hesitated. How badly did he actually want to keep following this echo of his sins, given how much pain and ruin it had already caused him? He considered for a moment the coward's path, of abandoning chase and heading back the other way and finding his only friend, Alessa, who seemed so at home in this mournful world. Behind him, the silhouette of the valet was rising. He stood facing south for a time, his fists tight by his side. Then four branch-like limbs expanded from his back, and without further hesitation, Reece entered the woods.

17
INTO THE WOODS

Although Reece suspected his pursuer could see perfectly well in the dark, he kept his flashlight off, if only to cling to the small hope of remaining concealed for long enough to gain a position of advantage. Then without warning the forest floor vanished from beneath his feet, and for one terrifying moment he was falling before he touched back upon solid ground and tumbled into the dirt. Reece scrambled to his feet and felt his way forward but found only a wall of soil ahead. It made no sense to remain in darkness if all he was doing there was waiting to be discovered, so he clicked on his flashlight. To his right stood the same earthen barrier. He'd fallen into some sort of trench, and from behind him his enemy soon emerged at its edge.

Reece bolted down the trench, the beam of his flashlight painting with broad strokes the root-strewn path. The sound of the hunter landing behind him was followed by a series of rapid-fire clicks, and its eerie discord continued as he ran, measuring all the while its distance behind him. Unable to abide ending so great a journey in a ditch, Reece gripped his knife in a tight fist, ready to make his final stand the moment death laid its hand upon his shoulder.

After some distance, the trench broke sharply to the right, and the embankment ahead flashed and turned to water, held back as though by a sheet of glass. Within the shimmering blue floated Amaya, smiling broadly. Her hair and skin were like sunlight and snow, and her eyes sparkled like sapphires. One after another, two large gems beaming with cyanic light burst forth from the embankment next to her, and each in turn faced up and to the right, lighting Reece's path. He slowed to a skid as he rounded the corner, but it was time enough to see Amaya push back with her hands and disappear into the depths. As he passed, a sound like cracking glass filled the atmosphere, and the dam burst behind him, sending water roaring forth and carrying the screeching demon down the trench as Reece emerged back onto the forest floor.

While under no illusion that he was out of danger, hope abounded that providence had not abandoned him. Someone wanted him to succeed, be it Amaya herself or whoever was making use of her image. But the demon wouldn't be far behind, so he continued his blind sprint, cutting long diagonals through the trees. After a time, the monster resumed his braying, but with his voice now distant, Reece was able to stop and catch his breath. He crouched and filled his lungs while listening to the sounds of the forest. The noise of crickets swelled and receded, and a breeze stirred the treetops.

With nature's chaos all around him, he focused on his steadying breath, and across what seemed a great distance, a light like that of a handheld lantern came into view. Orienting himself toward the light, Reece made his way forward with increasingly courageous steps, drawing ever nearer the flame waiting for him across the moonless expanse. Then as quickly as it had appeared, it was gone, and Reece again found himself unmoored on an ebon sea. He blinked several times, willing the beacon to return, but it was a different kind of light which next filled his eyes. It started with a flash of electric blue, then a chalky whiteness like the light of a film projector rolled across the trees, and Mia's voice resounded in his head.

"I've given you quite a poor impression of myself, Reece. I see that now. Shall I attempt to correct it? No, don't respond. Say nothing. My slave still seeks you. I have repaired only one connection within the pyramid, and that is my connection to you. He can't hear or see what I'm about to show you, so be still and silent."

Images of an ancient palace appeared in the darkness. There on her throne sat the woman from Mia's statue, dressed just the same and with an identical staff in her hand. The film continued alongside Mia's narrative. "I wasn't always a monster. I was once a woman, a queen of unrivaled beauty with the world beneath my feet. But a vengeful spirit struck me down, killing my children and transforming me into a serpent of the deep, ensuring that I would never be with child again. As an added insult, the malediction came with a caveat: 'Know the love of a hundred mortal hearts in this cursed form and become again as you once were.'

"Faced with such an impossible task, I spent many long years alone, growing ever more wretched and further from the hope of salvation, until I came at last upon a demon who ruled a remote island from within a stone tower. I seduced and conquered him, then split his remains into a black trinity. One third I banished to a holding cell in the form of a pyramid. The second I kept here in this world to act as my footman. The third I sent to walk the veil as a son of Nyx, entering your world as a living shadow to search for men with creative minds and vulgar hearts.

"One at a time I revealed myself to my captives. You already know what happens to those for whom the spell is broken, but please understand that I do it not out of a desire for cruelty, but out of necessity. The pyramid generates a great deal of energy, and it needs to feed. I cannot concern myself with what Balyxis does in that labyrinth. All that matters is that the energy it provides keeps the lantern burning until I reach my goal."

Balyxis. So, the demon has a name.

"Do you see how forthcoming I'm being, Reece? How honest? It's because I want you to believe me when I say that you really were supposed to be the last one. I admit it—I hid the truth from you. But it was only because I feared the truth wouldn't be enough. Instead, I tried to ply you with pleasure, then when that failed, with the threat of pain. They're crude tools, I know, but I figured they offered me a better chance than hoping your love might come in the form of mercy."

Images of Reece and Mia walking hand in hand the night before flitted across the forest. "I'm sure you can understand why I acted the way I did. And for my part, I see now that I should've trusted you with the whole truth. Maybe then you'd still be mine." Mia's voice had taken on a tone of whimsy. "Reece Holloway—my wild mystery man. The final piece of a beautiful puzzle."

"And now I'm on my knees in the woods, awaiting death at the hands of a demonic spider. What a difference a day can make."

"Shh," Mia said. "Balyxis draws near." Reece went rigid. The crack of a fallen branch sounded somewhere to his rear, and Reece's skin crawled with fear of the monster's touch. Mia's voice continued in his thoughts. "Be as still as a rabbit, and maybe he won't notice you." Reece obeyed. The sounds of clicking and the crunch of dead things underfoot crawled the void behind him. Then after a time, they passed.

It was several minutes before the sounds were far enough away for Reece to venture to draw a full breath, much less speak again. Once he did, he spoke with a new softness. "If I understand you correctly, and assuming any of this is true, once your curse is lifted you can turn off the machine?"

"Yes. Although the machine brings me great pleasure, I would leave it all behind to be myself again."

"And those in the white rooms would be released?"

"Yes. And the spirits locked inside the pyramid as well."

"Then I could've saved everyone just by submitting to you."

"You still can, Reece. You can be the hero who frees them all. You need only find the strength to adore what you hate, to unburden yourself of your most worthless treasure, for no gem sparkles more falsely than the will of man."

Reece gave his head a dour shake. It was a seductive lie, but one he couldn't bring himself to believe. "I'm not buying it. Nothing good can come of loving evil."

"Come now, Reece. Deep down you know that the world is far more complicated than such platitudes suggest. I'm offering you a safe return, no strings attached. Forget your petty morals and your wounded heart. I'll teach you to love me, and then we'll both be free. You've seen images of my true human face, but they can't compare to what I'm like in my original flesh. Let me show you how to love what is ugly, and you will inherit what is most beautiful. Let me be your queen, and I will make you my king."

"No. I don't want you in any form. Not for all the kingdoms in hell."

The woods were silent for a time before she spoke again. "Very well. I suppose one can't teach a dog the value of a diamond. So instead, I'll offer you a truce. Leave this forest now, and I will call Balyxis home. You will stay out of my way, and in return, I will give you something you want."

"Amaya. Give me Amaya."

"Amaya's not here, but her sister's still within my reach. A poor man's Amaya, I know, and a ghost at that, but are you not a poor man, Reece? Are you not poorer than you've ever been? You should accept my blessing with cheer."

Reece hesitated. A way out of this nightmare was more than he could have hoped for, but after everything Mia had done, he could neither trust nor forgive her. "Why do you want me to leave these woods? Why not just let me die here if I'm such a nuisance? You needn't make any deal with me."

"I like you, Reece. You're different. But it's clear you aren't a bird to be caged. So I'm giving you the chance to fly away, and as a gesture of my goodwill, I'm sending that lovely nightingale with you. Is it really so difficult for you to accept a gift from me? I'm offering you peace and pleasure. There is no catch. You will be her white room, and she will exist there only for you."

"It was you who killed her. Marco was just the murder weapon."

Suddenly, the forest burned red. "And what of it? She's better off here than she ever was with him. She's free, and he belongs to me."

However much easier it would make his life, Reece couldn't capitulate. He hadn't stepped into the water in search of Mallory but of Amaya. And he sure as hell hadn't entered the forest looking to make a deal with the Devil. Somewhere in the darkness that fire was still burning, and he was going to find it. Reece licked his dry lips in anticipation of what he was about to say. "I reject your offer, Mia. With all my heart."

The forest remained dark for a time. Then all at once, the trees flashed electric blue before fading to black again. "Another connection has been repaired, Reece. Do you want to guess which one that is?"

Off in the distance, the flame winked back into view. Reece sprang to his feet and bounded toward it, Mia's laughter carrying through the trees as he ran. With every step the beacon burned brighter, and the trees seemed to bend before him, urging him toward his goal. Then as he was closing in, something snagged his ankle, and he went tumbling down, landing with a hard crunch and knocking the wind out of his lungs.

Reece remained still and silent, allowing the pain from his fall to run its course. Having dropped the kitchen knife, he searched the bed of pine needles with his hands. When he failed to find it, he pushed himself up onto his knees, drew a deep breath, and reoriented himself to the flame. It was then Reece heard a sound of breathing not his own. He froze in place, his eyes drawn wide, but for naught in the pitch darkness. He unfastened the sheath of Marco's knife, then drew his flashlight and clicked it on.

Standing behind him was Balyxis, his eyes like eight blood-filled orbs, a single black dot floating in the center of each. With a series of clicks, he drew his jaws open. Pearly strands of webbing stretched between his fangs, and a cluster of spiders crawled out of his mouth and onto his face. Reece yanked the knife from its sheath and plunged it into the demon's neck, causing him to shriek in pain and slap Reece's hand away with enough force to make it go numb. The flashlight's beam darted this way and that, illuminating fragments of darkness, now and again passing over the screaming face of the demon. In the pandemonium, Reece dropped the flashlight and all went dark, save for the flame which swelled in the near distance. He broke toward it, knowing that another faltering step would be the end of him.

After reaching a small clearing, Reece came to a skidding halt. The flame was no more than a dozen feet ahead, hovering over an opening in a moss-covered knoll. Reece threw himself into the hole and crawled as fast as his hands and knees would carry him, tumbling at last down a slope and into a tunnel below. With no time to get his bearings, he got back on his feet and continued in a crouch toward a soft green light issuing from somewhere ahead. Low hanging roots brushed at his face, and Reece batted them away, the image of the demon's face covered in spiders still fresh in his memory.

Behind him, the sound of loosening soil announced his pursuer's arrival, sending Reece scrambling forward. There'd better be something useful at the end of this tunnel, or else all he'd done was bury himself in advance of his murder. By measures the tunnel became an emerald green, lit by lantern-like bulbs growing from the walls. Once Reece passed, the light faded and the shadows grew denser, until he found himself having to stop.

It was the end of the tunnel. Panic came over him in a stomach-flipping wave, until he realized the darkened space to his right was a passage further down. He would need to be swift—no mistakes. Shadows would not befuddle Balyxis, and every measure Reece was ahead was precious. He continued downward, slipping at times but never losing his footing, past patches of green and purple bulbs, each giving off just enough light to keep him oriented to the path ahead. After a while, the tunnel began to narrow, and claustrophobia gripped him by the throat. He didn't know what was worse, meeting a violent end or suffocating in a collapsing tunnel. Perhaps he would get a bit of both. The demon's clicks were drawing nearer.

Just as Reece thought the earth was about to close in on him, he clambered out into a vast moonlit cavern. The ceiling looked to be a hundred feet high, and below it a pool of water shimmered around an islet. At its center stood a tree, twisted and ancient but strong and very much alive. It was all trunk and thorns until the top, where a series of branches fed out across an opening in the top of the cavern. Beyond it, the night sky watched through the leaves, and at once he recalled the chalk drawing of a tree he'd seen behind The Eye of Night, as well as the engraving which hung over Alessa's bed. Each had depicted a tree without branches, save for those which filled its sprawling canopy.

Certain that this was what he'd been called to discover, Reece trudged into the knee-deep pool but stopped halfway to the islet as a growl filled the cavern. Balyxis was approaching the water. He grasped the hilt of the knife Reece had buried in his neck and yanked it out in one swift motion. Reece took an unconscious step back but stopped there. There was no use running. There was something valuable in that tree, and if he didn't stand and fight now, his blood would water its roots. Balyxis rushed forward, his blade held high like a psychopath on a killing spree. Reece's thoughts were a hopeless tangle. He was a prey animal, frozen in that final wide-eyed moment before crimson death.

With a final leap, the demon was upon him, and somehow it still came as a surprise to Reece when the knife sunk into his flesh. He couldn't believe it was happening, not even when Balyxis jerked the knife out of his body, and a stream of blood followed, catching the moonlight as it arced away and trickled into the water. His hearing had gone muddy, but it was clear the monster was laughing. It was a deep and sustained laugh, the kind you'd expect to hear from a villain in an old horror movie. Balyxis either couldn't or wouldn't speak, but he could certainly laugh, and his laugh was the most human thing about him.

Reece grabbed the demon's wrist, hoping to control where the blade landed next. He was incredibly strong, but Reece soon found that by locking his arm, he could at least prevent another strike from the knife, and keeping close prevented the demon from attacking with his arachnoid limbs. Balyxis grabbed him by the neck with his other hand and pushed his head underwater. Reece's right arm remained locked in place, but now he was drowning. He twisted his body and searched for the monster's feet with his free hand. It first closed around his right ankle. He let go and searched for his left. Once he had a firm grip, he pulled with all his strength, and Balyxis fell onto his side. Reece burst out of the water with a violent gasp, hitting the demon with his best punch as he was rising back onto his knees. Reece grabbed his enemy by the throat, and together they stumbled to their feet. The demon laughed again, seemingly enjoying Reece's spirited attempt at repudiating the inevitable. They struggled like that for a time, thrashing and sloshing back and forth through the water, the demon's knife-wielding hand gaining greater advantage as he raised it into position to deliver the fatal blow. The adrenaline was wearing off, and Reece was growing weak. He had given a good account of himself, but his enemy was just too strong, and he'd already taken too much damage.

It was then he saw the stone poking out of the water a half dozen feet behind Balyxis. Reece drove the demon back with all the power he had left in his legs. Then once he was in place, he hooked his right leg behind his enemy's and brought him crashing down headfirst onto the stone. Reece couldn't have hoped for a more accurate blow. The demon's head struck the stone with the force of a sledgehammer, and blood rushed forth, dispersing into the water. Balyxis loosened his grip on the knife, and Reece was able to shake it free from his hand. The monster tried to rise, but Reece placed a hand on either side of his head, plunging it down onto the stone again and again, using his every attempt at rising as momentum for another crushing blow, until finally the pupils of his eight eyes swam like tadpoles in pools of blood. His body shook in spasms as Reece wrapped his hands around his neck and dragged him off the rock.

Reece forced his head underwater and positioned his knee and all his weight upon the demon's chest. Balyxis bucked violently, sending crests of water bursting all around, and the water over his face bubbled and sputtered as he screamed in rage and terror, expelling hundreds of tiny spiders from his mouth. His sharp nails clawed at Reece's arms, peeling away strips of skin, but Reece maintained his grip and protected his neck by fastening his shoulders to his ears. Then the sputtering gave way to stillness, and the only movement was that of the spiders treading the water's surface.

18

THE CLIMB

As free as Reece had felt in the moment of his enemy's defeat, he now found himself imprisoned in screaming flesh. Although the knife seemed to have missed any major organs or vessels, its wound was steadily oozing blood. His face was a mass of stinging cuts, and strips of skin hung from his arms like tassels from a suede jacket. Worst of all, there was surely more pain to come.

Reece felt around under the water where the knife had fallen. Once he found it, he slipped it back into its sheath and snapped the clasp shut. Then he wiped the blood from his eyes and started toward the tree with stiff movements as if he'd been sunburned all over. "I suppose I'm meant to climb it," he said with a frown. "But of course I am." Reece surveyed the tree from its roots to where it disappeared into the night. It was a long way up and an even longer way down. Foot-long thorns grew in an ascending spiral. They would no doubt help him climb but would also present a danger, and he could hardly afford to open any more skin. Reminded of his bleeding, he peeled the wet shirt off his back, wrung it out, and created a makeshift bandage for his most troublesome wound. Once he was confident that the bleeding was under control, he found a starting point and pulled his way up onto the first thorn.

His chin nearly touched its tip, but his boots slipped on the bark as though he'd stepped in a puddle of oil. With arms quivering, he lowered himself back into a seated position against the tree and rested there for a time while looking out over the cavern. Natural shelves dripping with hardened calcite appeared to melt from the walls. Ahead, the hole through which he'd entered glowed in shades of purple and green. He could make his way back through the tunnel and out into the forest, but there he would once again be subjected to Mia's voice, and he wasn't keen on hearing what she had to say about this latest development. For whatever reason, she seemed unable to speak to him now. Offshore from the islet, a thousand tiny skittering legs marked the place where his enemy had fallen. Reece halfway expected Balyxis to come crashing up out of the water fully revived, but each passing moment rebuked the notion that he was anything but dead, his brains beaten to a pulp on a stone and starved of oxygen by the water which now filled his lungs.

A garland of stars was visible through the branches which filled the cavern's window to the sky. Its opening was perfectly circular and lined with stone blocks, like the inside of a well. Upon closer examination, it became clear that the branches were symmetrical on all sides. He had seen the same pattern in the mansion's rose window from where he'd viewed the stars the night before. "That can't be a coincidence," Reece said, struggling to his feet.

There would be no returning to the woods, at least not the way he came. Reece had been through too much for this to end any way but up. If only the climb would take him back home. This time he removed his boots and socks so that he'd be better able to grip the thorns beneath his feet. Stripped down to nothing but his jeans, he clapped his hands around the lowest thorn and pulled himself up, giving his weakness no time to find purchase before reaching for another. By the time he was twenty or so feet from the ground, it was clear that there would be no turning back. If he were to try and see his way back down now, it would likely be a quick flight with an unpleasant landing.

About halfway up, a deep and resonant breath resounded throughout the chamber. Reece flattened himself against the tree, peering over his shoulder to the spot where Balyxis had fallen. The demon lay still in the water. The pattering steps of a four-legged animal drew Reece's attention higher. Something unseen was moving along the cavern walls. In no condition for another fight, Reece called out to the invisible newcomer, his voice raw. "Whoever you are, I've got no quarrel with you."

The voice which replied was deep and raspy. "Nor do I have one with you, Mr. Holloway. I come only to shed light." An image of a dog with three heads and snakes growing forth from its body appeared as a projection along the wall. The monstrosity broke into a run, its muscular body rippling beneath its coarse, ragged fur. After a time it vanished, as though the projector had reached the end of its reel. When it reappeared, it was on the wall above the entrance. It watched Reece through six flaming eyes, each of its forked tongues exposed and dripping. Before Reece could speak, it broke into another run, the sound of its panting breath passing from one ear to the other as it circled him.

Unable to follow its movements, Reece rested his forehead on the tree, dizzy and nauseated. "If Cerberus would be so kind as to stay still, I'd appreciate it."

The hound laughed, its image flickering across the wall as it ended its chase. The beast then sat and began licking a massive paw with one mouth while speaking with another. "It's always good to be recognized. I wonder, Mr. Holloway, if you've heard the tale of the hero Theseus's descent into Hades."

Reece reached for another thorn and pulled himself up. "Of course I have. Theseus followed his friend Pirithous into the netherworld to steal Persephone from its king."

"A bold move, yes."

"Yes," Reece said. "And a disastrous one. Especially for Pirithous, who not only failed to capture Persephone, but never made it back out."

"Well, I wouldn't say 'never,'" Cerberus said. "But he was certainly there for a long and uncomfortable period." Reece continued his climb. It was difficult to accept that he was getting a lesson on the long-hidden details of Greek mythology from the hound of Hades himself. At this point the only thing that made any sense at all was to keep moving upward. As he climbed, Cerberus continued speaking. "Consigned to an eternity in the netherworld, Pirithous searched for a companion. Someone with whom he might suffer well. The man he found was one his own friend Theseus had killed—the fallen king Cercyon."

Reece halted his ascent. "I know that name."

"And he knows you, Mr. Holloway. Reece. May I call you Reece?"

"Sure," Reece said. "You know, you're far less of a beast than I took you for."

Again Cerberus laughed. "You will not know how much a beast I am until you're in my jaws. So, where did I leave off?" The image of the hound paced the wall at leisure, and Reece renewed his climb. "Oh yes, Cercyon. A man deserving of an eternity in Hades if ever there was one. Being a brutal type himself, Pirithous took right to him, and before long, those two were as thick as thieves. I won't bore you with a recounting of the centuries of their torment but suffice it to say the more savage of them, Cercyon, went to great lengths to protect his friend. Pirithous, being the cleverer of the two, spent his time hatching a plan of escape."

"Isn't preventing escape from Hades your job?"

Cerberus drew a long breath, and a guttural growl filled the cavern. "It is as you say. But nonetheless, Pirithous made it past me. And just between us, Cercyon would have too, if I hadn't had some unexpected help from a certain succubus who was following the pair in secret and who was more than happy to be the one to drag Cercyon back into the pit. You see, while he was still alive, Lamia had visited Cercyon in the night, and being the uncommon sort he was, he had managed to resist her."

"Lamia." Again Reece let his forehead fall to the tree. "It all makes sense now."

Cerberus stopped his pacing. "Oh, I meant no offense to anyone who might have failed in that regard. But in any case, he resisted her. And once he was in Hades, she made sure to drop in from time to time to remind him in creative ways of the price of that rejection. But after a while she grew bored of him, and as the violence of the world above passed from the age of sharpened metals to one of mechanized carnage, Cercyon joined in on the violence below. Through his native worth, he managed to gain the admiration of those in charge, and he became a tormenter of fallen souls."

Reece was growing dizzy. He'd lost too much blood. "As fascinating as this all is, I wish you'd get to the point."

"In time, Mr. Holloway. Sorry. *Reece*." Cerberus had spoken Reece's name with something of a hiss, and the snakes growing forth from his fur all stood up and hissed along with him. "Over the years Cercyon grew uglier, his flesh reflecting in measures the corruption of his soul. Not wanting to waste his immense talents on local work, we released him into the world to brutalize and destroy the wicked as they slept."

"A harvester of souls," Reece said, reaching for another thorn and pulling himself up. "No better than Lamia."

"Oh, he had no intention of being better. He only wanted to pay her the courtesy of a visit. It was the least he could do after all the times she'd visited him in the netherworld. And after decades of searching, he found her. She'd made herself queen of a strange island, a stopping point between life and eternity where one would never have thought to look. Unfortunately for Cercyon, she'd grown quite powerful with the help of a certain demon." Cerberus made a show of lowering his three heads and sniffing the space below. "Ah, there he is. Lying dead in the water."

"Not as dead as I'd like," Reece said. "Apparently there are two more of them out there."

"Yes. Lamia is a clever one, isn't she? And knowing this, Cercyon bided his time, setting up camp on a mountain overlooking her tower. One night while he was brooding over the expanse, a man appeared from the sky. It was his old friend Pirithous, imbued by the ages with powers the likes Cercyon had never seen. Pirithous fell to one knee, pledging fealty to the man he'd left behind, the same man who'd kept him from going mad all those centuries in the abyss. All he asked in return was that Cercyon change his methods. Pirithous would give him a portion of his powers, among them the ability to see within others the contents of their hearts. Together they would end Lamia's reign and retrieve her stolen souls."

Reece pulled himself up to another thorn. He was now in the stone-lined well of the cavern, just beneath the canopy. "And where do I come into all this?" The image of Cerberus jumped from the cavern below to the stone walls of the well and bounded around the tree in swift circles. Suddenly weak, Reece nearly let go, but managed to grasp the base of the tree's lowest branch. "I wish you wouldn't do that."

Cerberus slowed to a trot and then stopped. This space was narrower, and his image was now projected no more than a dozen feet from Reece. The snakes on his coat swayed together as though charmed. "Your role remains to be seen. I only ask that you do not trust them. Pirithous has his own reasons for scalping the souls Lamia has harvested. Both he and Cercyon belong back down below. They will no doubt tell you a different story about how you're the guilty one, about how corrupt your soul has become, and how ugly."

Reece had nearly reached the top. He could almost touch the branches which separated the world below from the sky. "But they wouldn't be wrong. I have sinned. I've committed great wrongs in any case, whatever you want to call that."

"Nonsense," Cerberus said. "You did only what any man in your position would have done. If you've committed any crime at all, it's of failing to be exceptional. I can tell you now, if you found yourself in the netherworld and decided to leave, I would step aside, for you do not belong there."

Reece held himself close to the tree and spent several moments in silence with his eyes closed. "And I guess I'm not supposed to find it concerning that the hound of Hades is advising me on spiritual matters?"

"I come to you undisguised because I have nothing to hide. I've given you the truth undisguised as well."

Reece opened his eyes and made a noise of derision. "Lamia gave me the honest monster routine as well, so you'll have to forgive me if I remain skeptical."

Cerberus's eyes blazed and Reece saw within them the swirling eternal pit. "You may believe as you wish. Just remember what sort of men you're dealing with when they ask you to do their bidding."

With that, the image of Cerberus faded, and Reece reached up and gripped the branches of the rose window, pulling himself onto the canopy. Once there, the branches filled in beneath him, leaving him kneeling on a platform of knotted wood. Across from him, a being shining with opalescent light was kneeling just as he was. Its shape was that of a woman, and as the marbled light grew thin across her face, Reece recognized Amaya.

A stream of tears cut a path through the dried blood on his face. He had found her, and she was okay. He couldn't have asked for anything more. But as he watched her shining image, it became clear that there was another who shared her place, kneeling with equal presence within the light. It was Mia. Before Reece could react, they separated into two individuals, kneeling side by side. Then in tandem their eyes opened, and the light which issued forth revealed their secrets.

19
AMAYA

The wind roared in Amaya's ears for only an instant. Then it was all pain and cold and panic. The breath she'd stored up in her final great sob had been knocked out of her lungs, and the desire to end it all had gone with it, leaving behind only fear and regret. She flailed about, her only sense of orientation that of rocking back and forth under the waves. The rumble of the machinery propelling the ship grew louder, and a fear of being hacked to pieces jumped to the front of her thoughts. Then the ship passed, and the rumbling died away, leaving Amaya as alone as she'd ever been. The burning in her chest wouldn't allow her to celebrate the miracle that she was still in one piece. It was time to breathe. Be it air or water, she had to take in something.

She opened her mouth and the ocean rushed to fill her lungs, but a painful spasm blocked its entry. This wasn't the way it was supposed to go. She wanted it to be over, and her

233

body was fighting a battle it had no chance of winning. Again she tried to intentionally draw water into her lungs, but the contraction of her throat made it impossible. She wasn't going to drown. She was going to suffocate. Warmth spread across her body, but rather than blackness she saw before her a crackling blue light, and beyond it her mother, reaching out to her as though through a rip in the darkness itself. It felt at first like Amaya was swimming toward her, but she soon realized that the hands which had alternately beaten and caressed her throughout childhood had already taken hold of her and were now drawing her out of the water.

When she broke the surface, she found that the dark shadow of a woman pulling her out wasn't her mother at all. The woman let go of Amaya's hands, allowing her to fall to the stone floor where she lay for a time, sucking in air and shaking with the impulse to cough. Then she grabbed Amaya by the arm and jerked her onto her feet, leading her forward through a space where the only illumination came from soft slivers of light built into the walls. "Wait..." Amaya said. She was struggling to speak, breathe, and cough all at the same time.

"No," the woman replied, and she pulled so hard Amaya thought she'd torn her arm from its socket.

She cried out in pain and fell flat on her stomach, coughing, whimpering, and muttering a useless procession of "please" and "wait." She searched through the veil of tears for the woman's face, but before anything could come into focus, the woman flipped her onto her back and dragged her by outstretched arms. It was then Amaya spied out of the corner of her eye the tip of a snake-like tail. She tried to scream, but the contracting of her throat in the water had left her voice all but gone, and her hoarse bellow soon turned into an intractable round of coughing.

After pulling Amaya up a short incline, the woman reached down and grabbed her by the throat, then lifted her off the floor and tossed her into the seat of a throne. "Sit, princess." She followed up the command with an amused chuckle, revealing even in the dimness the inhumanity of her smile, and with dawning horror, Amaya realized her suicide had been successful. She dared not even speak the name of the place she now was, but the evidence was right in front of her. Shrinking under the weight of her dread, she drew her knees to her chest, and her voice spilled out in a long, sorrowful wail. The creature watched with unconcealed glee, her lips drawn wide, laying bare the glistening white teeth of a shark. At once the throne lurched up from the floor, causing Amaya to emit a shrill cry and grip its armrests. This too delighted the monster, who said goodbye with a childlike flap of her fingers as the throne began to rise, and her cruel laughter followed until it disappeared into the ceiling.

Amaya's wailing faded into a whimper as the rock-walled elevator shaft closed around her. By the time she'd oriented herself, the throne was emerging through a hole that had opened above her. Her first view of her new surroundings was of a glowing mechanical pyramid. Then the throne turned and locked in place, leaving her staring at a blank wall. Once she no longer felt safety in inertia, she climbed onto her knees and peered over the top of the throne. Beyond the pyramid, a well-lit corridor peeked through a door a few feet ajar. She stood and made her way around the throne, stopping only to examine a statue of a woman seated in an identical throne on the other side. Her face was fully human and quite beautiful.

She lingered for only a moment before pushing the door open and stepping out into the hall. On either side, a series of screens displayed grinning male faces. After some hesitation, Amaya waded into their gaze. All was silent save for the sound of her quickened breaths and the water in her boots. Unconsciously she crossed her arms, rubbing them with her hands as she struggled not to look upon their leering faces. But the threat of danger demanded her attention, and what started as a cautious glance grew into a deeper inspection, leaving Amaya standing stock still and dripping across from one of the holographic faces.

Contrary to first appearances, the man was not merely staring into nothing. There was awareness in his eyes. Amaya took a step to the side, and a shiver stormed through her body. His eyes had followed her. She looked to the next screen, finding his gaze upon her as well. Desperate to hide, she hurried forward, her boots beating against the floor. They were all watching, each of them with the same lecherous grin.

At the end she found a set of stairs leading up to an open hatch. Beyond it laid the crimson light of the passage to the sponson. Never before had she felt such fervent hope. If only it might be real and not some evil trick. If only she might get a second chance. She made her way up, pausing upon the top step. The passageway was there before her, just as it'd been before she'd stepped out onto the sponson. She would soon follow it back to her berthing, to her bunk where she would close her numb eyes and awake in the morning with all this horror behind her, its details lost like those of a forgotten dream. She would have her baby with or without Reece, and it would be her greatest treasure.

Amaya stepped over the threshold, and after a flash of light, she found herself standing in a lab across from a man who looked like a doctor, wearing a white coat and round lensed spectacles. Bubbling glass vessels and instruments of brushed steel lined the walls. Behind the doctor, a table draped in surgical padding waited under a cluster of bright lights. Amaya spun away, hoping to retreat back down below, but the hatch had become a black mirror. Beyond her dim reflection she could see the doctor approaching, but that didn't stop her from screaming when he wrapped his arms around her, pinning her arms to her sides. She recoiled as his warm breath touched upon her ear. "No need to struggle," he said in an Italian accent. "There is nowhere for you to go."

It was impossible not to believe him. With Amaya's dream of escape so wickedly dashed, she wouldn't dare accept the promises of another mirage. All this was hers to endure. She could only hope that she would not have to endure it forever. A rote prayer she'd learned as a child entered her thoughts and repeated on loop, spilling out in a whisper. Her knees went weak, and the doctor lifted her and carried her across the room, laying her on the padded table. She flinched as he produced a scalpel, but with a gesture of his hand, he bid her be still and then cut her shirt and bra away. She tried to draw her arms over her chest, but he took her by the wrists and locked them in clamps by her sides. Amaya's eyes darted about the room as he raised one half of a metal shell, covering half the area from beneath her ribs to the top of her head. As he was closing the other half, her gaze fell upon a large glass cylinder standing before her, empty save for the amber slurry bubbling at its base. Then the shell snapped shut, casting her into darkness.

The inside was lined with a firm, leathery material, holding her in place and sealing the space between her ribs and lower body. A stream of oxygen flowed from above her nose, and Amaya drank of it greedily. Outside the shell, the lab's machinery buzzed and clicked, and for a time nothing happened. Then she felt her belt being unbuckled and she released a scream into the padding, but for naught as a set of clammy fingers dug into the waistband of her pants and underwear and peeled them from her legs. When the cool air hit her skin, her bladder released its contents, and she felt the warmth of urine collect under her rear end. The doctor spat some words of contempt and secured her ankles to the table.

Amaya searched for the colors she'd relied upon as a child when her mother had locked her in the closet. She nearly found them, but the smearing of a cold gel on her belly pulled her from her dream. The sensation soon faded, and numbness took its place. Next there was a feeling of pressure. Then after a long pause, something was roughly inserted, and her pain came out of its hiding place. Her screams came in pulses, fading into sobs until her lungs were full again and ready for another round. Looming above the pain, she discovered a renewed terror that it would never end, that this was the beginning of eternal punishment for plunging her and her unborn child thoughtlessly into the water. Then the procedure was over, and all she felt were the remnants of her throbbing hurt, along with a mild tugging and snipping.

Time passed in a haze. It was unclear how much of what she heard outside the shell was real and how much a trauma-induced hallucination. At one point she heard chanting, and a voice a species apart from any she'd ever heard before spoke at intervals, eliciting responses uttered in unison. Once they fell silent, a powerful jolt shot down her spine, lighting up every nerve, and at last she was able to slip into an altered state of consciousness.

She was thirteen years old and back in her bedroom closet. Her mother was having another one of her episodes. Amaya wondered who Mom thought was responsible for her sorrow this time, besides her, of course. She gave the door a little push. It didn't budge. Her mother had tied the twine tightly around the knobs. At least she didn't have to pee this time. Last time she had felt fit to burst after the first hour, and it had only gotten worse as the day had gone on. But she'd held it like a real trooper because if Mom had opened the closet and discovered a smell, there would have been hell to pay.

She searched for her colors in the darkness. What movie might they show her this time? Ah, *Prince Charming*. It was one she'd seen a thousand times, but it was a classic, so she had no complaints. There he was, playing video games in his underwear. Reece. Her Reecey Piecey. "Reecey Piecey," she muttered into the padding of her shell, and her lips stretched into a smile against its leathery material. It was cute how immature he was at times, but would she always find it so? No matter—there would be time later for the disappointments of middle age. Amaya watched herself flop down on the sofa next to him, a raspberry and lime soda in her hand. She propped her feet up against his leg, and with her free hand, she opened across her lap an issue of an Italian fashion magazine and flipped through Milan's latest as she sipped ice-cold soda through a straw. How vivid these colors were! It was as if they were a memory from another life rather than a dream of things to come. Perhaps that was what they were. After all, her prince rarely had a name, much less an adorable nickname.

The colors came apart and swirled in the darkness, then came back together in the shape of her ninth-grade math teacher, Mr. Mueller. He was standing next to her, smiling with warmth and praise for how hard she'd worked turning her D into a B. Amaya leaped forward and he caught her in his arms. When her lips fell upon his, both of their eyes opened wide in surprise like those two spaghetti-eating cartoon dogs. Amaya laid her head against his chest, her hands clasped behind his neck. His aftershave reminded her of…

Dad. There he was, sitting in his chair with a beer in hand (as usual!). Mom was cooking spaghetti from the smell of it. She was well today, and Dad didn't look angry at all. Reece was next to her on the couch, and they had the blanket her grandmother had knitted laid out across their laps. Under it, Amaya's hands were busy. Reece had a panicked look on his face as if he wasn't sure whether he could stay silent much longer. Amaya knew she should stop before she got them both into trouble, but she just couldn't help herself. No, on second thought, it wasn't Reece at all. It was what's-his-name from senior year. Reece would come later (ha!) once she was in the Navy. And she was in seventh grade now, so she wouldn't fall in love with Mr. Mueller for two more years. How strange and jumbled the colors sometimes were.

Outside the closet door, her mother was moving about the room, speaking to someone in Italian, which was odd because her mother didn't speak Italian. She called out "Mama!" but her voice was stifled as if something was pressing against her face. She tried to wipe it away, but the feeling remained. "Mama, please," she said, pushing against the closet door. She didn't like the colors anymore. They were too confusing, and she wanted to see the light. Finally, she heard the twine unwinding, and at once the door flung open.

The light from the cylinder, now filled to the brim with amber fluid, poured down into Amaya's eyes. She tried to sit up but found herself still bound by her wrists and ankles. After blinking a couple times, everything came into focus. A series of plastic tubes poked forth from crude bandages across her belly and fed into the base of the cylinder. Inside, a beautiful woman about her age floated naked. At first it was unclear whether or not she was conscious, but then she blinked, and the fluid began to drain, layering the sound of gurgling over the steady beep of the lab's monitors. Once the cylinder was empty, the glass rotated, and the young woman stepped out and made her way down a set of metal steps. The doctor met her at the bottom with a towel, and she raised her arms as he wiped the amber fluid from her body. All the while, she watched Amaya with a thin smile.

After the doctor had finished drying her, she snatched the towel away, then dabbed her neck a final time before casting it aside and approaching the table. "Mother," she said, brushing Amaya's damp hair aside. "You look like hell." The young woman pulled her own hair back, gripping it in a ponytail. "How do I look? A lot better than you do, eh? I wonder what Father will think." She let go of her hair and it cascaded back down over her shoulders. Then she turned her attention to Amaya's chest, reacting with mock surprise. "Oh! Is that for me?" Amaya struggled to raise her head, only finding enough strength to do so on her third attempt. Her breasts were lactating. "I'll have to pass," the young woman said. "As you can see, I'm already grown up." Then she snatched a surgical blade from beside the table and ran it across Amaya's throat.

20
FOAM-BORN

Reece's vision went dark, and he retched with violent heaves to expel the taste of blood from his mouth. The world spun as light crept back into his eyes. Then it slowed to a halt and appeared in sudden focus as a candlelit room formed around him. Its decor was a confluence of styles, but the unifying theme was one of subtle light and dark lacquered wood. It could have easily been a room in the mansion. It probably was.

The eyes of the women across from him were now closed. They were kneeling side by side on a platform that ran the length of the room, their matching robes flowing beyond its edge. There was no sign on Amaya's face that she was still suffering, and none on their daughter's, who appeared right at home in the shape Reece knew as Mia. He winced over what she might have seen as a helpless passenger in her own body. At the thought of his involvement, he resumed his retching, then wiped his mouth with a trembling hand, smearing saliva across his cheek. Mia had said they were only masks, that nothing in them experienced the world. Reece wove his hands together in prayer that at least on that count she hadn't been lying. When he opened his eyes, he found that his posture was one of penitence toward his daughter. It was her forgiveness he wanted, and he asked for it time and again, shaking his clasped hands before him.

"Forgive me, I didn't know."

"Forgive me, I was scared."

"Forgive me, it meant nothing."

A voice interrupted, saying "She can't understand you." While Reece recognized its singular timbre, he still felt as though he'd received an electric shock when he looked to the end of the room and found the host on his throne. To the giant's right stood his servant, looking as severe as ever. To his left was Alessa, the only gentle face among them.

Reece shifted, and he must have looked like he was about to rise because the servant said, "You may remain kneeling." Eager to demonstrate compliance, Reece settled back onto his heels. Never before had he felt so naked. He'd been stripped of most of his clothes and far too much of his skin, and his two greatest sources of shame were kneeling next to him. All was laid bare. "It's time I introduced myself," the servant said. "I am Pirithous. You've met King Cercyon, who I'm sure needs no further introduction. Alessa is our agent, living among the people in secret. Until today Lamia was unaware of her connection to us."

Alessa looked as though she wanted to step forward from the dais, but she remained in place. "I am sorry I could not speak freely before, but with our enemy able to see and hear through you, I had to be careful not to arouse her suspicion."

Her eyes told a different story than her lips. It was clear she felt responsible for Reece's grim circumstances, but Reece couldn't bring himself to blame her. She'd done everything in her power to stop him from going to the lighthouse, short of exposing their entire operation. "I'm sure you did everything you could," Reece said. He dropped the delicacy of tone as he addressed Pirithous. "But I struggle to see why you couldn't have said something. A few words would've gone a long way."

Cercyon leaned forward in his throne. "You were a trespasser, and you were given a trespasser's welcome."

Pirithous laid a hand on Cercyon's shoulder, and he relaxed a bit. "You must understand that we cannot take in those cursed by Lamia. The risk is too great."

A sense of frustration burrowed into Reece's head. "You didn't have to take me in. But you could've warned me that I was about to be enthralled to a succubus. If not out of regard for me, then to at least deny said succubus her crucial one-hundredth slave."

Pirithous took on the look of a man trying not to insult a child's fancy. "You're referring to her tale of needing the love of a hundred mortal hearts to lift her curse. I'm afraid she only told you that to gain sympathy. She knew you were closing in on us. Better to make a deal, if only just to get you out of the forest."

Reece frowned and shook his head. "Everyone here has so much to say about each other. As an outsider, I don't know who to trust."

"You should only be tempted to trust Lamia when her words demonstrate a commitment to the project of evil. After all, this is the creature who used the body of your own daughter to seduce you when any of her other masks would have done the job. As for me, you may choose to believe what you like, but this is the truth: the purpose of Lamia's machine is her own pleasure, just as she told you before she knew you were a threat."

Reece gave a disgusted wave of his hand and turned his face away. His gaze settled upon his daughter and then on Amaya. "Never mind her. Tell me about them."

Alessa answered. "What you see are replicas of their natural bodies, much like the ones the lighthouse produces." Again she looked as though she wanted to break ranks from the others. "Think of them as anchors, preventing the spirit from drifting away from safe harbor. Your daughter is in a dreamless sleep. And while she rests, she is kind enough to allow us to observe the one you know as 'Mia.' As for Amaya, she is living with you in the house by the woods. Her life is full of sunny days and peaceful nights."

An odd mixture of horror and relief flooded into Reece. On the one hand, they were using the soul of his murdered child as a listening device. On the other, Amaya was protected and at peace, and living with him of all people. Bitterness gripped his heart. Amaya's devotion to him had been greater than he'd ever dared believe. His eyes remained dry, but when he spoke there were tears in his voice. "Did I do this to her?"

"Lamia and Balyxis did this to her," Pirithous said. "But your weakness opened the door for them."

Reece's melancholy burned away like alcohol under a flame. "What was I supposed to do? I was frozen, unable to lift a finger. Are you asking me to believe a better man would've been able to fight back?"

"No. I'm asking you to believe a better man wouldn't have had to."

Reece clenched his jaw. "Cerberus told me you'd do this."

"Of that I have no doubt," Pirithous said. "How is the old boy anyway?"

"Eager to be reunited with you two. But enough about him. Tell me what the point of all this is. Have I really come all this way to stand trial for my shortcomings?"

"This isn't a trial, Reece. I'm merely pointing out your fondness for the wayward hand so that you might understand how it is you and your family got here." Pirithous raised a finger to head off Reece's bourgeoning dissent. "There's no disputing it. Lamia wouldn't have come for you if it weren't so."

Reece rose up onto one knee, then onto his feet.

"Sit down," Cercyon said.

"No," Reece answered. "Now tell me what you people want from me."

Cercyon's eyes burned with indignation. It was clear he wasn't accustomed to disobedience. Beside him, Alessa's face radiated heartache. She apparently didn't like how this was going. Pirithous stepped down from the dais and took a few steps forward. "You've seen what they did to Amaya. Don't you want revenge?"

Reece tightened his fists by his sides. "Go on."

"Using your daughter's soul as a key, we can take back control of her body, ejecting Lamia in the process. But it would be for naught as long as Balyxis controls the black mirrors. That's where you have given us an unexpected gift. When you killed Balyxis's terrestrial form, you made a connection with him, one which will allow us to send you into the pyramid where one of his other two forms resides."

Reece laughed. "You want me to fight him again? In the shape I'm in?"

"You needn't fight him. You need only keep him busy while our agent works."

"And what agent might that be?"

"Amaya."

A growing anger soon eclipsed Reece's impulse to laugh at how absurd the proposal was. "After everything she went through in there, you want to send her in to die all over again?"

Pirithous's expression remained sober and his voice calm. "She will not die again. I will walk her through it, just as Alessa will walk you through the pyramid."

Reece felt his sanity pushing against its breaking point. None of this could be real, yet he was compelled to experience it anyway. "And what will happen to my daughter's soul once it's no longer of use to you?"

"Once her role is complete, we will send her on her way. Take comfort. She's going to a better place."

"I would take comfort if any of this made sense. Why would Lamia go after my unborn child when she had Amaya right there in her hands? Not to mention this island is full of bodies she could've taken for a lot less trouble."

"Lamia's masks have certain requirements. Not only must they be uncorrupted by death, but she must take them at a time when their will is still too weak to resist her. That's why she disposed of Amaya once she'd claimed the prize growing within. She was simply no longer of any use. As for the island's ghosts, they serve another purpose. If the men in the white rooms are Lamia's priests, the ghosts are her faithful. Their unspoken charge is to continually reject their own humanity, and in return, their bodies never age. Without knowing it, they bow down before Lamia's altar each time they gather in the town—flesh debasing flesh, their fruits given into the waiting maw of the devourer."

"And I suppose I can save them all if I just go along with your plan."

"Their salvation is not up to you," Pirithous said. "But you can help us defeat the ones who keep the light from their eyes."

Reece cradled his head in outstretched fingers and then dragged both hands down his face. "I cracked that pyramid open and saw for myself what was in it. It's just a damned machine, full of circuits and wires like any other. How am I supposed to get inside?"

Pirithous took a few more steps forward until he was no more than an arm's distance away. Once there, he lowered himself to one knee with his hands turned upward. Brightness shone from his palms, and a bar of white light formed between them, coalescing into a xiphos, its blade burning with an emerald fire that radiated no heat. He spoke without raising his eyes. "Only spirits may enter the pyramid. If you agree to do this, you must forfeit your life."

Reece took two steps back, his gaze locked upon the xiphos, which seemed to be quietly singing to him. "Forfeit my life? But I've come so far."

Cercyon groaned. Pirithous kept his eyes on the floor. "And yet it will be for nothing if you don't go all the way. But I understand that this is a lot to ask. If you prefer, I will send you back across the veil, and you can do your best to leave all of this behind you. But I beg you to make the right choice, to end your journey with a noble sacrifice."

Reece took some time to gather his thoughts. Once he did, he spoke with newfound purpose. "A few minutes ago I said I didn't know who to trust, but that's not quite true. I don't trust the succubus, that's for sure. Nor do I trust the watchdog of Hades. And no offense, but I don't trust its two most infamous absconders either. I guess that leaves the nice, quiet girl I met at a bar, who opened her home to me and gave me a bite to eat." Alessa blushed and lowered her eyes. "We'll leave aside the part where she drugged my tea and cast a spell on me, because I know her heart was in the right place. So, what do you say, Alessa? What should I do?"

"I cannot make this decision for you, Reece. I can only tell you that what Pirithous says is true."

Reece considered the choice before him for only an instant and then allowed himself a little smile. There was a strange comfort in giving up on his hope of going back home, especially in the moment of its offer, for in that moment he understood why he never could—why no one ever could. "Okay," Reece said. "I'll do it." Pirithous laid the sword at his feet and then took several steps back before raising his eyes again. Cercyon was watching with what looked like quiet contempt. "What's my next move?"

"You will need to wake Amaya. As much as she has suffered, you must make her remember what happened so that she'll understand her role. We'll be gone when you return. The sword alone will be waiting." Reece nodded his acknowledgment, and with a wave of Pirithous's hand, the room dissolved into nothing.

When the world took shape again, Reece found himself standing in the sun-drenched kitchen of the house at the edge of the woods. Amaya had her back to him and was stirring a pot of stew. The smell of vegetables and herbs hung thick in the air. She was wearing a bohemian skirt of earthen shades, and a coil of fabric held her golden hair in place. Reece took a step forward and the floor creaked, prompting Amaya to turn and flash a victorious grin. "Can't sneak up on me."

"Wouldn't dream of it," Reece said. He was already losing the fight to keep emotion out of his voice. "Whatever you're cooking sure smells good."

Amaya dipped a wooden ladle into the pot and held it up to his mouth. "Careful, it's hot."

Reece blew on its contents before taking some of the liquid in through pursed lips. Real or not, it was delicious. He hadn't eaten anything since the food Alessa had given him. "Tastes great, love." The final word came out mangled, and Amaya adopted a look of concern and set the ladle down on the stovetop.

"What's eatin' you, hon?"

"Come sit with me for a moment," Reece said. He led her over to the table and they took a seat across from each other. There he held her hand between his, searching for an entry point into this impossible conversation. If only he could skip past this part and go straight to dying. "Are you happy here?"

"Of course I'm happy here," she said, laying her free hand upon his. "It's everything we always dreamed of."

Reece cleared his throat and stilled his quivering lip. "Where do you think we are, Amaya?"

Her eyes were awash in puzzlement. "We're..." She looked around the room. "Well, we're at home."

Reece's leg bounced with nervous energy under the table. If he wasn't careful he was going to come apart at the seams, and that wouldn't do either of them any good. "I'm sorry, but I'm afraid we can't stay here."

Amaya's puzzlement turned to alarm, and the foot of her chair scraped against the floor as she moved away from him in her seat. "That's crazy talk, Reece. Of course we can stay here. We live here!" She was growing increasingly agitated.

Reece had no way of knowing if he was doing any of this right. He cursed Pirithous for sending him in so ill-prepared. "Think carefully, Amaya. How did we get here?" Seeming to lack an answer, she searched Reece's eyes for a reason for the question. It was time to take the next step. "Do you remember being pulled out of the water?" Upon hearing that, she snatched her hands away from his, folding one over the other and bringing them in close to her body. Her eyes broadcasted suspicion. Reece expected his next words would be the shot that killed her illusion. "Do you remember going up the elevator? There was a man, a doctor, waiting for you in a room above."

Her eyes went out of focus. Then without warning, she leaped from her chair, nearly causing it to tip over. "We should eat. The vegetables will get soft if we cook them for too long." Amaya went to the stove, slid the pot from the burner, and killed the flame. Reece approached from behind and laid a hand on her elbow. She snatched her arm away, fixing upon him a set of eyes that begged him to leave well enough alone. Were it possible they could spend an eternity together in that house, through endless days of sunshine and cool nights pressed together in bed, it would be well enough indeed. But their time was short. Reece felt as though God had conferred the knowledge of good and evil on only one of humanity's parents, and it was now his burden to tell the other. It was the hardest thing he'd ever had to do.

"We have to go back there," he said in a half-whisper. "We have to make them pay for what they did to you. For what they did to us. And make sure they can't do it again."

For the first time since they'd met, Amaya looked at Reece with hatred. She understood. She remembered. And she hated him for making her remember. Then once again, her eyes went out of focus, and she wrapped her forearms around her belly and sunk to the floor. A whimper soon grew into a sob and a sob into a wail. Reece tried to console her, but every time his hands drew near, she slapped them away. She went on like that until she sounded like a child who'd screamed herself hoarse but had gained too much emotional momentum to stop. Not knowing what to do with his hands, Reece fastened them to his hair. Of all the horrors he'd faced since stepping into the water, this was the worst. He searched the room for some way to communicate with those who were watching. Finding nothing, he took to shouting at the ceiling. "She gets it! She understands!" Amaya looked at Reece in terror and confusion. "She's had enough. Pull us out!" Amaya clapped her hands over her ears and curled into a ball, her back expanding and shrinking as she sobbed into the floorboards. "God damn you, Pirithous, pull us ou—"

In the blink of an eye, Reece was back in the room, kneeling in the same place he'd started. Everyone was gone but Cercyon, who was leaning back in his throne, picking one of his large square fingernails with the tip of the xiphos. "She understands," Reece said again, his voice now small and soft. After receiving no reply, he said "I believe that's mine."

Cercyon drove the tip of the blade into the arm of his throne. "I'll tell you what. Best me in single combat and you can have it back." He leaned forward and joined his wrecking ball hands together.

Reece shrunk under the weight of his chagrin. "You know I can't do that."

"You might as well try. You're dying in this room one way or another. And it's not going to be as noble as Pirithous would have it. Nobility is what your memory gets after you've finished the job. Until then, you're still just one of Lamia's slaves." The giant extended his hand to the right side of the room. There on the wall hung one of his mirrors, and in its reflection, Reece looked as diseased and corrupted as he had in the mansion the night before. "I know you," Cercyon said. "I know every self-serving argument you can produce. 'Forgive me, I didn't know. Forgive me, I was scared. Forgive me, it meant nothing.' Yes, you didn't know. At least not the full extent of Lamia's misdeeds. But you knew she was responsible for Amaya's ruin. Yet you consented. And yes, you were scared. But let's not pretend that's all you were feeling." Reece opened his mouth to protest, but Cercyon cut him off before he could speak. "You forget that when you were defiling yourself with her you were gazing into my eyes as well." Cercyon lowered his chin, and the candles around him dimmed. "And lastly, I will not hear another word about how it meant nothing. You've been reaching out to Lamia your entire life, and you'd be hers this instant had the hand of providence not brushed against your blindly grasping fingers."

Once he'd finished speaking, the candles dared again to cast the fullness of their light. After a period of silence, Reece gave his reply. "You're talking about the presence by the vineyard." Reece met Cercyon's eyes and spoke like a man who knew the final door was closing on his existence. "I get it now. You don't hate me because I'm cursed. You hate me because something greater than you reached out to save me." Reece settled down onto his heels. "I'm not going to fight you, Cercyon. But I will be dying with nobility whether you like it or not. So go ahead and do your worst."

Cercyon watched him quietly for a time, then rose to his feet and stepped down onto the floor. His foot struck the wood with a powerful thump, and Reece flinched with each additional step the giant took as though he were firing a gun for the first time. Cercyon placed the palm of his hand against Reece's face and wrapped his fingers around his head as if he were grasping an apple. Reece expected that at any moment he would twist his wrist, snapping his neck and sending him instantly to blackness and beyond. Seconds ticked by like that as he awaited his transport to the pyramid. Every breath was more desperate than the last as he fought for air against the rough skin of Cercyon's hand like a man on the gallows taking panicked breaths through his hood. There was no reading of last rites to let him know when the end was coming. Only the executioner knew which moment would be his last. Then at once, he brought the mystery to a close.

The feeling of pressure lasted only a moment before the crunching of bones demanding Reece's full attention. He felt the crown of his skull and both jaws snap all at once. Reece latched his hands onto Cercyon's wrist, and for the short period in which he was still able to hear, he heard himself cry out into his killer's hand. Dislodged teeth carved apart his tongue, and his voice drowned in blood. Knives of broken bone cleaved into his brain, and he saw a vision of his mind being cut into strips and laid crossways in golden layers. Then for a time, everything went black.

When the light returned, Reece was falling in slow motion toward a vast sea. At a certain point, he stopped in midair and watched his body continue without him. His face was an unrecognizable mess, more grotesque even than the monstrosity which had been the malformed Marco. One of his eyes had been sliced open by bone fragments. The other, lidless, watched him in panic until finally the body landed with a crash, sending water rushing about it in a crimson froth. Reece hovered over the water, watching with pity as everything he was sank beneath the surface.

Once the waters had calmed and no remnant of his body remained, white foam began to form. It percolated with growing intensity until a head crowned in swirling tendrils of hair breached its surface. Reece's disembodied form settled upon the water, watching as a statuesque beauty rose from the spot where he'd fallen. Her skin, white to the point of bloodlessness, glistened with a thousand sparkling drops. Her eyes, lacking any hint of darkness, glinted like diamonds.

Waves leaped all around her in arching crests, and her robe was the ocean itself. A sense of awe over what he'd helped create washed away Reece's self-pity. There was no surface on which to fall in adoration, nor did he have a body to lower before her, but it was clear the foam-born saw him, and she looked upon him with love. Turning her head, she gazed out into a distant fog where a white light shone some distance above the waters, and riding a roaring wave, she departed in its direction.

21

A HEALING FLAME

Darkness had fallen again. There was no more ocean, no more salty air. Only a world without sensation. Then from the numb void a feeling of warmth enveloped the place where Reece's head used to be. Experience was still without form, but what he perceived to be the fragments of his skull seared at their edges like they were being welded together. Then by measures, a species of half-dead sensation returned to the rest of his body, following the same pattern of warmth displaced by sizzling heat. To his surprise, he found that he was able to open his eyes. The space around him seemed immeasurably vast, an endless hollow licked by the tongues of the flickering fire which ran the length of his body. Reece lifted his head. He was hovering in midair with Alessa standing over him. Her hands were engulfed in flames, and under their light, she searched his naked form, stopping whenever she passed over a wound and sealing it with her touch. Reece laid his head back down and gritted his teeth, all of which were miraculously back in place.

"It is unpleasant, I know. But you must understand that it is for the best."

"Yes," Reece said. While he was for the moment obliged to agree, he genuinely believed her. "Am I in the pyramid?"

"No. You are in a hidden place. I am creating a body for you so that you can be like me once you return. Dead but reborn in flesh."

Reece turned the phrase over in his mind. "That's unexpected. In my final moments, Cercyon implied that I'd be nothing more than a memory once this was all over. I didn't think he wanted me to get a new body."

"You are correct, he does not. But what he did to you was not part of the plan, so I too am taking liberties."

"That's mighty brave of you, Alessa. Thank you. Especially considering how your king still sees me."

"I am confident that once this is over, he will see you differently. Perhaps one day soon he will no longer have to see such things at all."

"What a pity that would be," Reece said. "He seems to enjoy it."

"Although he would never say so, I believe it is a burden for him. I suspect that is why Pirithous gave him that portion of his powers—because he could no longer bear it himself. It is difficult to love humanity when you see everywhere the ugliness inside them. He needed someone strong to carry that burden. And King Cercyon is strong. If anyone can bear it, it is him."

"To be honest, I don't much care about his burden or how he sees me. You're a different story though. What do you see when you look at me, Alessa?"

"I see a broken man in need of fixing, and that is my present task."

Reece's body seized as she laid a fiery hand upon his shredded arm. "Is that all you see? A man in need of repair?"

Reece heard only the whisper of fire in the silence which followed until Alessa joined in with the hum of a bittersweet melody. After a few bars, she replaced her hum with words sung in Greek. Then they faded back into a hum, as though the lyrics were only a dim memory for her. Reece lifted his head a few inches and watched from the bottom of his eyes as the fire cast shards of dancing light upon her face. Her eyes met his as she sealed his stab wound. Reece groaned through gritted teeth, but on the other side of his pain, he discovered a strange sort of manic cheer, and a laugh worked its way out of his chest. "I did not think that would tickle," Alessa said. "But I am glad you found it so."

"Just thrilled to be alive. Where does a person learn skills like these anyway?"

"The power was a gift."

"Well, lucky for me you have it," Reece said, wincing. "I'm glad you care what happens to me, even if your king doesn't. And how about Pirithous? I can't quite get a read on him."

"He is a complicated man. But as far as his intentions toward you go, he means for you to be destroyed along with the pyramid."

"That's fair," Reece said. "Annihilation is what I expected."

"It does not have to be that way." A sense of frustration was becoming apparent in her voice.

Reece thought for a time before speaking again. The last thing he wanted was to upset her, but after what he'd experienced at Cercyon's hands, an egress from conscious reality was no longer something he feared, and he found that he could only tell her the truth. "I'm happy to do my part and disappear, Alessa. I've seen too much to want to see much more."

"You have seen nothing. Pirithous has been through more than you can imagine. He rose from the depths of Hades to become what he is today, passing through much darkness to arrive at the light. He suffered and became something better than his suffering."

"And yet he sends me into the pyramid with no way out."

"It is a disappointment to me as well, but it was not a decision born of cruelty. He simply does not want any of Lamia's thralls to remain after our task is finished."

"A pragmatic choice," Reece said. "And one I can't argue with."

Crackling flames leaped up into the darkness, and Reece's body tensed. When Alessa spoke, her voice betrayed an anger not yet fully embraced. "You defeat yourself."

Reece's body relaxed. "Sad to say I've made a career of it." He decided a change of subject was in order. "So, what's your take on Lamia's tale of needing her hundredth slave to lift her curse? Your bosses don't seem to think there's much to it."

"I do not know," Alessa said. Her voice was calm again. "It has been so long, I do not know if any of them truly remember what they were. All I know is what they have become. I owe everything to King Cercyon, but if I am being honest, he has not made ideal use of his many years. That is one of the reasons Pirithous is here. Together they have done much work to arrive at this moment."

"That's why I'm afraid for you, Alessa. What happens when they see how you've misused your gift?"

The flames flickered out, and all went dark. Then one by one, blacklights winked into being, and Reece found himself lying on the bar in The Eye of Night. Alessa cupped her hand behind his neck and helped him up into a seated position. Reece examined his body and found that he was wearing a fresh set of clothes. He lifted his shirt and examined his wounds. Not even scars remained. Alessa came around to the other side and helped him down onto a stool. There she looked him over, and once she was satisfied with her work, she pulled him into an embrace. Reece melted into the warmth of her touch. He wrapped his arms around her back and gripped her shoulders as if letting go might send him tumbling back into the dark. When Alessa spoke, her voice hummed against his neck. "Do not worry about me. I know what I am doing."

Reece pulled back far enough to make eye contact. "You don't want to experience Cercyon's wrath. Take it from me."

"And I will not." Alessa took Reece by the hand and guided him off the stool. "Come with me." She led him to the right side of the room, and the model of the town lit up as they approached. Hundreds of lights burned in hundreds of tiny windows. They came first to the section of town where Alessa lived. "I awoke here in my room, remembering nothing of my life before. I simply got out of bed, and like a moth to fire I was seduced by the pleasures of the town." Alessa swept her hand over the bar district, and the figures moved about on their tracks. "I made friends quickly, just as I always had. We indulged our senses every night and slept the days away. In time, some of them became pregnant, and I learned that not everything is permitted in our endless carnival. Once with child, we go to the lighthouse to be 'unburdened,' and we make this trip without exception. I thought this strange at first, but I soon came to view it as ordinary. It is amazing what you can get used to."

"The myths do say Lamia is a devourer of children."

"It is more complicated than that, but consumption is a fine enough way of thinking about it."

They continued until they were standing before the model of Cercyon's mansion. "One day I received an invitation to a special party. I was so happy to be invited that I traded whatever I could for the materials I needed to make myself a dress." Alessa glanced at Reece with a look of whimsy. "I still have it, hanging in my closet." She leaned in close to the model and Reece leaned in with her. "Once I was in Cercyon's great hall, I looked into his mirror and saw reflected for the first time someone I loved. Memories came flooding back. Many were unpleasant, but they seemed too distant to hurt me anymore. The face in the mirror no longer belonged to the sad girl who died with a needle in her arm. King Cercyon cared for me, and I soon found that he cared for me even more than the others. That is why I know he will not harm me. And neither will he allow harm to come to me at the hands of Pirithous. I will, of course, be stripped of my powers, but I never wanted such things anyway."

Next, she led Reece to the model of the lighthouse, and her expression became grim. "This monument to evil is the home of the demon's lantern, and of the pyramid which keeps it burning so brightly. It is here the souls attracted to this island are re-embodied. You might say this is where I was born."

"I was born in a bar," Reece said.

Alessa smiled. "Yes, you were. Happy Birthday, Reece."

Reece peered into the lighthouse's windows. "I don't understand how a thing like Lamia can create life."

"She cannot create life. She can only create bodies, and only counterfeits at that. Life comes from somewhere else."

"Counterfeits perhaps, but counterfeits that can reproduce. What are their children like?"

Alessa gazed into the painted sky beyond the model. "I cannot say. None have been carried to term. But if we are successful, we may yet find out."

Reece placed his hand on Alessa's shoulder. "We will be." He tried to gauge her response. She looked worried. "So tell me, what's the plan?"

Alessa led him back to the bar where they both took a seat. "It is as Pirithous said. He will transport Amaya's soul to your daughter's body, forcing Lamia back into her own. As the girl's mother, Lamia will not be able to take it back from her. Their bond is too strong."

"And what can I expect inside the pyramid?"

"Chaos. The pyramid is an unpredictable place, likely even more so in its current state. Physically you will be on your own, but I will be able to see what you see, and I will do my best to guide you. I will not be able to send any weapons or tools with you. Your spirit goes, nothing more." She took both of his hands in hers. "I will do everything in my power to pull you back out before King Cercyon destroys the pyramid. With any luck you will make it back to this body, Lamia will end up dead, and Balyxis's final form will be trapped within the veil, condemned to spend an eternity watching from the shadows, powerless to effect change."

"You're speaking my language," Reece said.

Alessa took on an earnest expression. "Reece. I will not force you to go. I can take you away from here if you want."

Reece shook his head without hesitation. "Amaya needs my help, and I'm not going to let her down again." Alessa's expression changed to one of relief, and she guided him off the stool, then onto the floor where they knelt across from each other. She drew Reece into a final embrace, and he lingered there for a time, the scent of her hair carrying him back to the memory of her apartment. He saw her again on the bed, sunrise painted upon her skin. "I'm looking forward to seeing you in your dress once this is all over." When he pulled away, Alessa joined her hands behind his head, cradling the base of his skull in her palms. Her eyes flashed like new pennies catching the sun. With a sudden rush, Reece decoupled from his body and watched it fall limp into her arms. Then the floor opened beneath him, and his spirit sank into the abyss.

Reece climbed up off the floor of what was by all appearances some version of the lighthouse's grand foyer. Gone however was the opulence, the gold picked clean as if by a swarm of thieves, and the once plush carpet mottled and singed like something had leaked all over it and was subsequently burned. He was wearing a pair of dark, cotton trousers and a matching shirt. On his feet he wore a pair of work boots. He was dressed like a prisoner, and in this mechanical brig not even the lighthouse was safe from the island's native blight.

A set of double doors stood in place of the black mirror between the twin staircases, and the winding staircase to the ceiling was gone entirely. Behind the double doors is where Reece would find the room where he'd been enthralled to Mia, though no amount of imagining could produce a picture of what it might look like now. Alessa's voice faded in and out like a voice on a radio with a broken antenna. "Do you hear me, Reece?"

"I do." Reece smiled despite his surroundings.

"Thank heavens. For a moment I was worried that I would not be able to reach you. It is difficult for me, and I will need to concentrate. You may lose me at times but know that I am always near."

"I appreciate that. So, what's my next move?"

"Locate Balyxis, then get a safe distance away and do something to get his attention. Make him angry if you can. You will need to draw him away from h—" Alessa's voice trailed off, leaving Reece in silence. With nothing else to delay him, he made his way forward and pulled open the double doors. On the other side, he found a tunnel of slick, glistening flesh which quivered under the sudden rush of air. He closed the doors with haste. *God, please don't let that be where I'm supposed to go.*

Reece backtracked to the foot of the stairs and reexamined his surroundings. Finding nothing else of interest, he made his way up the steps to Mia's bedroom. The design on the frosted glass door was different from before. Rather than a goddess of the sea, the door depicted a man holding a little girl in his arms, her hands locked around his neck as she looked upon him with love and admiration. Behind them, sunbeams burst forth in a fan of perfectly spaced rays. Reece turned the knob and pushed open the door.

Simulated moonlight brightened the facade of an arched window in the back of the room, casting a ghostly pallor over the carpet. From the light of a rotating projector, animals ranging from golden ponies to electric blue whales traversed the walls on a blanket of stars. On the bed lay an oversized rag doll, its legs splayed open and its head surrounded by a halo of yarn hair. Its gray button eyes stared fixedly at the ceiling.

His presence was no secret—that much was clear. Reece stepped back out of the room and closed the door as gently as if the glass might shatter at the slightest tremor. His movements were those of a man who had already snapped but who was taking pains to postpone the physical manifestations of his psychotic break. Halfway down the stairs, it started to spill over into his body, and a plaintive moan worked its way out of his chest. Balyxis must have already known he was there, unless the pyramid itself was able to torment without need of an operator. Reece stopped in the center of the room and made every effort to compose himself. His eyes fell again upon the path between the stairs. Better to face that unholy flesh than to spend another moment looking upon such a vile mockery of the life he'd lost.

Reece threw open the doors and entered the carnal pit. The slick pink floor quivered with each step, and blue veins pulsated along the walls. On the other side, he found himself in the room where he'd been enthralled, though there was now nothing in it which might identify it as a living space. The bed and the vanity set were gone, and the floor was a metal grate pocked by holes the size of golf balls. At its far end, a ladder rose through an opening in the floor.

As silently as possible, Reece lowered himself into a prone position and placed an eye against one of the holes. The room below swelled with crimson light. Balyxis hovered over the pyramid, his arachnoid limbs moving like branches in the wind. Across from him stood one of the black mirrors.

Reece held his breath and pushed himself back up into a crouch, then moved cat-like to the front of the room before replacing his body just as carefully back on the floor. From this new vantage point, he was able to get a better look. Along the wall stood a row of cages housing the bodies of men propped up on metal frames, their heads wrapped in cocoons of silk. The only sign they were alive was the movement of their chests and the patches of silk which sucked in against their mouths as they breathed. One of them started convulsing, and Balyxis turned his head in his direction. He raised his arm, then extended a gnarled finger, and the man fell still. The demon then withdrew his arm and returned his attention to the black mirror.

By all appearances, Balyxis was unaware of Reece's presence, lending credence to the theory that the pyramid itself had conjured the vision of Mia's room. Reece returned himself to a crouch and moved along the wall so slowly that his muscles ached from the effort. Once he reached the ladder, he made his way up, all the while taking pains not to make a single sound, nor to transmit the slightest vibration.

Reece stopped where he judged Mia's room to be and looked over his shoulder. Etched onto the corroded metal was a child's chalk drawing. It depicted a little girl holding hands with a man and a woman. The woman had yellow hair, and her dress was the color of the sundress Amaya had worn on the first day of their vacation. Reece clenched his jaw and squeezed his eyes shut. This was no time to give in to emotion. Steadying himself, he continued to the next level, arriving through a hole in the pocked metal floor. In front of him stood a door. Reece climbed off the ladder and stepped through it into the space beyond.

The entire floor was one large room brightened only by the moonlight outside the windows. To his right were stacks of empty shelves and closets full of bare hangers. On the far end, a procession of broken mirrors reflected a floor littered with shards of glass. To his left, a row of mannequins stood in what remained of glass cases. Some wore wigs and badly applied makeup. Others wore nothing, and a few were without limbs or heads. Only one case was empty. A man with his back to Reece was running his fingers over the lips of one of the mannequins as if longing for someone only he could see. Reece had made no sound, but as though sensing his presence, the man turned, fixing upon him a set of bright yellow eyes. It was Marco. He lurched forward, his blinking eyes vanishing and reappearing like fireflies. "Reece?"

Reece's blood rushed in his veins. Speaking to the dead was macabre enough, but there was something particularly unsettling about meeting a man you'd just killed. Then Reece remembered that he was dead too. "Marco. I guess your queen wasn't waiting for you with a reward after all."

For an instant anger flashed on Marco's face, then it became drawn, and he looked away as if in shame. "No, she wasn't. She was angry that you beat me. Angry enough to fry me right there in my vault. How about you, Reece? If you're here, you must've gone back to the lighthouse."

Reece held his hands out by his sides. "What can I say? I couldn't resist."

Marco gave him a knowing nod. "I guess the nuns at the orphanage where I grew up were right all along. We all get what we deserve in the end."

"Well, I can't speak to all your crimes. But for what it's worth, you didn't kill Mallory. Mia did."

"Maybe. But that wasn't the first time I gave Mal a beating. If I'm innocent, it's only because when I was teaching her, I always managed to resist the urge to teach her all the way."

"I never said you were innocent. Far from it."

Marco faced the windows and moonlight fell upon his profile. "I wasn't always such a bastard, you know. When I was a kid back at the orphanage, I paid attention. I did my best to memorize 'the good book.' Not sure I understood much of it, and what I did understand I sure as hell didn't believe. But the way I saw it, if it wasn't a path to heaven, it was at least a way out of hell."

"Yet here we are," Reece said. "If only we'd been better, eh?"

"Not sure I could've been better. There was always something rotten in me, even when I was doin' my best to be good. Mia just put that rottenness to use. She has a real talent for figurin' out what you're capable of, then giving you that last little push over the edge."

Reece crossed his arms. "Yeah, well sometimes she gets it wrong."

Marco grinned. "Sure. Keep telling yourself that. In any case, we're not gonna talk ourselves out of regret by sayin' we couldn't have done any different. Wishing you'd done different is too much a part of bein' here. I guess that's why Balyxis hasn't had a go at me yet. Oh, I'll get my time down below—we both will—but for now we get to walk these halls and think about everything we lost. It's tempting to say that the regret is the worst pain of all, but I don't think we'll be sayin' that once he gets his hands on us." Marco turned away from the windows and faced Reece. Outside, the clouds passed in front of the moon, and the room fell into dimness. Suddenly Marco's yellow eyes were the only feature Reece could make out against the backdrop of his silhouette. "I may not have took so well to scripture, but there's one verse I always liked. One even a dummy like me never forgot. Wanna hear it?"

Reece swallowed hard. "Sure."

"*Do not let your heart turn to her ways or stray into her paths. Many are the victims she has brought down. Her slain are a mighty throng. Her house is a highway to the grave, leading down to the chambers of death.*' And that there is why I can't just chuck aside my regret. Because I knew. I always knew. And she got me anyway." A scuffling on the floor above drew their attention upward, and for a time both men stood quietly with their eyes raised to the ceiling. Then Marco made a move in Reece's direction, causing him to step back toward the door. "No, Reece, don't run." He closed the distance and took Reece by the arms. "I'm not gonna hurt you. But there're others here who will. Others who've been here a lot longer than us. I've already seen worse violence from them than anything I saw locked up. We gotta stick together. Watch each other's backs. We're not enemies anymore, understand?"

Reece gripped Marco by the shoulders. "We're no longer enemies. But that doesn't make us friends. Nonetheless, I'm going to get you out of here. Then you'll go to wherever it is men like you belong. But in the meantime, I'm afraid you're going to have to go down below a little sooner than expected." Before Marco could express his puzzlement, Reece spun him around and drove him backward toward the ladder. His look of shock morphed into one of rage, and he reached for Reece's throat. Reece pushed with all his strength, sending him reeling through the door. His head smacked against the ladder, and then he folded knees-to-face in a sickening crunch as he tumbled down through the opening.

A series of thumps filled the chamber before his body landed on the basement floor. With a running leap, Reece bounded onto the ladder and scrambled up to the next level. Once he was back on solid ground, he peered down the ladder into the basement, where Marco's body lay twitching. Within an instant the demon's face appeared, glaring back up at him.

Two sets of spindly legs reached up through the opening and raised his body onto the ladder, and Reece rushed through the next door, muttering a broken prayer.

22

REBIRTH

Amaya came back into the world through a churning mist of recollections. She saw faces she recognized but to whom she couldn't attach a name or significance. They were like the faces of people gazing down into a baby's crib, immense and all-encompassing but without identity. She saw home in all its forms: a room where a man with a kind smile called her to bed; another inhabited by brightly colored animals, all of whom were dear friends; and finally, a room where there was nothing to see at all. It was in that dark envelope of warmth she felt safest, for no matter how glistening, all that brought light to her eyes brought with it the fires of destruction.

The mist cleared, and she opened her eyes to the base of a tall glass cylinder. The left side of her face throbbed against a metal floor grate. After pushing herself up onto wobbly arms, she ran her fingertips over the area of pain and felt the pattern of the grate impressed into her skin. A series of bruises mottled her arms, and when she lifted her head, she felt an area of soreness around her throat like someone had choked her. What sort of beating had she taken?

Amaya gaped at the cylinder, distant memories rising and disappearing like the streams of green bubbles percolating within it. Its color reminded her of the bottles which had always been overflowing from the kitchen trash. She couldn't say whose kitchen it had been, but she remembered thinking that despite their odd scent, anything that color must taste like something akin to sweet green apples. Until one evening, the man of the house had given her a taste, and she'd discovered that not only did it fail to meet expectations, what she spat into the kitchen sink wasn't green at all.

"Can you hear me, Amaya?"

The words had emerged from a buzzing in her head. Amaya glanced about to be sure she was alone, and when she spoke, she discovered a fear of her own voice, as though it were connected to something she didn't want to see. "Yeah. I can hear you."

"Good. My name is Pirithous. We know each other better than you remember, although I expect your memory of me will soon return. For now, please understand that you're in danger and that your survival depends on how well you follow my instructions. Do you understand?"

"Yeah," she said again, her voice catching the edge of a sharp breath.

"It looks like you're on the sixth level of the lighthouse. Search the memories left behind in your body. Do you recognize this space?"

Amaya did as he asked. A series of glass cylinders in metal frames lined the walls, bundles of shining black hoses protruding from their sides. Some appeared to boil within. Others bled an icy fog which dissipated against the floor grate. In a few she found partially formed adults, little more than skinless muscle and sinew, lidless eyes, and branches of bare nerves like the limbs of a tree in winter. In others, babies no bigger than a lemon rolled about on a cascade of bubbles. Amaya approached one of them, hypnotized by the chaotic jostling of the ball of flesh within. Its shiny black eyes caught the light time and again, twinkling at her with each graceful turn. A red light flashed at the top of the cylinder, and its skin parted into ulcers. An amber fluid issued forth from its body, sinking to the bottom of the cylinder and disappearing into the vents of a rotating ring. Then a blue light flashed, and within seconds its flesh began to heal. When the focus of Amaya's eyes shifted, she found herself startled by the faint ghost of her reflection in the glass. She studied her features and found their familiarity unsettling in the same way that hearing her voice had been.

"I understand how new and interesting everything must look, but please try to focus."

"Sorry," she said, turning from the cylinder and continuing her survey. The chamber she was in was three levels high. The level above contained more of the same, cylinders of liquids and human bodies in various stages of development. The space below blinked and hummed like a symposium of machines. In the center of the room, an operating table stood half covered by a metal shell. Creeping panic climbed Amaya's spine, and only the commitment to her assignment prevented her from losing her composure. "Yes, this is the sixth level. Level two of the lab."

Before Pirithous could respond, a monitor flashed to life, revealing the image of a man hunched over the exposed electronics of a pyramid. One of his eyes was magnified to grotesque proportions by a lens extending from a metal band around his forehead. His face was damp with sweat, and he spoke nasally Italian in a hurried cadence. Amaya understood little of what he said, but between his mannerisms and the few words she was able to catch, it seemed he was conveying a mix of good and bad news.

"Nod your head like you understand," Pirithous said. Amaya complied but felt like she must have looked like a deer nodding before the headlights of an oncoming car. Once the man had finished speaking, Pirithous said "Repeat after me: 'Capisco.'"

The man's face and voice had rattled her. Too many memories were returning at once. These were more recent, and she much preferred the echoes of a distant past. She said "Capisco," but it sounded less convincing than when Pirithous had said it. The man on the screen lifted the magnifying glass and stared into the monitor. Without taking his eyes off Amaya, he reached for a remote control, and with the push of a button the screen went black.

"That did not go well," Pirithous said. Amaya opened her mouth to speak but ended up saying nothing. "No matter. We will proceed as planned. You'll need to get to the nearest control panel and unlock the door."

"Who is he?" she asked after finding her words. She was still watching the blackened screen.

"His name is Acerbo. He was a doctor in the Second World War, during which he behaved shamefully. He is our enemy's number one human familiar. But forget about him for now. Do you know where in this room the control panel is?"

"It's down there," Amaya said, indicating the black mirror on the level below. "But it's protected. The one inside will attack me if I try to use it."

"Have no fear of that. Your ally in the pyramid is drawing the demon away as we speak. Now go below and release the locks. King Cercyon is waiting outside."

Amaya made her way down the stairs. Once at the bottom, she took a moment to examine the room. The memory of her time with Acerbo was becoming clearer, like a corpse rising to the surface of a lake, revealing the crime which had taken place nearby. She saw herself in her old body, strapped down to the table and squirming in her own piss. The woman whose body she was now in crossed the room to where she lay, passing through her like a ghost. Amaya raised a hand to her throat. This pain was different. Sharper. She closed her eyes, willing the ghosts of her past to leave her. When she opened them again, she approached the black mirror and placed her feet before it with deliberation. Acerbo had been standing in this very spot, waiting for her to come stumbling through with the desperate hope of salvation written upon her face.

Beyond that, she recalled things her old body had never seen but of which her new form held fragments. She saw the spider gazing from the mirror, speaking to her in a language of arcane symbols transmitted through thought alone. The specifics were lost, carried away by a mind that was no longer there, but she could see the symbols forming and disappearing in what was left of her memory, and their content was that of the most ancient thief, the ever-destructive imperative to steal, kill and destroy.

"Amaya…"

"Yes. I'm going." She stepped forward, two fingers extended. A static charge issued between her fingertips and the screen, nothing more. Her frame relaxed, and a tiny sigh escaped her lungs. Maybe the demon really wasn't there. Maybe the mirrors really did belong to Acerbo now. "It's not working. Acerbo must've disabled the mirrors from the control room."

"He is a clever devil," Pirithous said. "It's no wonder why Lamia prizes him. You'll need to take the control room. Find a weapon you're comfortable with, and please be quick about it. You may defeat Acerbo, but if Lamia finds you—"

"I know," Amaya said, moving toward a tray of instruments near the operating table. On it she found an array of knives, hammers, and drills. Some were merely crude tools. Others spun and whirred at the click of a button. One of the knives featured a keen, spiral blade that twirled on its handle, catching the light of the cluster of lamps overhead. Amaya flipped the switch, and the blade came to a stop. The now empty cylinder overlooking the operating table called her back to a dead past a final time. Her original body was gone, and the one she was in now had been dragged into maturity and subjected to outrageous misuse. More importantly, it had been stolen from someone who never got a chance at life. But it was hers now, and for their ruined lives she would not shed tears, but blood, and enough of it to cleanse this tower of its horrors forever.

Amaya tucked the blade into the stack of leather straps that ran down the front of her black corset dress and wrapped her fingers around the handle of a shining steel hammer. Then she passed through the glass doors and entered the helical staircase that snaked around the tower. The stairs were for those not authorized to pass through the mirrors. This body had no memory of taking them before, and once she regained access to the mirrors, she would never need to take them again. As she descended, the walls and ceiling of the staircase shimmered with what looked like neon scales. At the end of a great winding distance, she emerged onto the second-floor landing and made her way around toward the stairs which led down to the grand foyer.

Pirithous's voice returned. "Acerbo has no doubt locked himself in the basement behind the black mirror. You'll need to find a way to draw him out. Search your memory. Is there anything you could use?" Amaya stopped outside the French door and gazed into the frosted glass. Her body had ugly memories of that room. Not only of herself but the others like her, ripped from their mothers and grown into living perversions of their humanity, then used in unspeakable ways. She shifted the hammer in her hand until it seemed a custom fit, then smashed one of the panels and stepped through the opening onto a bed of crunching glass. Without stopping, she made her way up the spiral staircase and into the room above.

The entire floor was one large room brightened by fixtures mounted along the walls. To her right were shelves full of luxury items and closets packed with dresses. On the far end, a succession of mirrors reflected a chain of plush islands and benches for trying on shoes. To her left, a row of women stood in fluid-filled cases, their eyes shut. Amaya made her way toward them, the hammer once again shifting in her hand.

23
FIGHT OR FLIGHT

Prayers for deliverance froze in Reece's throat as he entered the space beyond the door. Blackness came and went at a frenetic pace under the flash of a strobe light. He was standing before a maze of cages stained with blood. Controlled violence had taken place here, and more was on the way. He moved forward in a crouch, trying to put as much distance as possible between him and Balyxis. After a time, the door swung back open, revealing the demon's flickering silhouette. He stepped forward and closed the door behind him with a nudge from one of his bone-like appendages. Once he stepped forward, Reece saw through the cages that he had taken on the appearance of Dan Collins.

"Where are you, Holloway?" Reece remained silent, moving low and away from Collins along the cages. "You're not still looking for that DiMartino chick, are you? She's as dead as they come, my man. Forever wed to ol' Davy Jones."

He paused and looked around, grinning as though his words were bringing him great pleasure. "Lucky for you, eh? Would be rough to get stuck with some Deck slut's crotch spawn." Collins covered his mouth with his hand and then removed it. "Oops. I forgot that's the word that gets your fists a-swingin'. Well, maybe those are just the words I should be using then. After all, we left some business unsettled in Marseille, and you were too much of a coward to show up and finish it in Valletta."

Collins's head moved with an uncanny stutter under the strobe light as he checked every cage. Once he was in position, Reece cast at him a heavy hook and chain attached to a rail on the ceiling, then scampered away until he reached a different part of the room. Collins avoided the attack by simply leaning back at the waist, and he froze in that position, an arrogant grin plastered across his face. After a time, he stood erect and continued speaking. "How like you to punch and run, Holloway. No wonder DiMartino had her head on swivel." Collins's eyes widened, and he took on a look so seraphic it bordered on madness. "I knew her, you know. In the biblical sense. One night I was involved in an altercation at a bar in Koper, and one of our boys got a bottle broken over his head. I didn't throw any punches myself, but because I was there, the officer of the deck wanted to get my statement about what went down. By that time I was already in my stateroom, so he sent the watch to fetch me. Imagine my surprise finding a piece of ass like that knocking on my door in the middle of the night. Normally I would've considered the consequences, but I was still a little drunk, so I asked her to come inside and help me get dressed. You know, Holloway, if the timing lined up a little better, I'd wonder if that sprout of yours wasn't actually mine. I mean, let's be real. My swimmers are no doubt a far sight stronger than yours."

The demon's words were getting to him. They sounded so unrehearsed he was having trouble dismissing them. Reece needed to get away. He crept low along the final row of cages, hoping he wouldn't find a dead end on the other side. Once he turned the corner, his mind seized, and his extremities began to tingle. Hanging from the door was a rusty padlock.

Reece fought his way out from under a wave of panic and searched for another egress point. In the flashing light, he caught a glimpse of a vent along the bottom left side of the wall. He lowered himself to the floor. Screws secured the vent in place, but in its deteriorated state he was able to pull the covering out enough to get his fingertips behind its edge. In his mad struggle they slipped free, shearing away skin and sending blood dripping down his fingers. With no time to tend to his wounds, he worked them back in, all the while casting frenzied glances back through the cages. Collins had reached the final row. "Time for our rematch, Holloway. Make sure you don't hold back. Your eternity depends on it."

Reece pulled until his arms shook, and the screws dislodged from the crumbling wall. He pushed the vent cover aside and dropped to one elbow, releasing a flurry of kicks until the cover on the other side gave way. The space was so narrow Reece was barely able to wriggle through. There was no telling if the demon would be able to follow or what would be waiting for Reece on the other side, but in that moment, it felt like his life's greatest triumph.

Once through, Reece found himself in a dimly lit hall with doors to his left and right. Some were barricaded shut, while others were sealed to their frame by nothing more than years of corrosion. His only option was an open door at the far end, but the room proved a grim barrier to the success of his plan. The walls were bare, and the floor was smooth concrete littered with bits of glass and other refuse. At its far end, the body of a man lay upon a stone slab under an open window. His flesh was speckled with bruises in various stages of healing, and his clothes were caked with dried blood. To make matters worse, it soon became clear that they weren't the only ones in the room.

Reece froze as if he'd been touched in a game of freeze tag. Someone was standing against the right wall. His head was wrapped in silk like those in the basement, and little tufts of it stuck out as though he'd been picking at it. A set of bare legs were visible beneath his white smock, and from the looks of his feet and the bloody pattern of footsteps around him, he'd been walking in broken glass. Reece felt torn between wanting to run and wanting to help this pitiful man, but he hadn't the power to do either, so he backed up with caution, trying not to step on anything which might further signal his presence in the room. After a few steps, Reece felt the heel of one of his boots sink into the floor. He'd nearly stepped into a hole. It was about the size of a manhole, and there was no telling how deep it went. He switched direction, backing up toward the window where the body lay.

The moment his back was against the wall, the corpse awoke. He gazed at the ceiling for a time, his eyes bright like yellow lanterns. He sat up on the slab and cradled his head like a man waking up with a hangover. Then after a few moments, he swung his legs over the side. Reece flattened himself against the wall, daring not even to swallow for fear the creature might hear. He squeezed his eyes shut. All his hopes were now set on providence.

"What are you doing here?" asked a gravelly voice.

Reece was frozen stock still as if he might fool the breathing cadaver into thinking he was merely one of the room's fixtures. He waited in terror for the man's follow up question, but the next voice he heard was Alessa's. "This is not a very good plan, Reece. You must open your eyes." She sounded almost as scared as he was.

Reece opened his eyes and found that the creature was still facing forward. By all appearances, he was watching the man with the silk-wrapped head and was unaware of Reece's presence. When he didn't receive a response to his question, he raised his arms and slammed his hands down on the slab. "Answer me!" His voice had grown several times larger and was dripping with rage. A muffled sound emerged from the silken cocoon, and its wearer's knees wobbled like they were about to collapse under him. With a roar, the creature stood from the slab and stomped across the room, then rained a storm of blows down on the other. The smaller man fell to the floor, patches of red growing across his silken mask. Beyond the doorway, the shadow of Balyxis was moving down the hall.

"Leap down into the hole," Alessa said. "Now, Reece. There is no time to think!" Reece obeyed, crossing his arms and jumping down into darkness. He fell for only an instant, then his feet hit something solid, and it shattered under his weight. When he hit the floor of the space below, he felt a sharp pain in his ankle, and he tumbled into a pile of shattered concrete and plaster. Reece coughed the dust out of his lungs and climbed back onto his knees. He'd fallen into a dim room with no windows. The only light was that which spilled from a lone candelabra.

His ankle throbbed, but he was able to bear weight on it. He didn't dare examine the skin under the torn parts of his clothing. There wasn't much he could do about those cuts and scrapes anyway. "I sure could use your healing touch right about now, Alessa."

"Sorry, Reece. I am unable to help in that regard. You must find a way out of that room. Balyxis might follow you down through the hole."

Reece scanned the room but wasn't able to see much, so he retrieved the candelabra from the rickety wooden table, then flipped it over and kicked one of its legs until it broke off. Now at least he had a weapon. He searched the perimeter with the light from the candles, finding little of interest until he came upon a section with words etched into the wall.

Without a care that she was somebody's daughter
Reece knocked her up and tossed her in the water

Alessa chimed in before he could comment. "It is a psychological attack, Reece. You must not let it get to you." But it had gotten to him, and his old guilt reached up from its burial plot, joining the throbbing pain in his body in its demand that he place his back against that wall, sink to the floor, and wait there come what may. "Keep looking," Alessa said. "There must be something more useful."

Reece carried the candelabra to the far wall. At its center, he came upon a framed painting that ran from floor to ceiling. He leaped back, a shudder running from his shoulders to his feet. The painting depicted Cercyon sitting on his throne, his expression as grim as ever. In his arms, he held a nude woman curled up against his chest like a child being carried to bed. She was attempting to conceal her face behind her hand, but it was clear from her eyes alone that the woman was Alessa.

"It is a lie," Alessa said. "You must not believe any—"

Her voice was gone again, and at once Reece's body ached with greater clarity. The demon of doubt was struggling to get back inside, tearing open his chest and snapping its jaws at what remained of his heart. He couldn't let it in. He had enough demons to deal with as it was. *The words on the wall are a lie, and so is this. Burn it. Burn the lie and never think of it again.* Reece touched the painting with the candle's flame, then tossed the candelabra to the floor and stepped back. Fire crawled the canvas, eating it away in blackened patches until all that was left were Cercyon's eyes watching him with hatred.

Once the last of the canvas had burned and the smoke had cleared, Reece found before him the opening it had concealed. Judging from his position, it should have led back into the room with the mannequins, but instead he found himself passing through a set of beaded curtains into some ruined version of the strip club where he'd met Mallory. In place of the couches and tables, metal cages like the ones he'd seen in the basement stood in haphazard rows, each facing the stage. Within them stood men propped up on frames, their faces wrapped in silk and their bodies shivering. There was no music, just a long breath that stretched out over the minutes, punctuated in bursts by blasts of distorted noise from the speakers. Reece weaved his way through the cages, examining each in turn. He stopped before one of them and tried to get the attention of the man inside. Its inmate gave no reply beyond a quickening of his breath.

A projector in the back of the room flashed to life, and Reece shielded his eyes. Blue waves danced across the stage, and before long Mallory emerged from behind the curtain, two sets of arachnoid limbs protruding from the back of her red negligee. "How about a private dance, Reece?"

Reece gripped the table leg like a batter awaiting a pitch. "How about you go fuck yourself, Balyxis?"

"Now is that any way to speak to a lady?" Mallory leaped down onto the floor, and the men nearest her began convulsing in their cages. She then took to terrorizing Reece with false lunges, causing him to stumble and clumsily dash from cage to cage in ever more desperate attempts to keep her at bay. "You know, there's one thing I never understood, Reece. When we first met, you told me you'd been seeing my sister for seven months. But a couple days before she took the plunge, she called me up and told me about a man she'd met at a bar in Marseille—a Frenchman who'd taken her on a romantic drive, then screwed her brains out on the hood of his car." She paused for effect, watching Reece's response. He struggled to hide the pain from the wound she'd ripped open, and there was no telling whether he was having any success. The blare of distorted noise sounded again, and he cringed beneath it. "Amaya was always so eager to tell her poor, backward sister about her adventures, yet she never mentioned you. Funny, that. I suppose you were little more to her than a name on an apartment lease. Our little princess did always hate sleeping on the ship with the peasantry. So she entertained your dull whims without mentioning them to anyone, not even to throw it in my face that she'd captured the heart of an officer, while I was stuck with what she'd left behind once she'd grown tired of Marco."

Reece roared and swung the table leg as hard as he could. Mallory raised her hand and caught the weapon mid-swing, then jerked it away from him. Before Reece could turn and run, she twirled it around and brought it crashing down between his neck and shoulder, breaking his clavicle. Reece moaned in pain and stumbled away, rounding one of the cages before making for the stage. As he clambered up, Mallory threw the table leg and it bounced off his back, knocking the air out of his lungs. "Run like hell, Reece. And be sure to keep me entertained. Because once I get bored, you're finished."

Reece stumbled through the curtains and toward a door backstage. Pushing it open, he found himself back on one of the pocked metal platforms with the ladder straight ahead. He stepped forward and gripped the ladder. The path down now appeared like an infinite fall, with platform after platform telescoping down forever. *No matter how deep an abyss you're in, there's always something below it.* He looked up and found only two platforms above. With no choice in the matter, he positioned himself on the ladder and did his best to climb with one arm.

Once he reached the next level, he nearly stepped off the ladder but then stopped himself. This is where Balyxis would expect him to go. He judged the next platform to be several levels higher. If he could make it, it would buy him a solid lead as the demon searched the space below. Reece continued his climb, pumping his legs until he thought they might give away. Sweat dripped from his brow and burned his eyes. In time he looked up through the stinging blur and saw the final platform nearly in reach.

At once the sound of roaring distortion returned, and despite his arm's weary protest, Reece pulled himself up and rolled onto his side, drawing his knees to his chest. Footsteps echoed on the ladder below. With no way of knowing whether he'd been seen, all Reece could do was lay frozen in the fetal position. After a time, the demon's feet touched down on the floor below, taking several steps before the door creaked open. Then the steps fell silent, and the door slammed shut.

Reece climbed up off the floor and steadied himself against the wall. "Alessa. Are you there?"

Her radio static voice whispered in his ears. "I am sorry for my absence, Reece."

"It's okay," he said. "Did you catch what happened below?"

For a moment she was silent, and he thought he'd lost her again. "Yes. I hope you are not taking his lies to heart."

"I'm trying not to. But he has a real talent for breaking a guy down."

"I know. But we must keep moving. By all appearances, this should be the dining level. Maybe you will find something there to defend yourself."

"I don't know—that didn't work so well last time. At this point I think I'd rather just find a bite to eat."

"I do not think there will be any food. But I promise, when you return, I will cook for you whatever you want."

"I'm going to take you up on that, Alessa. I'd love to have some more of that amygdala."

"Amygdalota," she said, and Reece could hear the smile in her voice. "You will have more amygdalota than anyone has ever had."

Reece smiled back and rested his head against the wall. "How's Amaya doing?"

"Hard at work, but I am afraid the door is not yet open. You will have to keep Balyxis busy for a while longer."

"Roger that," Reece said, and without further delay he passed through the final door. The lower floor of the dining level was empty save for a small collection of tables and chairs draped in sheets. A set of wide steps in the middle of the room led to the second floor. As Reece was making his way up, he noticed that one of the wrought iron spindles was standing askew, and with some effort he was able to pry it loose. It was sharp and heavy and would make a far better weapon than the table leg had. At the top, he arrived in the great hall. Marble columns ran the perimeter of the room between windows each taller than a man, their curtains drawn open so that the entire space was drenched in moonlight. On the face of each column was a gothic sconce, their candles melted into nubs of wax. On the right side of the room, a spiral staircase ascended into a circular recess in the ceiling. At the center stood a table with two chairs where a mannequin awaited her dining partner. Reece remembered that one of the glass cases on the mannequin floor had been empty and wondered if perhaps one of the damned had hauled her up here, hoping to recreate a treasured moment.

Reece made his way to one of the center windows on the far side of the room and looked out over the water. Bolts of red lightning fell to the horizon, turning the ocean to blood. Some distance from the shore, he saw his old ship, and tears fell from his eyes. Could a rescue be underway? If he could manage to board the ship, would he awaken to a time before any of this had happened? No sooner had he finished the thought than two massive whales breached the surface, arching up into the sky as lightning crackled in clouds of rolling crimson. They landed one after another, smashing the ship into three parts, each of them sinking into the sea. An immense wave followed, crashing into the rock face and sending hundreds of tons of water rocketing into the sky. Through all of it Reece hadn't moved a muscle. He just stood there sucking tears into his nose, his jaw set firmly in place. The pyramid does nothing but take. Now it was his turn to take something from it.

With no time left to spend on lost causes, he threw the mannequin over his shoulder and carried it to the window. Then he removed his boots and set the mannequin upright in them so that it was standing behind the drawn curtain. Reece stepped back and examined his work. The curtain was just sheer enough so that the moonlight revealed only a faint outline of its body. He would just have to hope that Balyxis thought he was stupid.

The sound of the opening door below was Reece's cue to hide. He positioned himself behind one of the columns and waited there in stillness, gripping his makeshift spear. Reece could hear downstairs the sound of Balyxis yanking sheets off of tables, and he flinched at the noise of a chair clattering across the floor. Then the critical moment came when his footfalls landed upon the steps. They were slow and deliberate, like the nocturnal dripping of a broken faucet, echoing through the silence. Finally, the demon's feet sounded upon the marble floor. Reece followed the sound to the middle of the room.

A mocking snicker filled the air before he spoke. "Je te vois, Reece." For a time there was neither sound nor movement, and then his footfalls began anew. Reece shifted to the far side of the column as the demon drew near. "Reeeeece." The utterance came out as more of a breath than a word, and it filled the entire chamber. A flash of red lightning cast the demon's shadow upon the back wall. His four spider's legs were raised and ready to strike. Then his footsteps stopped.

Alessa's voice came rushing back. "He has seen the full shape of the mannequin, Reece. Either run or strike, but you must do something now!"

Reece leaped out from behind the column, his bare feet patting across the floor. When the demon turned, Reece saw the face of the interloper. He sunk the spindle just below his sternum, and the interloper's human arms grasped it while those of the spider tore into Reece's flesh. Lightning flashed again, and at once his face was that of Balyxis. He roared in pain and his jaws flung open, spraying venom into Reece's eyes. Blinded, Reece only heard the breaking of the glass, and while he felt the wind whipping against his flesh, he was not able to see the ground as it rushed up to meet them.

24

SEE NO EVIL

Amaya had found it easy, surprisingly easy—disturbingly easy, in fact—to drill through the eyes and into the brains of Lamia's masks, ending once and for all their usefulness to her. She had spared only one, the prettiest of them (who thankfully also happened to be the lightest) for the next stage of her plan. Moving the body was an exhausting endeavor. She tried a few different methods, finally settling on the pack strap carry she'd learned in the Navy. Although once she reached the spiral stairs, she had no choice but to just let the body tumble to the bottom. Pirithous stayed quiet throughout the procedure. Perhaps he didn't like what he was seeing. Or perhaps he simply had nothing to add.

Once on the landing, Amaya positioned the body halfway over the railing and took a moment to catch her breath. Acerbo was no fool, except to the extent that every man is a fool when they're in love, and odds were he was head over heels for all of Lamia's masks. He would no doubt abandon his intellect and come running the moment he saw through his monitor one of his queen's masks lying inert outside the mirror. He would have to. Everything depended on it.

Pirithous finally chimed in. "Are you ready for this?"

"Of course. If you have anything more to say to me, say it now. I'd like for us to keep radio silence once I'm inside. No distractions."

"Good luck," Pirithous said, and his voice faded from her mind. With nothing more to delay her, Amaya grabbed the body's legs and flipped it over the railing. It landed with a crunch and settled into a contorted pose, its spine twisted and its closed eyes directed toward the black mirror. Amaya climbed over the railing and crouched on her heels upon the lip which extended beyond the base rail. Adrenaline surged through her body, and the air she took in seemed only to satisfy the hunger of her lungs by half. It was vital she got this right. After all, she was taking revenge for two.

The space below flashed blue, and Acerbo spilled out from behind the mirror, falling to his knees blubbering and rattling off spurts of Italian to a dead woman who could hear none of it. Then at once he fell silent and let go of the body. When he looked up, Amaya saw on his face an expression of deep regret, but by then she was already falling toward him, a hammer clenched in her fist.

It was hard to say where it landed first, because after the first strike a second followed immediately, and then a third, and Amaya lost count as a series of cuts opened on Acerbo's face. His spectacles slid across the floor, bloody and shattered. Every couple blows he screamed, and that caused Amaya to become even more excited, so much so that if Acerbo had dropped dead on the spot, she likely would have continued beating him for quite some time. But he held on for dear life and managed to push her far enough away that he could stumble back through the door. He staggered down the stairwell, his hand leaving a bloody smear along the wall. Amaya stashed the hammer in one of the straps of her dress and retrieved the spiral blade. She powered it on, walking behind Acerbo at a leisurely pace as he blundered down the hall. The faces on the screens stuttered in a broken freeze frame. "No need to struggle, Dr. Acerbo. There's nowhere for you to go."

He peered back over his shoulder as he lurched toward the final corridor, his face streaked with blood and tears. "What did you do to her?"

"I killed her," Amaya lied, leveling the spinning blade at him. "And now I'm going to kill you."

Once in the final corridor, Acerbo made a dash for the control room. Amaya sprinted after him, throwing herself against the door as he tried to close it and knocking him on his back. He climbed back up off the floor and lunged at her, and her knife made a meal of his chest, ripping away both fabric and flesh. He struggled to control the blade, but Amaya slipped from his blood-slicked grasp, cutting him time and again. In a last-ditch effort, he threw all his weight at her, causing her to stumble backward and pinning her underneath him. With what strength he had left, he raised his arm and brought his elbow down upon her face, slamming her head into the floor.

A net of images more like dreams than memories broke Amaya's fall into unconsciousness. She saw a man whose face she knew but couldn't quite place. He was strong and full of love and smiled as he pulled her by the hands across a sunlit beach. She laced her hands behind his neck and drew him close, her nose taking in his scent. Running her fingers up the back of his head, she searched for a handful of his wavy hair, but to her horror, she found only bald skin.

A wave of pain rushed through her body as a fist landed on her ribcage, taking her breath away. Snapping from her dazed state, Amaya pushed her face into her attacker's neck and bit down hard, ripping a chunk of his flesh away as he pulled back. She spat it out onto the floor, gasping as she fought to refill her lungs with air. Once her focus returned, she found Acerbo sitting against the wall, his hand held tight against his neck and his legs kicking at nothing.

She wiped the blood away from her mouth, and then pulled herself back up into a standing position. With knife in hand, she positioned herself over the pale and terrified monster wriggling on the floor. Grabbing him by one leg, she pulled him away from the wall until he was lying flat. "Shh, shh," she said, falling to her knees beside him. She laid a hand over his eyes and his breaths became shallow and quiet. "What happens next happens to you in darkness." With a flick of the switch the blade began twirling again, and there on the floor, Amaya finished her work. Once she was done, she tossed the knife aside and drew in a full breath, slicking her blood-soaked hair back against her head.

"You were magnificent," Pirithous said.

"Thanks."

"King Cercyon is outside the door. Will you let him in?"

"Yeah," Amaya said, clambering back up onto her feet. She approached the main panel, and with a wave of her hand, it sparked to life. Eight shimmering orbs appeared, and she punched in the code.

"Thank you, Amaya."

Once again, Pirithous's presence faded from her mind, and Amaya took the time alone to allow herself the luxury of weariness. She looked upon the body of Acerbo—evil, vile Acerbo, whose insides were spilling out all over the shiny floor. What had he been working on? She peered down into the network of circuitry within the pyramid. It was this device that had allowed Lamia to broadcast her stolen body to a hundred lecherous slaves. Her ire rekindled, Amaya retrieved the hammer and brought it down upon the pyramid until it was spitting sparks.

There had been no sudden stop at the bottom. There had been no bottom at all. It was as if Reece had been snatched out of the air and dropped into a vacuum. Sight returned to his eyes through the blur of saltwater. A woman with dark hair was pulling him from the surf and onto the sand. "Are you okay?"

Reece fell to his hands and knees, coughing and sputtering until he was able to form intelligible words. "I think so," he said between gasps.

"You almost drowned."

Reece looked up and saw Alessa's face in the moonlight. Some distance behind her, Pirithous was standing with his arms folded. "Did I make it out of the pyramid?"

"I'm afraid not, Reece. You fell from the lighthouse into the water."

Reece looked over his shoulder and found that the lighthouse had undergone some changes. Large chunks of it were missing, and what was left was framed in a reddish glow from a fire raging beyond the harbor. "That doesn't make sense. There's no way I could've fallen that far."

Pirithous wore a look of contempt. "Well, you did. And now you have to get back in there and finish the job."

"Unless you want me to do it," Alessa added, placing her fingertips upon her chest.

Reece dismissed the notion with a wave. "No. I'll do the job. It's just that I thought I'd already done it."

"And you have!" Alessa said. She helped him up from the impression he'd made in the sand. "You've done a wonderful job. Splendid, really. But now we need you to do one last thing."

Reece rubbed his face with his hands. "Okay. What is it?"

"We need you to go back into the control room. There you'll find a cord connected to the pyramid. You must carry the other end of that cord to the top of the tower and plug it into the lantern. Very simple. Understand?"

Reece looked the lighthouse over again. "I understand the instructions. I just don't understand why you want me to do it. I did what you asked."

"Yes, and as I said, you did a splendid job. But you see, King Cercyon is coming soon, and he's going to destroy the pyramid once and for all. If the two are connected, once he destroys the pyramid the lantern will be destroyed as well. Then there will be nowhere left for Balyxis to run to. Gone forever. Kaboom." Alessa mimed an explosion with her hands.

"Okay," Reece said. "I'll do it. But what if I run into him again? I don't think I can get the jump on him a second time."

"Highly unlikely," Pirithous said.

"Yes, highly unlikely," Alessa agreed. "He didn't make it as far as you and was splattered upon the rocks. Though you never know how long that sort of thing will last in a place like this."

Pirithous shrugged, his arms still folded across his chest. "It's all subject to change. Still, you'll probably be fine if you hurry."

Alessa drew Reece near and gave him a peck on his cheek. "For luck." Reece nodded and started off toward the lighthouse. Once he'd covered a dozen feet or so, he looked back at them. Alessa had her hands folded in front of her as though in prayer. She bore the imploring expression of someone whose entire hopes rested upon another, which made Reece feel heroic. Pirithous still had his arms crossed, but he granted Reece what he took to be a respectful nod.

Setting off again, Reece made his way up the zigzagging steps and into the courtyard, and when he arrived at the front door, he found that it was already open. The face carved into the molding was no longer that of a woman, but of Balyxis, his eight smooth and featureless eyes watching Reece as he passed through the doorway. The door between the staircases had been blown off its hinges, and the tunnel of flesh had been burned. The smell of singed flesh hung heavy in the air, and Reece fought the urge to be sick.

Once through, he made his way down the ladder and into the control room. The cages were now empty. Coiled on the floor was a roll of cord, glowing florescent green. One end was plugged into a socket built into the pyramid. Reece grabbed the other end and tied it around his waist, then made for the ladder. When he looked up, he was struck by a sense of vertigo. Gone were the metal floors between levels. It was all ladder straight to the top. After taking a moment to ensure that the cord was securely attached, Reece began his ascent.

25
CHAOS

A maya stood before the touchscreen panel, scrolling through the black mirrors with flicks of her wrist. The images stuttered and tore, and red and blue lines combed their way from top to bottom. Even though the audio was corrupted, she could hear what must be King Cercyon's booming steps as he went from room to room. Occasionally she heard the cry of one of the handful of men Lamia allowed to move freely about as her servants. A howl erupted off-camera somewhere on the training floor. Then after a breathless silence, a man's mangled body shot across the room and bounced off the wall, landing in a heap. Without the demon or a functional connection to the white rooms, these were merely men, and they were dying as men do.

A lump formed in Amaya's throat as Cercyon entered the frame. It was beyond certainty that she had no buried memories of this man, for she never would've forgotten

317

someone so imposing. He approached the body and watched it as it twitched on the floor. The image on the screen tore, and once it came back, the destroyer was staring directly into her eyes. Amaya felt a pressure in her ears as though she'd instantly risen to dizzying heights. Then the screen tore again and went black, and the pressure was released. There was majesty written upon the features in her reflection. Her hair, no longer slicked with blood, moved about her head like rolling blades of fire. A smile formed upon her lips, and the face in the monitor smiled back. When the screen flashed back to life, only the dead body was visible in the frame. Cercyon had moved on, and it occurred to Amaya that it was perhaps time for her to move on as well. The storm had arrived, and her role was complete. Pirithous was out there somewhere waiting for her. Dim memories of his kindness in a bright place above a forest were beginning to fall into her mind like the first leaves of autumn.

The sound of footsteps echoing down the hall broke her from her spell. They were not the thunderous steps of Cercyon, but of someone much smaller and moving with purpose. With a wave of her hand the screen went black, and she retrieved her blade from the floor. She stepped into the doorway just as one of Lamia's thralls rounded the corner. He froze in place when he saw her. "My queen! What happened here?"

Amaya braced herself against the doorframe. "Never mind that. Why have you come?"

The man looked puzzled. "Is this a test, my queen?"

"Yes, it's a test. Now answer my question."

"The enemy's inside. You ordered me to come open the white rooms so that the others could help defend you, and to find Dr. Acerbo so that he might help you prepare the final rite."

Amaya searched her body's memory but found nothing. Perhaps this final rite was not something Lamia thought she would ever have to do. "Which is?"

"Why, to merge with the one inside the lantern of course." The man's puzzled look was growing into one of suspicion.

"Well done," Amaya said. "You've proved that you are who you say you are. One can never be too careful with the enemy inside the gates." She winced as if in pain. "One of them has already attacked me, but as you can see, I fought back." The man tried to look past her into the control room, but she moved her head with his, blocking his view, then gave him a soft look and fluttered her lashes. "I need someone reliable to escort me above. Can I count on you for that?"

An expression of joy came over the man's face, and he held out his arms like someone reuniting with a loved one after decades apart. "Yes, my queen. Of course." She stumbled forward and fell into his embrace, her face only inches from his. It wasn't until the blade began whirring behind him that the joy faded from his eyes. Then they reflected only horror as the knife drilled through the base of his skull and into his brain. Once his light was gone, Amaya ripped the blade free, and he crumpled to the floor.

"Did you hear that, Pirithous?"

"I heard it, and I'll get word to the king. You've done everything expected of you and more. Come up to the ground floor. I'll be waiting."

Although Amaya ached to be free of the tower, she couldn't leave without seeing the place her abusers had lain with her image so many times. She returned to the control room, activated the panel, and released the locks on the doors while leaving the inmates in stasis. Once back in the hall, she placed pressure on one of the doors with the palm of her hand, breaking its smooth surface. A low hum issued forth, followed by the sterile odor of a morgue. She pulled out the drawer and found a man lying in it. His face was without expression, and if he was breathing, it was too shallow to see from the movement of his chest. Amaya turned away in disgust. Few had ever known the sensual rewards he'd reaped from her ill-gotten body. Yet even fewer would feel envy upon seeing his naked form set so starkly against a backdrop of pure absence. His excess was all that remained of him. *What a sad, pitiful man.* There was no need to wait for the judge. These gallows birds had received their sentence, and their executioner was already there.

Amaya closed the drawer and went back into the control room, bringing the panel up a final time. She navigated its cryptic menus, pulling up the diagram of the white rooms and drawing across them the symbol for current. Then she raised the voltage to the highest setting.

On her way back to the stairs, she tried not to watch the faces on the screens as they contorted in pain, their flesh blackening and flaking away. One by one, the screens went blank until there wasn't a man left to watch her complete her journey. She climbed the steps past the smear of blood Acerbo had left on the wall. Once at the top, she dropped her knife, and it clattered back down below. Pirithous was sitting at the foot of the staircase that led to the second floor. He stood when he saw her, and at once Amaya realized what a mess she must look. Pirithous looked her up and down, his expression of friendly ease growing into one of compassion. "What have I done to you, Amaya?" Once he'd finished speaking, his gaze fell to the floor.

She approached and lifted his downcast face with the tips of her fingers, then ran her hand through his hair. "You pulled me out of a dark closet."

While no one had hindered Reece's climb to the top, the journey itself had been nearly enough to defeat him. He sat crouched against the wall on the platform of the dining level, rubbing his screaming shoulder in the hopes of moderating its rage. The climb had felt impossibly long, as had the cord, which seemed to grow every time he felt he was losing slack. It was clear now that the cord would be exactly as long as it needed to be to connect the pyramid to the lantern.

Once he'd rested some, Reece slid himself back into a standing position. But as he did, the cord around his waist came loose, and the metal connector banged against the floor before taking off back toward the ladder. Reece lunged forward, throwing himself prone on the platform and catching the cord with one hand just as it was about to begin its free fall back to the control room. He lay like that for some time, breathing away his pain and panic into the floor. "That would've been bad," he said, climbing back to his feet. He refastened the cord around his waist, making sure it was as secure as possible before heading through the door.

The dining hall was unchanged, save for the strong wind which blew down the stairs. *That's a lot of air for one broken window.* Reece ascended with cautious steps, one hand still resting on the cord around his waist. Once he reached the top, he saw that the entire wall had been destroyed, and large sections of the ceiling lay in heaps of broken stone. The spiral staircase still stood attached to a section of what remained. Reece climbed it, emerging onto the roof of the lighthouse's main structure. A smaller tower loomed over the center of the open space, its windows tinged with golden light. Reece went to the side and looked over the edge. Kapsali Beach lay below. He struggled in the dark to find Alessa and Pirithous, but there were no signs of movement. Offshore the waters looked troubled. Something was brewing out there. Reminded of the urgency of his task, Reece returned to the tower and tugged on the handle of the metal door. He had expected resistance, but to his surprise it not only opened, but it fell right off its hinges, landing with a deafening report.

This was the chamber Reece had seen through the mirror in Mia's pit. Candles sparked to life all around him as he entered, casting light on the arcane symbols carved in a spiral across the stone floor. At the top of the tower hung an amber structure like a honeycomb-patterned chalice without a stem. A stone staircase ran along the wall, terminating at a door in the ceiling. "When in doubt, go up." Reece began his ascent, and after a certain distance, he noticed that the symbols on the floor were lighting up red concurrent with his progress. Once he was nearly at the top, he stopped to examine the honeycomb structure. From below it had looked to be made of glass, but from where Reece now stood, he could see slight oscillations in its surface. Whatever it was, it was organic.

The final symbol lit up as he completed his ascent, sending a rumble through the chamber and releasing the lock on the door. Whoever was in charge had cleared him for entry. He felt again how it had been for him during his first hours on the island—as if he were in a dream, and no matter how strange the people and events surrounding him, he could find no cause for any serious concern. Reece pushed the door open and climbed into the space above.

Storm panes set in metal frames enclosed a lantern of bronze and polished glass. It expanded and contracted as though it were breathing, and its lenses rotated in billowing cascades. At its center, the primary lens cast its gaze out over the expanse. Every so often a glimmer of light, almost too quick to be caught by the eye, flittered in through the windows, and Reece saw for an instant the face of a man moving like oil on water across the lantern's surface. Then it dissolved, and its colors sank to the bottom and disappeared. At first this happened across several well-spaced intervals, then more frequently, until the room was bright with ghostly flashes.

Once the period of brightness had passed, Reece recalled his charge. A metal socket formed on the lantern's frame, and he removed the cord from around his waist. The sound of static roared and faded in his ears. It was familiar, but he was unable to place its source. When he moved the connector toward the plug, the static came roaring back louder than before. Somewhere behind it an unintelligible voice was speaking with urgency.

Before he could make out what it was saying, Alessa arrived with Pirithous behind her. "This is it, Reece. The end of Lamia's reign of terror."

"Alessa. What are you doing up here?"

"We couldn't make you do this alone, Reece. Now that we're all here together, it's time. Complete the connection. Put an end to Lamia and her demon forever." The light from the lantern came and went in swells, casting brightness and shadows over Alessa's face. Behind her, Pirithous watched Reece with what looked like hunger in his eyes. Alessa placed her body against Reece's and drew his mouth into a kiss. "It's time for us to be together. We need only finish what we started."

Reece looked down at the connector in his hand, and a feeling of panic like the one which had gripped him outside Mia's room washed over his body. He may have been too confused to know the truth, but he was pretty sure he could still identify a lie, and there were two of them standing right next to him. Reece extended his hand and offered the cord to Alessa. "Now that you're here, how about you do the honors?"

The tiny muscles in her jaw were working like mad. "No, Reece. That honor is yours alone."

"Well, I don't want it. This wasn't Alessa's wish, and I'm certain that wasn't her kiss." Pirithous had unfolded his arms and was looking at Reece with fire in his eyes. "How about you, Pirithous, or whoever you are? Care to give it a bash?" At once the spell lifted, and Reece saw before him Lamia and Balyxis. "That's what I thought," Reece said, laying the cord just below the lantern. He started toward the door and Lamia moved to block his path.

"Do you really think I'm going to let you walk out of here?" Tiny flames of light rolled over the scales of her flesh. Her eyes were as opaque as black marble.

"Yes, I do. Because the truth is you aren't here at all. And I'm pretty damn sure you can't lay a hand on me as long as I know that." Reece stepped forward, and Lamia became as mist, allowing him to pass through her. Balyxis was all that stood between Reece and the doorway. The demon spread his jaws as if to launch his venom, but Reece continued forward unabated, passing through his body as he dissolved, his roar fading into the ether.

Alessa's voice returned to Reece's thoughts the moment he left the chamber. "I am sorry they used my image to trick you, Reece."

"Not your fault. I was never really all that convinced anyway. Lamia just isn't you. If I hadn't received a face full of venom, I would've seen that from the start. I suppose I should be grateful though. She yanked me out just as I was falling to my death."

"I believe you have only serendipity to thank for that. There was another attack on the pyramid just before your fall. That is what altered your outcome. After that, all of Lamia's hopes rested upon getting you to repair the connection from within."

"To serendipity," Reece said, walking to the tower's parapet and gazing off into the ocean. About five miles from the shore, a flock of what looked like thousands of birds circled the blood red sky over an area of disturbance in the water. It ebbed and swelled, sending ripples of waves in every direction, until at last an object appeared. At first it looked like a whale was breaching the water's surface, but the object continued to rise. Great volumes of water roared down its sides, and it became clear that a mighty iron crest was advancing toward the firmament. Soon after, the helmet of an ancient Greek warrior emerged, sea green from eons in the deep. A pair of eyes like emerald suns blazed from the darkness beneath the helmet. Though still miles away, the rumbling of footsteps along the ocean floor were already sending tremors through the lighthouse. Reece watched in awe as a neck appeared, followed by a set of shoulders which shrugged off the weight of countless tons of water, sending it pouring down like a waterfall over a muscled breastplate and into the roiling mist.

"Alessa, can we talk about the gargantuan Greek warrior rising out of the water?"

All was silent on her end for a time. When her voice returned, she spoke with urgency. "King Cercyon has been alerted to Lamia's plans and is en route to the basement to destroy the pyramid. You must get out of there, Reece."

"Gladly. Just tell me which way to go."

"Down. Just get out of the lighthouse."

"That sounds doable. How long do I have?"

"I do not know. The way you experience time within the pyramid is unreliable, and since half my attention is there, one can assume I am also an unreliable judge. I only know that once King Cercyon destroys the pyramid, you will be out of time. Take care, and although you must move quickly, be mindful of the ones below. They are presently without guidance, but they may still attack on sight. Be swift and silent, Reece." Cercyon was now nearly halfway out of the water, and the lighthouse trembled with increasing intensity. The birds swarmed about his helmet in a wild tumult. Reece turned and looked up at Lamia a final time. She was watching him from the lantern room, the rage and hatred gone from her eyes. She looked like a woman condemned.

A series of quakes strong enough to move the floor beneath his feet punctuated Reece's journey back to the ladder. Once there, he made his way down as quickly as possible, holding tight with his good arm whenever the building shook. There were no more platforms, but as he passed the doors of each level, he found the golden eyes of the damned gazing out at him. Many appeared to be new to this world, and they looked at him with terror and confusion. The more seasoned of them watched Reece with hatred. One leaped from the door and onto the ladder, nearly knocking Reece off. Reece managed to shake him loose, and the man slipped down several rungs. Hanging by one arm, Reece brought his foot down upon the man's face until he slipped free and plummeted below.

By the time Reece had nearly reached the bottom, his arm was so tired that he could scarcely bear to hang on another second, so he dropped the final distance, landing hard upon the pocked metal floor. Ahead the tunnel of flesh was closing, and as Reece crawled toward it, the bodies of the damned fell like hail behind him, slowly at first, then in a roaring torrent of flesh and bones shattering against the unyielding steel.

Reece scrambled to his feet and launched himself into the tunnel. The charred flesh constricted around him, and for a moment he was convinced that he could go no further. But its grip loosened with each thunderous step of the titan's approach, and Reece was able to work his way through to the other side. He gasped for air as he squeezed out the other end and tumbled down onto the carpet. By now, Cercyon was so close he could hear the cacophony of the countless birds which swarmed about his helmet. Bolts of red lightning touched down on the land outside the open door, and the foyer pitched and rolled like a ship battered by a storm. Reece climbed to his feet, and as he ran for the door, a sound like crushing blows raining down one after another split the atmosphere. Through the chaos, a broken message emerged. "Co-- back -- me, Ree--. Pl--." Then the sound of a great tearing carried Reece back into silence.

26
FALL

The reservoir above the ceremonial chamber expanded and contracted with all the vigor of a dying lung. A couple of times, Lamia thought she saw the shadow of the demon seed stirring within it, and her tongue began moving again, and her mouth opened as she craned her head back, her face held skyward like a nestling begging for food. But each time she was denied her meal. At this point, her chances were looking grim. Without the power of the pyramid, the lantern could not give birth to its seed. And without the seed, Lamia would not have the strength to defeat her enemy. She stretched her arms out in desperate appeal, like a true believer awaiting the baptismal water. The mouth of the reservoir puckered softly, sending a thin stream of mucus dripping down onto her neck. "Please. Please." She clapped her hands back together and repeated the incantation.

A groan issued from within the reservoir, and with hope renewed, she unhinged her jaw, letting the top portion of her head fall back until it was level with the bottom, creating a glistening lawn of bone-white spikes. Her forked tongue danced at its center, enticing the infant out of its womb. The candles flickered, and the sacred symbols blazed with infernal light. From deep within the reservoir, she heard the infant's cry, and excited breaths rose from her gullet in a machine gun staccato.

Then the crying stopped, and the flames of the candles fell still. The two halves of her head rejoined like a Venus fly trap closing over its prey, and her eyes once again settled upon the reservoir. Its golden shine had faded, leaving behind a sallow pallor. The silence was louder than anything she had ever heard. Her final hope lay dead in the reservoir, and she would soon follow, becoming nothing more than a hated memory.

"Enough with the self-pity," she said aloud. "I've failed to erect a suitable defense. It's time to consider retreat." She weighed her odds of leaping to the waters and judged them to be somewhere between slim and nil. More than likely she'd end up as nothing more than a stain outside her fortress for her enemies to jeer at. *That's no death for a queen.* It felt strange contemplating death after so long steeped in the waters of immortality.

A sound like thunder ripped her from her thoughts. Her enemy had arrived, and he was hammering the door off its hinges. Soon he would be standing over her, alight with the glow of his own arrogance. She cast one last glance above. What a sweet twist of fate it would have been for Cercyon to find his prey imbued with infernal power and suddenly more than his match. But instead, her savior lay lifeless in a honeycomb bladder under the fading light of the lantern. How quickly fate's tides turn. How suddenly the waves come crashing down.

The door fell right on cue, landing on the floor with a boom. Lamia kept her back erect, not wanting to give him the satisfaction of seeing her cringe before him. "Ah, my venerable executioner has arrived!" she said in their native tongue. She remained facing away, coiled within her tail. As was his custom, Cercyon conveyed his contempt for her by saying nothing. Naturally, he would give her this infuriating silent treatment. "*I know you,*" he would no doubt soon say. *Of course you know me, you cur. You've hounded me to the ends of eternity.* And for what? A little torture? As if he wasn't guilty of the same crime a thousand-fold. Lamia listened as his steps measured the distance he'd taken toward her. When he stopped, she judged that there was still a safe gap between them. He wouldn't kill her just yet. After such a long wait, he no doubt wanted to savor the moment. Perhaps before ending it, he would even bring in an artist to commit her humiliation to canvas, then bask in the delicious irony of hanging it in the study she'd wrecked only the night before. Seeking an end to the agonizing silence, Lamia spoke. "I suppose you're not going to tell me how you got in."

"I'm not here to give explanations. Or to listen to them."

Lamia uncoiled and spun to face him, her black eyes shining and her jagged teeth bared. "I suppose you're here to listen to me beg then?" She forced a laugh. "You're going to leave this tower a disappointed man."

"I doubt that."

"You gloat only to mask your impotence, Cercyon. But you cannot hide the reality that you are far from my equal. I built an empire here and enslaved a demon as old as humanity itself. I captured men who probably would have ended up damned anyway and gave the ones worth their salt an eternity worth living. This whole island is full of lost souls who now have somewhere to call home because of me. And what have you done? You've spent years projecting your own sins onto others and punishing them for it. And now you've teamed up with Pirithous to strip the people of this island of the only good thing they've ever had. Am I evil? Yes. Unequivocally. But I built something that works, while you play at being holy with your old cellmate. Once a king, now a servant." Lamia spat on the floor in contempt. "People don't want what you offer, Cercyon. They don't want to see the light. They will gladly choose to live in darkness for an eternity if it feels good, and I make it feel good. All they have to do is play the game, and all you had to do was stay the hell out of my way."

In the aftermath of her speech, Lamia's chest heaved and fell with hungry breaths. Cercyon's expression had not changed. "You may enter now," he said in English. Behind him, two figures appeared in the doorway. One was Pirithous. The other was the body she'd been evicted from, somehow reanimated. That Pirithous had come to witness her fall was by no means unexpected, but she could not fathom how her mask was moving about on its own.

"Your darkness is a place of sorrow," Pirithous said. "In time, all who embrace it see that. And those who never asked for it see it much sooner."

Lamia laughed. "You've reanimated this flesh puppet as some sort of rebuke?"

Amaya took a step forward. "I remember what you did to me, you monster. I remember watching you step down from that cylinder in this very body." She held her hand out in front of her. "And you cut my throat with a knife held by this very hand."

Lamia whipped her tail, audibly splitting the air. "I took what I needed from you and put you out of your misery quickly. That's what mercy looks like, child. This ogre you now follow has never showed an ounce of mercy in his entire existence."

Pirithous folded his hands in front of him, bowing his head as though in prayer. After a moment, he spoke again.

"Cercyon has been redeemed. He has made mistakes, but he is penitent. Are you?"

Lamia laughed again, and this time it wasn't forced. Her cackle echoed throughout the chamber from the floors where her runes had gone cold to the reservoir above where the seed of her demon lay stillborn. "Penitent toward whom? You?"

"No, Lamia. Not me."

Cercyon made a sound of derision. "You're shouting into the wind, Pirithous. This thing is beyond redemption."

"I am not a thing, Cercyon. And I am not beyond redemption. I am simply not in need of it. I have crossed countless veils, and all I have ever seen is an endless nightmare sprawl. And through it all I have survived and have helped others survive. And damn the withered husks of those who couldn't hack it. And that includes you, my king." She pointed an accusing finger at Cercyon. "Vengeance is a weak man's poison, and you've imbibed so deeply that there'll be nothing left of you once the bottle is empty."

She then turned her ire back upon Pirithous. "And you are even more pitiful. You made yourself a legend by getting past Cerberus and escaping Hades. And what do you do with that? You harass me with no greater goal in mind than to rescue your mad friend from an eternity of self-imposed torment. He did nothing with nothing, as anyone could have predicted. But you, with all your gifts, spend your days pursuing this pointless vendetta."

"I'm merely a servant delivering a message. Cercyon has listened and has understood. You say everything's an endless nightmare sprawl, but it's only because you've been moving sideways. You're fond of saying that there is always something below, but have you really never considered that there may likewise always be something above?"

"You disappoint me, Pirithous. There is no paradise but what you create with your own hands, and I have created it right here on this island with only a few handfuls of harvested flesh." Lamia turned her attention to Amaya, her eyes glinting with mischief. "Speaking of flesh, yours was quite the fan favorite, girl. Never before had the faces on those doors looked so pleased."

Pirithous dropped his gaze and took Amaya's hand in his. "Your depravity knows no bounds, Lamia."

"Ah," she said, a grin breaking across her face. "So, this mask wasn't merely reanimated for the purpose of throwing it in my face. I didn't know you were such a collector of used and broken things, Pirithous. Tell me, how does it feel to be the last man in line?" Her voice sparkled with the joy of malevolence.

Pirithous raised his eyes from the floor, locking them onto hers. "We are all waiting in line for something, Lamia. And there's something you've been in line for far too long."

The bravado which had been burning like a lit coal cooled in Lamia's chest. She had taken her stand and had made her speeches, and none of it had mattered. Her fire was going to be snuffed out, and there was nothing she could do about it. She tried to spit on the floor, but her mouth had gone dry. Looking from face to face, she found them unchanged. Despite all her wild bluster, they were going to go on, while she faced oblivion or worse. And her pride would not allow her to reach out for a single low hanging branch as she made her way down the river to that eternal fall, for all the forest was her enemy. At once, resignation fell like sunlight upon her face, and she addressed Cercyon. "Do what you came to do."

Cercyon stepped forward, the floor of the chamber vibrating with every step. Once he was standing over her, Lamia opened her mouth to speak, and Cercyon raised his hand. To her horror, she obeyed his call for silence. "I know you," he said before placing the palm of his hand against her face and wrapping his fingers around the back of her head. Enveloped in darkness, Lamia breathed through her nose, awaiting her moment of transport to either eternal night or somewhere beyond. She thought of all her great pleasures and of her many triumphs. Among her conquests, Reece Holloway stood starkly against the blackness of her thoughts as though he were clothed in neon. She would never understand how, but he had somehow managed to set her world crumbling beneath her feet. She tried to clear her thoughts, of Reece and all the others, so that she could face her execution like a queen. But something remained, even after everything else had been swept away. Lamia had long supposed that when her day of reckoning came, she would face it without fear. On that count she had been wrong.

27
RISE

Reece was shaken from his slumber by the rocking of his bed beneath him. When his eyes came into focus, he found himself gazing up into an overcast sky. The freshly dug sides of a square pit were rising all around him. Men he recognized as Cercyon's servants flanked him on either side. They were clothed in robes and were hard at work lowering his bed into the ground through a system of ropes and pulleys. At center stood Pirithous, draped in the vestments of a priesthood unknown to Reece. He was dipping a bundle of sticks in a bowl of water and shaking the droplets into the pit, all the while chanting in a language Reece couldn't place. On either side of him stood Amaya and Alessa, their heads bowed in solemn repose.

Once the bed touched down upon the earth, they severed the ropes, and their slack fell to the soil in a series of thumps. Everyone chanted in harmony while Pirithous looked skyward, his arms stretched out before him. When the chanting stopped, they lowered their heads in silence. Only Alessa's eyes remained open. After a time, the congregation began their departure, but her eyes remained on him until finally Pirithous placed a hand on her shoulder and led her away, leaving Reece with only the face of the heavens to look upon. On the left side of the pit stood a row of tenements like the one Alessa lived in. Sunlight broke through passing clouds, sweeping patches of orange and gold across their walls—slowly at first, then faster as the days came and went with increasing speed, reflecting upon them the passing of ages. Houses sunk into their foundations, and wood rotted and fell to the ground, only for the buildings to arise rebuilt anew. And so the cycle continued, the sun rising and setting and casting the land into light and darkness, warmth and cold, and through all of it, Reece lay forgotten outside of time.

Eventually, he grew tired of watching, and the world disappeared behind his eyelids. From somewhere in that brown expanse, he felt himself rising. The skin of his back broke contact with the bed sheets and a swirling breeze swept him away. Reece struggled to open his eyes but found that his eyelids were too heavy to lift. Then as gently as he'd been raised, he was set back down, and a layer of earth was laid atop his body. It was there in the damp of the soil that Reece was able to do his highest quality thinking. His concentration only broke in the moments when he could hear Alessa above, tending his earthen blanket while speaking as one does over the grave of a loved one about the mundane details of their day. He had no idea if she'd be able to make him grow again, but there was such kindness in her trying that he was tempted to want to live just so she wouldn't have to see her efforts fail. If he did break free from his roots and rise again, he would do so a new man. The earth had shown him everything he was and everything he could be, free from self-deception. To have found such wisdom in the grave would have been his life's greatest travesty. Life truly is wasted on the living.

One bright day Reece opened his eyes and found that he could see. Most of his body was still beneath the soil, but sections of it had broken the surface, like a man floating on his back in a pool. Alessa was kneeling over him, hard at work pruning the vibrant green sprouts which had grown along his nerves and broken through his skin in search of light. Once she'd finished her pruning, she got him up to speed on the details of her day as she kneaded the soil around his body, the sun beating down upon her browning face. After a while she rested, wiping the sweat from her brow with her forearm and revealing a set of nails caked in dirt. Finally, she produced a watering can, and Reece closed his eyes as she showered his body in coolness.

The next time Reece awoke, the night was crisp, and the sprouts which rose from his body were a lovely shade of green under the light of the moon. A passing deer as white as clouds stopped next to where he lay, and upon seeing it, Reece laughed like a small child seeing a new family pet for the first time. The deer craned its neck downward and looked at him with curiosity, sniffing him at first and then breathing him in deeply through its cold, wet nose. Reece felt his consciousness disperse and all went dark. Then the deer lifted its face to the moon, releasing billows of white vapor from its nose, and Reece flowed up into the night. From there, he saw Alessa's garden with his body lying at its center, now almost fully emerged from the soil. A short distance away stood the house at the edge of the woods. It had undergone some repairs, and a warm light burned in one of its windows. Behind it lay the forest, its canopy blanketed in countless tiny points of light like fireflies.

Rising higher into the sky, Reece saw that the windows of the lighthouse had gone dark, and its lantern no longer conveyed its beam onto the sea. Across the distance, he saw Cercyon's mansion. A line of candles marched up the path from the town below. Through the windows of his great hall, he could see dancers locked in a twirling embrace. Reece felt himself drawn to the rose window, and he materialized in flesh among them. His left hand was laced in Mallory's, and his right was upon her waist, and they spun in unison to music that seemed to come from all directions at once. Upon the dais, Cercyon sat on his throne, his hands folded in front of him. He no longer looked like an ogre but like the man he'd been before the torment of Hades had warped him. Pirithous stood to one side and Amaya to the other, gazing into each other's eyes. When the music stopped, Mallory's hand slipped from Reece's and she stepped back, laughing with joy. When at last she returned her eyes to his, Reece bowed, and she curtseyed in return, pulling the edges of her white dress up from the floor. It was then Reece saw his reflection in Cercyon's mirror. He looked strong and healthy, and a finely tailored jacket hugged a set of shoulders that looked capable of bearing the weight of the world. The smile upon his face was one of ease, as though nothing else could take its place.

The mirror grew brighter until it was shining with pure white light, and the next time Reece opened his eyes, he found himself in bed. He was unable to identify the room, but the items within it spoke of a succession of places he'd once called home, and the presence of Alessa's wooden tree engraving next to the bed suggested she was somewhere nearby. Shadows sifted through the trees, creeping in through the window and flitting about on the closet door, where a dress the color of pine needles hung from a wire hanger. The character of the light grew from morning to midday and then settled into the orange of evening all in the space of a long breath. Then the shadows of the night filled the room, and from within the dress, limbs sprouted like branches. It filled in as though flesh were growing within it, and from its collar emerged a head draped in hair the color of leaves crumbling in winter. For a time, the figure dangled there without moving, then its mouth drew open, revealing an eye which seemed to hold within it sunset's remains. From behind the figure's eyelids two mouths appeared, and when they spoke, their sound issued forth as separate voices speaking as one. "I have been watching you sleep for so long, Reece. Will you ever come back to me?"

"It's cool here in the soil," he said. "I've been having such lovely dreams, and nothing hurts anymore."

"I am glad you have found some peace. But your sprouts are withering, and mushrooms are taking their place. I have been plucking them away, but it is a troubling sign. If you become one with the earth, there is no telling where you might go. It is your choice, of course, but I would rather you stay here with me. There is still much for us to discover together."

Reece laid his head back on the pillow and listened to the sounds of the night, his eyelids growing heavy. "I think I'll sleep on it, Alessa."

And sleep he did, with memories of what had passed and visions of what might be blending and weaving until he could no longer tell them apart. And when he awoke, the color of light in the room suggested midday. The dress was missing from the closet door. Only the wire hanger remained. Reece sat up in bed and inspected his body, finding no sign of his injuries. New clothes lay clean and pressed over the back of a chair. He planted his feet on the hardwood floor. Then he dressed and made his way down the stairs, feeling no need to steady himself along the banister. He was well and strong, perhaps more so than he had ever been. He followed the aroma of toasted almonds into the kitchen where he found Alessa pulling a tray of amygdalota from the oven. As if sensing him behind her, she turned to face him, and a smile broke across her face. She ran her hands down the front of her forest green dress and performed a graceful twirl. "I wore it today because I knew this would be the day you awoke."

"You certainly do have a knack for teasing certainty out of the unknown. How will I ever keep anything from you?"

Alessa let out a little laugh. It was the first of its kind he'd heard, and his heart leaped at its sound. "You do not need to worry, Reece. My gift has been passed on to Amaya. I knew you would awake this morning through nothing more than the intuition I got from my mother. She always understood these things."

Reece looked around the kitchen and found his joy over being awake tinged with the memory of sorrows. To his right he saw the table where he'd broken Amaya from her spell, and he wondered if he was now being cared for in the same way in that uncanny world above the forest canopy. "I saw so much after the pyramid. I don't know what was real and what was a dream. I don't even know if this is real."

"You are safe with me now, Reece. And many more are safe because of you. Things will be different now that the lantern has withered. Without its draw, the people will disperse and make new homes. I believe that in time new life will grow throughout every hill and valley of this island."

"That's great for them," Reece said. "But what about you? Where do you stand with your king?"

"He has accepted what I did, bringing you back from the pyramid. I believe Pirithous mostly blames himself for granting so much power to one of the ghosts. Their love for me remains though, and they are grateful for all I have done." Alessa looked around the room, satisfaction written upon her features. "They even gave me this house." Her gaze then fell to the floor, and she bit down on her lip as if she wanted to ask him something but was nervous about what the answer might be. After an audible breath, she looked back at Reece. "It can be ours if you like."

Alessa's eyebrows sat high on her forehead as she awaited his response. Reece crossed the kitchen and took her hands in his, searching the dark bronze of her eyes for a view of his future. Within them he found only mystery, and he decided that was enough.

www.ingramcontent.com/pod-product-compliance
Lightning Source LLC
Chambersburg PA
CBHW010735310726
48971CB00010B/2841